FATA MORGANA

THE UPGRADE SERIES #5

WESLEY CROSS

JOIN THE UPGRADE SERIES

To receive free books, get behind the scenes stories, and be the first to hear about new releases—sign up for the newsletter.

See the back of the book for details.

PUBLISHER INFORMATION

This is a work of fiction. Names, characters, businesses, places, events, and incidents are either the product of the author's imagination or used in a fictitious manner. Any resemblance to actual persons, living or dead, or actual events is purely coincidental.

Published by
Cerberus Prints
PO BOX 90399
Brooklyn, NY 11209

PROLOGUE

Sahara Desert, Algeria

"Is this how it ends?"

Helen Chen's chapped lips cracked as she spoke and she winced, regretting opening her tortured mouth. She shivered and pressed her aching, freezing body against Mike Connelly's warm shoulder. The night was taking a firm hold on the desert. The temperature that hovered in the oppressive nineties during the day went into a free fall as the sun went down, and by the time the shining path of the Milky Way stretched across the black sky, it dropped below zero.

A brutal sandstorm that lasted for two days had forced them to take shelter at the foot of a black sandstone formation whose jagged peaks made it look like a crumbling medieval castle. The rock polished for millennia by wind and sand created a natural alcove and the two of them huddled there for almost forty-eight hours, sipping on the last of their water and trying their best to keep the sand out of their mouths and eyes. The wind finally died out in the last thirty minutes and now the desert was eerily silent, except for the occasional rustling of the sand sliding off the dunes. They needed to be going now, but neither of them had enough strength left to get up.

"Let's go," Connelly finally said, ignoring her question, his voice a scratchy grumble.

She watched him stand up on shaky legs and fix the makeshift sling that supported his left arm.

"Come on." He offered her his good hand. "We have to keep moving."

She didn't answer and grabbed onto him, letting him pull her up. Her joints screamed as she straightened herself, and Chen wobbled hard enough to fall over, if not for Connelly's grip.

"We'll find it."

"I'm not sure," she said, forcing herself to take one step and then another, falling behind him.

"Tuat is somewhere close," he said, referring to a string of small oases that lay to the south of the Grand Erg Occidental in Algeria. "It has to be."

She kept silent, concentrating whatever was left of her energy on making her legs move, planting her feet into the cold sand. They had thought they saw an oasis before the storm came. It was southwest from the route that Connelly wanted to take, but the vision of the green leaves and something blue in between was so convincing and their water ration so low, they had gambled and altered their path. Their spirits were high as, for a few hot, exhausting hours, it seemed they were getting closer and closer to a sanctuary. But then the pressure had dropped, the wind changed, and within minutes the promised land disappeared into a hot, arid air. Then came what the locals called a *simoom*, a massive dust storm.

As her limbs moved mechanically, Chen looked up into the dark sky. The Sahara wasn't a friendly place, but Helen had never once in her life seen that many stars. She took a long breath, her headache subsiding, replaced by something that almost resembled a mild euphoria. Most people don't get to choose where to die, and to draw her last breath under the vast sky full of stars didn't seem to be the worst way to go. Content, she concentrated on moving her feet again, resigned to her fate. It didn't matter if Tuat was close. Mike Connelly must have known that as well. They were not going to last through the night.

1

Manhattan, New York

"Mike? Can you hear me? Come on, wake up. We've got to go."

A meaty, sweaty hand not-so-gently patted him on the cheek and Mike Connelly opened his eyes. There was a blur of a face a few inches from his own, and then the hand came into focus, striking him again, even firmer this time. A sharp pain twisted Connelly's guts, and he turned over, a pressurized stream of vomit spraying the gray concrete floor below him. He spat, trying to get rid of the vile taste in his mouth.

"Connelly," the man insisted. "We can't stay here."

He turned, his vision not quite keeping up with the movement of his head. Nausea came back, but this time he was able to keep it down.

"Chuck?" he managed. "Where's everybody?"

"I've no idea." Kowalsky grabbed him under the armpits and pulled. A column a few feet away from them cracked with a sharp snapping sound, an ugly fissure snaking down from the ceiling all the way down to the floor. "But if we stay here much longer, we might never find out."

"Where's Jason?"

"Are you deaf? I don't know," Kowalsky snapped as debris trickled down from the ceiling of the garage. "Move."

Connelly climbed to his feet and looked around, surveying the garage. The cars on this side of the parking lot looked like they were hit by a giant wrecking ball. There was destruction on either side of where he was, but as he looked closer, there was much more damage to his left than to his right. It seemed he had been caught by the edge of the blast, and perhaps that was why he was still breathing. He looked ahead and froze. A few yards from him, half-hidden in the shadows from the flickering lights, lay a large, dark pool of blood. The image of the glowing assassin swinging the blade in a controlled, precise move was burned into Connelly's mind. Killing the man he had sworn to protect.

"We can't do anything if we are dead." Kowalsky tugged on his elbow, moving him away from the dark spot and toward the exit. "Come on."

He let Chuck guide him toward the exit, and a few moments later, they emerged onto the street. A row of cars parked on the side of the road in front of the tower were on fire. A large column of smoke was rising from the carnage, wrapping around the building like a hungry boa constrictor squeezing the life out of its prey. The snapping sounds of automatic fire cut through the veil of city noise every few seconds.

"Damn it," Chuck spat, and let go of him. "My car. We'll have to go on foot. Can you run?"

"I'll manage."

As they started toward the end of the block, a man clad in a Black Arrow uniform turned the corner, an assault rifle in his hands, his eyes lighting up as they met Connelly's. Mike's hand slapped the holster, only to come up empty, his trusty Mark 23 missing from its usual place. The mercenary swung the rifle around, but before he could level it, Chuck's Chiappa barked and the man fell to his knees, clutching his chest, and then collapsed on his side.

"Good shot," Connelly said, heading for the fallen man. "I need to grab that rifle."

"Slow down, cowboy." Chuck grabbed his shoulder, stopping him in his tracks. "These guys are the least of our problems. I'm much more worried about the bots."

"Bots?"

"Yeah." Kowalsky slowed down and pressed himself against the side of the building as they approached the end of the block. Then, without stepping out on Sixth Avenue, he peeked around the stone edge of the building. "One of those spider-looking things. See for yourself."

Connelly waited for Chuck to move back, and then he risked a glance down the street from where the Black Arrow mercenary had come a few moments ago. There, in the middle of the sidewalk, right under the neon "Soup and Sandwich" sign of a local cafe, was a strange glistening object. It had a gunmetal-gray cube-shaped body, each side about five feet long, which dangled suspended between four spindly telescopic legs that gave the entire bot the arachnid appearance. The top face of the cube was split open in the center, each side creating a shield angled at a forty-five degree angle. Between them, a short, fat barrel of a weapon was swiveling back and forth. Connelly had never seen a weapon like that before, but he had no doubt he didn't want to be on the receiving end of its charges.

"Where are you?" he heard Kowalsky say in a harsh whisper behind him, and when he turned, he saw Chuck holding a phone to his ear.

"Who's that?"

"There's a murder bot in the middle of the street. Don't come charging down Sixth," Kowalsky said, ignoring his question. He stayed silent, listening for a few seconds, and then continued. "In that case, stay as close to the right as you can and pick us up by the corner building. The one that looks like the Flatiron Building. Try not to make too much noise."

"Latham?"

"Yeah." Kowalsky pushed him away from the side of the building and looked out again. "Lucky bastard. He missed all the fun because of the traffic and now he gets to be our savior. Let's do it. Walk fast, but do not run. Maybe that'll work."

They crossed Broome Street, trying to gain as much distance from the bot as possible before crossing Sixth Avenue. Connelly risked a quick glance over his shoulder. The bot seemed to be preoccupied, swiveling its barrel up and down the empty street.

"There." He pointed to the triangular evergreen hedge in front of the narrow building. "Let's take cover."

"Not a single car," Kowalsky muttered as they took position behind the bushes. "He's going to stick out like a sore thumb."

There was a distant roar of an accelerating car and a few moments later, a black town car appeared, speeding up Sixth Avenue. The windshield was poked with bullet holes and its right-side mirror was hanging on a wire, clattering as the car roared toward them.

"So much for not making too much noise," Kowalsky said.

Connelly watched as the bot stopped moving around, its torso swinging toward the upcoming vehicle. The end of the barrel flashed piercing blue, but Latham seemed to have anticipated the shot, the car swerving madly on the empty road. A massive explosion ripped through the bus stop a few feet away from where the car had been, launching the plastic booth up in the air. It flipped a few times like a leaf in a hurricane and then smashed into the mailboxes at the corner of the street.

The car flew over the intersection, and Connelly and Kowalsky were running toward it before it came to a full stop.

"Floor it."

Latham stepped on the gas pedal and the vehicle lurched forward, pressing the passengers into the seats. They swerved again and another explosion momentarily lifted the back of the car into the air, the engine whining as the rear wheels hopelessly spun, looking for friction. Then, a moment later, it came down with a crash, Kowalsky cursing under his breath as he and Connelly grappled around for support.

"I hate those things," Latham yelled as they turned onto Spring Street, putting some buildings between them and the bot.

"I told you," Kowalsky said. "Don't make too much noise."

"The city is overrun by Black Arrow," the driver replied as they screeched into another turn. "They are putting roadblocks everywhere. I used my old Guardian ID three times. It worked. Twice."

"What happened the third time?"

"That happened." Latham pointed at the holes in the windshield. He lowered the speed and moved to the right lane. "What's worse, it's not just the mercs. Bots are everywhere, too. Mostly these boxy ones, but I've seen a few others. And most seem to have the same weapons. It packs a punch. I saw one lighting up a minivan. Shredded the thing to pieces. Thankfully, it's slow to reload."

"It doesn't matter. We won't be able to fight them. We don't have that kind of firepower. Do you think we can still get out of the city?" Connelly glanced through the back window. It looked like they lost the bot. At least for now.

"I think so." The car slowed down even more. "They started downtown and are moving methodically north. The GWB should still be open and once we are on the other side, we are home free."

"I need to go back to the city," Connelly said. "I need to look for Jason."

"About that." Latham's eyes flashed in the rearview mirror. "I'm not sure if you had been fully debriefed on this yet, but Chuck and I came across a treasure trove of information."

"What kind of information?"

"Old Otomo factory somewhere in Africa," Chuck said. "Jason thought they were planning on making sentinels but didn't think they would pose a serious threat. It looks like we might have underestimated the danger. Now I'm starting to think that the bots that we see today in the city are the first platoon of the incoming army."

"We will lose the war, before it even begins," Connelly said.

"Exactly. We don't have the exact location for the factory, but Latham and I think we have enough clues to point us where to look."

"Are you going?"

"No," Chuck said. "You are."

"I can't. I have to find Jason. There's no time for me to run around the world looking for a factory that may or may not be supplying the bots. My job was to protect him. I failed in this job. The least I can do is to find where his body is."

"Listen." Chuck put his hand on Mike's shoulder and gave it a gentle squeeze. "Let's not make any assumptions. I know it's not easy, but I want you to think logically. We have two pressing issues. First, we need to find Jason and the others. Second, we need to blow up a factory that might be printing the vehicles of our demise. For those two issues, we have two candidates: a special ops soldier and a detective. Now, tell me, Mike, what is the rational thing here to do?"

Connelly turned away and stared through the window for a few seconds, seeing nothing.

"All right," he finally said, turning back. "We are going to Newark, then."

"What's in Newark?"

"I might know a guy."

2

Manhattan, New York

"*L*et them pass," Kowalsky said, taking a hold of Latham's elbow. He leaned against the building and chewed on an unlit cigarette as he watched an armored truck with Black Arrow markings slowly roll down Avenue C. There were no road-blocks in Alphabet City, but the trucks carrying mercenaries in black uniform and foot patrols seemed to be everywhere.

"For your protection, please abide by the city's curfew. No civilian pres-ence is allowed on the streets of New York City after eight p.m. without Black Arrow transit passport. Anyone stopped without papers will be detained for further questioning. For your protection, please abide by the city's curfew..." The loudspeaker repeated the message over and over as the long barrel of a machine gun mounted behind a dual shield swiveled left and right, reinforcing the message.

Kowalsky and Watkins had made a few stops in New Jersey, picking up supplies and the USB drive with the data on the Otomo factory in northern Africa before heading for the port of Newark.

After meeting with Mike's contact at the port and arranging to put Connelly on the ship headed for Tangier, they spent the night at Latham's cousin's house on Staten Island. The next morning, they made their way back into the city, first driving to Queens, and then taking the Pedestrian Walkway across the Manhattan Bridge. From there, they headed for the safe house Kowalsky claimed he had used in Alphabet City.

"How do you know the place is even still there?" Latham asked.

"I don't know for sure," Kowalsky said, peeling off the wall and starting to walk again. "But the chances are pretty high. When I was still on the force, the NYPD occasionally used empty apartments in the projects for temporary base operations, safe houses, and so on. The buildings belonged to the New York City Housing Authority, also known as NYCHA. There was no need to haggle with private landlords for access. As long as the place was available, we could set up shop any time. Some were temporary, but some, like the place on Houston, were used on a more permanent basis."

"What makes you think the NYPD isn't there anymore?"

"They had stopped using this apartment a few years before I left. It was in limbo. Technically, the police department still had the paperwork with NYCHA for the continuous use of it, but there was no need and it got buried in a bureaucratic pile of docs nobody cared to go through. Especially in the era of big budget cuts. The more time had passed, the less chance it was going to be used for anything else. It wasn't unique—I've seen at least a dozen places like that."

"What about squatters? Surely in a building like this, people will notice the place is empty."

"They'd stay away. Word travels far here, and everyone knows the police could use it at any time. Even after a long while."

"I hope so."

"There it is." Kowalsky pointed ahead of them at what looked like a few narrow five-story buildings pressed together like a stack of pancakes. "It's on the fourth floor."

The front wall of the building that, at some point in time, was painted in bright white was covered in grime and soot. Surprisingly, there was almost no graffiti, as if the dirty surface was too repulsive for street artists even to consider as canvas. A few homeless men were camping under the awning next to the entrance, the stench filling Kowalsky's nose and forcing him to breathe through his mouth. The men watched the two enter the building with suspicion, but none attempted to engage or beg for food or money.

"Elevator?" Latham raised an eyebrow. "There's a light."

"Only if you want to celebrate next Christmas in there," Kowalsky said and headed up the chipped cement stairs. "That light is probably the only thing that still works."

The lack of graffiti outside was balanced by the heavily tagged walls of the stairwell. Curse words, crudely drawn pictures of genitalia, and love messages covered most of the surface. But crowded by the ugly scrawls in a few places, there were a few genuine pieces of art. A solemn profile of a samurai. A silhouette of a dancer. The face of Jim Morrison reflected in a broken mirror.

The apartment was locked, but Kowalsky quickly defeated the rusty mechanism with a set of picks. He swung the door open, letting Latham into a faded yellow kitchen. The air was stale and cold. A large wooden table sat in the middle of the room, surrounded by a few black plastic chairs. A plastic curtain with faded flower prints separated the kitchen from a bunk bed on the other side.

"Holy cow, it's cold in here." He walked across the room, opened the oven, and turned the knob. There was a hiss of gas, but no spark. "And there's no light. You've got a lighter?"

Watkins took off his backpack, unzipped its side pocket, and produced a disposable blue Bic lighter.

The oven ignited with a whoosh and a few moments later, the heat started to spread through the small apartment.

"I'm taking the bottom," Watkins said, examining the bed. "The mattresses are older than my grandma, but they will do."

"You wish. I found the place to stay. I call where I sleep. You'll be on the second floor, buddy. Let's set up shop."

They unpacked their gear on the table and Kowalsky unfolded a large computer screen and clipped it to the kitchen wall.

"Let's check the outside surveillance first," he said, logging into Orion's cloud server. "Let's see who planted those bots right under our nose."

"Sounds like a plan." Watkins took a seat on the other side of the table. "How do you want to split it?"

"Let's start twelve hours before the attack. I'll take the northern and western sides, and you take south and east."

"Okay." Watkins looked up from his tablet. "Listen, I know you are not a fan, but now that we are treading some dangerous waters, I think you should consider bio patches."

"You mean that poisonous fake skin stuff that you wear all the time?"

"It's a crude description, but yes."

"I don't know. Every time I see you put that shit on, I can't help but think that if I had them on, I'd sting myself when I went to take a leak."

"You're such an idiot sometimes," Latham said. "These are weapons, just like your beloved Chiappa. You don't go to the bathroom with a revolver in your hand, finger pressing on a trigger, do you? Same here."

"But they are literally on your skin."

"Yes. But they are not active all the time. That is not how it works. Some chemicals are benign as long as you don't mix them. For example, you can store organic solvents and nitric acids with no issues. But if you mix them in a one-to-one ratio." Watkins leaned over the table. "Boom. The mixture explodes. Or you mix bleach and ammonia and you get phosgene gas, which is many times deadlier than chlorine. Didn't you do baking soda and vinegar experiments when you were a kid? Chemistry is a wonderful science, my friend, and now that we are outnumbered and outgunned, we should take advantage of every tool at our disposal. If not for those fake skins, as you put it, I wouldn't be here."

A shiver ran down Chuck's spine. Watkins, of course, was referring to the time when, while still working for Alexander Engel, he had been captured by Victor Ye and his goons. He was strapped to a table and was going to meet a gruesome death, if not for a paralyzing graft in his hand that allowed him to overpower his torturers and escape.

"I'll think about it," he said and started the video. The street in front of the Orion Tower appeared on his tablet's screen, and Kowalsky hit the FF button, as he watched the cars and pedestrians going about their business at an exaggerated speed like in a Charlie Chaplin movie. He concentrated on the part of the road where he had found the sentry and kept skipping the recording forward until he saw it.

"There," he said, slowing the video to a normal speed and bringing it to the large screen on the wall.

A garbage truck with city markings pulled up to the curb with a man riding outside of the cabin. He jumped off when the truck came to a stop and, after glancing up and down the street, put a small object on the surface of the road. A moment later, the air around him flickered, producing a hologram image of a few white plastic barricades with orange stripes. The man stepped out of the image, went to the back of the garbage truck, and pulled the lever. The small boom of a crane extended from the bowels of the truck, carrying a matte-black cube. It lowered the cube in the center of the illusion and folded back into the dark insides of the truck.

"This is slick," Watkins said. "We don't have tech like this."

"No, we don't. Maybe you are right."

"What?"

"About using every trick we can. Show me your poison toys."

Watkins stretched his lips into a smile and pulled out a small plastic container from his backpack. He popped the lid open, exposing a matrix of cells, each with a small plastic vial inside. Containers had small hand-written inscriptions on their sides and color-coded labels on top. Most of the labels were yellow, a few were red, and two of them black.

"This is my basic setup. Something I always have with me on the go. I had a much bigger collection at the tower, but alas."

"What's with the colors?"

"The yellows are neutralizers. They will momentarily paralyze the victim and render them incapable of defending themselves."

"The reds will hurt and the black will kill, I'm assuming?"

"No. The red ones will kill more or less instantaneously. The black ones." Watkins carefully took the two vials with black labels and put them in front of Chuck on the table. "They will kill too, and you will feel like you are being burned alive the entire time."

"Damn." Chuck picked up one of the glass cylinders and looked at it to the light. "You came up with this?"

"No." Watkins averted his eyes. "Engel has a whole lab dedicated to things like this. I just happened to understand them more than some of the other people who used them."

A phone vibrated in Kowalsky's pocket and he pulled it up, his face getting flushed as he recognized the number. He answered the call and put it on the speaker.

"Chuck?" the woman's voice said. "Is that you? This is Helen Chen."

3

Rigel Compound, Upstate New York

Steven Poznyak scraped the last of the buckwheat off his bowl and rubbed his stomach. It rumbled in response. The small round room that served as Poznyak's living quarters was at the lowest level of the former missile launch control center. The furnishings were spartan. There was a simple twin bed at the back of the staircase leading to the two upper levels. On the other side, he had a sturdy, solid wood desk with a single drawer next to a minibar and a microwave. He gave the little refrigerator a wistful look. He pictured an oily paper bag sitting right on the top shelf. A properly grilled medium-rare burger bulging through the brown paper and a side of truffle fries, hot enough to burn his fingers.

He swallowed and opened the door. A small wooden box of potatoes was sitting at the bottom of the fridge and a large red onion and two medium-sized carrots on the second, next to a lonely bottle of beer. Poznyak sighed and closed the door. Buckwheat would have to do.

Rigel Compound, named after the brightest star in the Orion constellation, seemed to have been getting dimmer by the day. Since the orbital strike that took down one of the generators and injured a dozen people, things progressively took a turn for the worse. When Orion's team took control of Project Thor's weapons and eliminated the risk of the compound being overrun by Engel's forces, the morale briefly improved. But while Black Arrow couldn't attack the installation for the fear of retaliation, it didn't stop them from harassing the site, ambushing supply convoys and all but besieging the compound.

Now, fuel was running low, forcing Poznyak to re-route its limited supply to the most vital of the compound's projects. The cold room, that among other things, housed the frozen body of Rachel Hunt, was a constant source of stress. The sarcophagus was a power-hungry device, and Steven shuddered every time he thought about a possible power failure. But an even bigger problem that started to loom over the entire community was the dwindling supplies of food. There were some sympathetic farmers in the nearby towns that occasionally sent a truck or two under the protection of night, but those were rare as Black Arrow punished anyone daring to interfere with their business. A few folks at the silo organized foraging parties which replenished some of the meat stock at Rigel with fresh venison, but it also came at substantial risk of running into nearby patrols. By now they were rationing food, and Poznyak struggled to find a solution on how to move forward.

His computer beeped, flagging an important message, and he sat up straighter, looking at the screen. It was a video file that came from Helen Chen's account. He hadn't heard from her since the attack on the tower and now, staring at the familiar name, he had a rush of scenarios racing through his head, one scarier than another. Was it a dead man's switch kind of message? Designed to be delivered if the owner of the account was no longer among the living? Or was it a hostage videotaped by someone who gained access to Chen's private network by forcing her to give up credentials?

"Play it," he finally said out loud, his voice shaky. The face of Helen

Chen filled the screen. Her face looked fine, if paler than usual. She wore a black leather jacket over a gray hoodie and she seemed to stand somewhere in a public place, an out-of-focus sign in French on the wall behind her.

Steve, she said, looking into the camera. *I'm sorry if getting this video spooked you. I'm fine and unhurt, at least for the moment, which is more than can be said about a lot of other people. I know Connelly is alive, but know nothing about Max or Jason, as we got separated during the attack on the tower. If you hear anything, please send me an update. I'm going crazy not knowing. I might not respond to your messages, but I will get yours.*

She paused, collecting her thoughts, and Poznyak thought he heard a PA system broadcasting a message in the background.

I'm at the airport, Chen continued, as if reading his mind. *In Quebec. You must be wondering what the hell am I doing in Canada and how I got here, but the less you know, the better. Chuck can fill you in if you see him in person. I think this link is secure, but who the hell knows. Keep that in mind if you send messages, too. Don't say anything that can get anyone compromised. All I can tell you is that I have to travel somewhere to help Mike.*

"Pause," Poznyak said. He stood up, and started pacing back and forth, a short manic semicircle between the bed and the table. He went back to the fridge, pulled the bottle of water out, and took a few greedy gulps. It helped, if even for a moment. "Continue."

I don't know how long I'm going to stay there. She paused, as if considering her last sentence, and then continued. *To be honest, the odds of coming back aren't great. That's why I wanted to talk to you about two important issues. The first one concerns Orion, so if...no, when Max and Jason return, you should talk to them about it immediately. It's about Orion's intellectual property. The attack wasn't just physical; we got hacked as well. A huge portion of our IP that deals with augmentation is now out in the open. Not everything, but close. What's worse is that it's now everywhere. I've seen packets and packets of information going out to China, Japan, Russia, Europe. It's all over the place. There's no putting this genie back into the bottle. I give it three months before we see replicas coming out of every corner of the world. I don't know what that means and part of me is happy it didn't just go to Engel, but the other part of me is terrified. Because I can't fathom what the future holds with so many people having access to this technology. Some, I'm sure, will use it for good. But many won't. I think the world as we know it today will unrecognizably change. Which brings me to the second reason I wanted to talk to you. I want you to pay attention. This is of paramount importance.*

"Oh boy," Poznyak said out loud and sat back in his chair. "If all our tech secrets being stolen was just an opening act…"

I have an AI, Chen said. *And when I say AI, please take my words seriously. I don't mean a sophisticated program or a system that acts in a human-like manner. This is an actual self-aware intelligence that is capable of independent thought. It's not an opinion; it's a fact. Max and Jason both talked to her and came to the same conclusion. It is alive, Steven. It, or rather she, calls herself JC. It's a long story why, and I'm sure she'll tell you in great detail if you would like her to. There are a few things you should know. JC is the key to Rachel's revival. We can't do it without her.*

A crease crossed Chen's forehead as if she was displeased with herself. *At least not in the foreseeable future. But while she's capable of helping us, I am not fully certain what her ultimate agenda is. In some ways, she's like a genius child who has never been outside. She's read a lot of books and watched thousands and thousands of hours of video. Shows, documentaries, and so on. She has a penchant for crime shows. Her knowledge is vast, but she lacks real life experience. And this is, and I cannot emphasize it enough, our only advantage over her. Sometimes when I talk to her, I feel like a mother, trying to raise an adopted child who happened to be a genius. Some other times I'm terrified, because I think she might turn out to be as friendly as Skynet from the old Terminator movies. You are going to have to figure out how to walk the line between befriending her and not getting tricked in the process. For now, I think it's prudent to take every precaution to make sure she can't escape. I've built a Faraday cage. Make sure to engage it every time before you bring her online. You'll find the detailed set of instructions in the left drawer in Max's desk. For Rachel's procedure, you'd need to connect her to the quant, which means whatever hardware limitations she has now will be gone. Make sure Max knows that is about to happen and take extra measures. Max and I had discussed them before. He can bring you up to speed. It's important for you to know that I've had this conversation with JC, and she knows she is indispensable for the task.*

Somewhere in the background, the PA system came to life again, the announcement unintelligible to Steven. Chen glanced back and then checked her watch. *It's my cue. I have to go, Steven. Please send me updates. Hopefully, I'll see you all again soon.*

The video jerked as Chen moved the camera away from her face and then stopped.

"What time was the message sent?" Poznyak asked. If he knew when Helen had taped the video, he could try to at least figure out which flights were scheduled to depart.

"Time stamp has been removed from the file," the computer replied.

"Clever girl." He couldn't help but smile. He'd have to deal with the anxiety of not knowing where she was headed. But if somebody could hijack the message, they wouldn't know where she was going either.

"Turn it off," he said and headed for the stairs. Max Schlager's quarters were directly above his, on the second level of the former control center. Like Steven's, the place had a twin bed hidden behind the stairwell. There was a door leading to the blast lock area, which also served as a communal shower and bathroom for all three levels. A big ergonomic chair with a multitude of gadgets attached to it was positioned in the middle of the space in front of a curved desk flush to the round wall. There was a giant monitor attached to the wall above the desk, surrounded like Saturn by its rings, with several smaller monitors of varying sizes. The main monitor was turned off, its smooth surface a still lake of the darkest shade of ink. The others were on. Some were showing live video feed from a few cameras installed in different spots of the complex. Others ran lines of code that he couldn't even pretend to understand.

Poznyak sat down in the chair, observing the monitors, his hands naturally falling on top of the split keyboard divided between two armrests. Then he reached down into the left drawer and pulled out a notebook page with a few lines of neat Helen's cursive. He read it in silence and then glanced at the big screen. A shiver ran down his spine.

"All right," he said, flipping the switch mounted on the chair and watching the steel cage locking him in. "Let's see what we got here."

4

Tangier-Med Port, Morocco

The edge of the sun's fiery disk peeked over the horizon, turning the sky yellow in the east and sending pink and orange streaks across thin wispy clouds. It shone through the forest of loading cranes and cast long shadows over the turquoise water of the Strait of Gibraltar as the MCC *Oswald* came to a full stop. Mike Connelly adjusted the heavy backpack on his shoulder and glanced at the shore. He had never been seasick, but after eight days on the ship, half of them spent during the storm that caught him off guard, he was eager to put his boots on solid ground again. By noon, the air would warm up to a balmy sixty-five degrees, but now the fresh breeze was brisk and Connelly zipped his leather jacket all the way up, warding off the cold.

"Can't wait to get off?" Tarik smiled, as if reading his mind. Tarik Mehdi had served as a chief officer on the *Oswald* for the past fifteen years. Three captains commanded the ship during the same time and most of the crew considered Tarik to be in charge.

Connelly had no idea what the deal was between Rovinsky and the port officials, but Tarik provided him with a small but comfortable cabin in the stern part of the ship, didn't ask questions, and even kept him company most of the days during dinner time on the mess deck. Those conversations served as a pleasant distraction and, under different circumstances, he would have enjoyed the trip. But most of the days he thought back to the fateful attack on the tower, playing it over and over in his head and trying to understand if he could have done something different to protect Jason. So far, if there had been an answer, he couldn't find it.

"It was a great journey." He returned the smile. "You were a gracious host, and I'm grateful for your hospitality. But yes, the shore looks good."

"This trip used to take over two weeks, not that long ago. Now it rarely takes over six days. If not for the storm, we would have been here two days ago. As for hospitality, it wasn't trouble at all. Anything I can do for Jim," Tarik said. During his long talks, he had mentioned Rovinsky a few times, and he knew the man well.

But his references had been vague, and Connelly didn't think it was appropriate or even important to press for details.

"Thank you anyway."

"Good luck, my friend." Tarik extended a hand. His handshake was warm and firm. "You've got my number. If you need a lift on the way home, let me know. Now hurry, unless you want to go through customs. Mohammed will take you through the port to the other side, and then you're on your own."

"Goodbye."

Connelly made his way to the pier and nodded to a bearded middle-aged man, who immediately started away from the ship. A long, white rectangular building loomed in the distance. A large sign next to the building had an Arabic lettering in the top half. On the bottom it said Tanger Med Port Center in block English letters.

"Where are you taking me?"

"Car," came the laconic answer. The man pointed somewhere beyond the building. "Driver take you any place."

"Okay," Connelly said.

"Don't talk," the man said. "See people, look down, understand?"

"Yes."

They walked in silence for a few minutes, past the endless rows of containers stacked on top of one another. Finally, containers gave way to a long parking lot and a white wire mesh fence behind it. Mohammed pulled on Connelly's arm, making him squat behind one car as they watched a guard in a yellow reflective jacket slowly walk on the path running along the fence.

"Quick now," the man urged.

They jogged, keeping their profiles as low as they could until they reached the fence. Then Mohammed ran ahead along the wall, lightly tapping on the poles as he went.

"Here," he said, stopping. "Help me."

Confused, Connelly got closer to the wall and only then saw it. The joints where the mesh met the poles were cut and replaced with hooks. The hooks were painted white to match the wire. From a few steps away, without knowing where to look, it was impossible to see that the wall was compromised. Together, they pulled the section of the wall up. Mohammed went first, and then held the wire until Connelly was on the other side. Then they lowered the section of the wall back into place.

"Run now. Guard come back soon."

They sprinted up the hill and away from the wall. Connelly kept glancing back, but the guard was nowhere to be seen and soon they were over the hill and away from the view.

The car, a beige Volkswagen Jetta, had been waiting for them near the gravel service road. Next to the vehicle was a woman dressed in a black *abaya*, a traditional dress covering the entire body. The *niqab* and dark aviator sunglasses hid her face.

"Here," Mohammed said, trying to catch his breath. "She take you."

"Thank you," Connelly said. He watched the man wave his hand and walk back to the port. Then he turned to face the black-clad woman. "Hello. Do you speak English by any chance?"

"A little," the woman said in a familiar voice. She pulled down the aviator glasses and niqab, revealing her face. "It would be weird if I didn't."

"Holy smokes." Connelly stepped forward and scooped Helen Chen into a hug. She hugged him back and for a few seconds they stood there, not willing to let go of one another. Finally, he stepped back. "How?"

"Chuck," she said, as if the name alone could explain everything. "Let's get going."

He put his backpack into the back seat and a few moments later, they were on the N16 road, heading south.

"Did you see Jason?" He asked the question that had been burning him.

"No," she said, her eyes not leaving the road. "The last thing I remember, there was some kind of blast and I got thrown back. When I came to, I was lying in front of the collapsed ceiling that blocked my way. A few inches more and we wouldn't be having this conversation. I crawled back and got out through the east entrance just in time. There was chaos, and Black Arrow was everywhere. And murder bots."

"Yeah, one of them tried to introduce itself to me and Chuck, but thankfully, Watkins drove us away before it did. I'd never seen anything like this."

"I had."

"Oh yeah? Where?"

"Awhile ago." She threw him a look he couldn't read. "In Hong Kong. They were guarding a place I was trying to break into. They are deadly, but thankfully aren't too bright. Hong Kong is where I had my first run-in with Black Arrow, too. Anyway. I made my way out of the city and found a place to lie low and try to find anyone who was still active. I got my lucky break when I called Chuck. That's how I knew you were coming here. For the past five days, I've been digging around—"

"Wait, five days?" he interrupted her. "How did you get here? You took a plane?"

"Yes. I've got skills." She smiled, but the smile faded too quickly. "It wasn't all smooth, though. I had to get out of the country first, and that wasn't easy. I got a few close calls, even got grazed by a bullet once, but who dares, wins, isn't what you guys say?"

"SAS say it," Connelly said, "but yeah. Wait, you said you got shot?"

"Grazed," she said, lifting her right arm and letting the sleeve of the dress fall, revealing a fresh, angry scar on her forearm. "Not shot. Just a scratch. Once I was on the other side of the border, it was easier. I made a few calls and hopped on the plane to Madrid. From there I made my way on this side of the Gibraltar."

Connelly watched her face as she drove, her jaw set, her piercing blue eyes not leaving the road. "Why come here to help me?"

"Chuck," she said simply again. "He convinced me that destroying the factory here in Africa will mean winning or losing this war. I thought the stakes were too high to leave you here alone. Did he tell you about Nikko and how he escaped?"

"Yes," Connelly said. "That was one horrible story. But he thinks we might have a lead."

"The man who drove Zara and Takara to the port?"

"Exactly."

She pulled the cloth off her head and shook out her hair. "While you were cruising across the Atlantic, I did some digging. The human trafficking cartel that kidnapped Takara doesn't exist anymore. Apparently, a few other women escaped and went to the police. The cops took down the entire ring a few days later."

"That's great."

"Yes," she continued. "Not only that. Because the story was big, it was easy to put some information together and soon I knew where to look for people who used their services in the past. There were only a few of them in Tangier and out of those, only one matching Takara's description. He's an old textile merchant, named Nabir El Amrani, and lives on the edge of the Medina with three women who I suspect had come from the cartel before it was shut down. He is extremely wealthy, at least for now. State-of-the-art security system and two teams of guards protect him twenty-four hours a day, seven days a week. I left him alone while waiting for you."

"I sense that wasn't the case for the other guy." Connelly chuckled.

"No," she said without smiling. "The other guy *was* wealthy. Now he's rotting behind the bars in Rabat being questioned by the *Direction Generale de la Surete Nationale* for conspiring against the king and tax evasion. I dare to say he has some rough road ahead of him. His money mysteriously disappeared and found its way into bank accounts of the women he had abused over the past few years."

"Nice work." He reached out and touched her shoulder. "I'm happy to see you, and I am grateful that you've come all this way to help me. But I'm also worried, because I think it's going to be extremely dangerous."

She shrugged. "We have to do this, Mike. No matter the cost."

"I know." He took away his hand, his cheeks hotter than the temperature of the car would have warranted.

"I watched the house," she said, unperturbed, "and I think I know who the driver was. He works for the supply company and technically isn't connected to the house, but I saw him chat with the women on a few occasions, even though he is not supposed to. I'm pretty sure he's our guy. We'll know soon enough."

The road snaked away from the coast and soon there was nothing but rolling hills on one side and sparse woods on the other. The humming of the engine, the rustling of the tires on the gravel road, and the rhythmic rocking of the car combined into a powerful, hypnotic cocktail and Connelly's eyelids grew heavy. He leaned his head on the headrest and fought to keep his eyes open.

"It's a long drive," Chen said. "Rest now. The answers are coming."

5

Manhattan, New York

Chuck Kowalsky lowered his head and raised the cardboard with the words "Will work for food" as the four-men Black Arrow patrol got closer.

"This is a spectacularly bad idea," he heard Watkins mutter to himself.

"Probably," he agreed. He was hot and cold at the same time. The wig, a fake beard, and the filthy coat he stole from a homeless man's tent next to their safe house in Alphabet City made him sweat, and the freezing wind immediately whisked away the heat. They were sitting at the corner of Varick and Broome Streets, and Watkins somehow created an even more pitiful image. His partner was sporting a pair of boots coming apart at the seams and was wearing a secondhand raincoat he had dragged through the mud a few times. Watkins raised a paper cup with a few coins in it, pointed it at the approaching men, and shook it.

"Filth," said one mercenary and spat, landing a sticky glob at

Chuck's boots as the patrol passed them. "Should line them all up against the wall. No one will miss 'em."

"Like I said," Watkins whispered as the patrol continued down the street. "A terrible idea."

"I don't have any other ideas," Kowalsky snapped, watching the men. "We need to see the place again. This is how it works. You go back to the crime scene and investigate. This is where it happened. We might find something."

"All right, Sherlock. Lead the way, then."

Kowalsky stuffed the sign under his arm and stood up, grimacing as the blood rushed into his frozen legs. The windows on the first floor were shuttered and so far, only a few of them were properly boarded up and reinforced by rows of two-by-fours. The rest of them loomed like some dark, prehistoric caves. He sprinted toward one opening and, casting a quick glance up and down the street to make sure nobody could see them, dived into the dark belly of the building. They walked as far as they could risk it without turning on the flashlight, glass crunching under their boots, and then Kowalsky pulled out a small flashlight, keeping it pointed away from the entrance.

"Over there," he whispered as the small pool of light darted across debris-strewn floor and illuminated the Exit sign above the service door. He turned off the light.

"What are you doing?" Latham whispered. "We are going to break our necks without the light."

"It's clear enough," he whispered back. "Let's not risk it. Put your hands on my shoulders and don't drag your feet. We'll walk slowly. We can take as much time as we need."

He could hear Watkins mumble something to himself but couldn't make out the words, and a moment later, he felt the hands of his partner on his shoulders. He stood for a few more seconds, letting his eyes adapt, and then moved in the door's direction.

It wasn't pitch black. When he strained, he could make out the straight lines of the columns and the rectangular frames of the doors as they passed them, one by one. He kept his hands out, feeling his way through the space, and stopped a few times as his fingers touched the cold concrete surface of the columns. Finally, when he thought they covered enough distance, he risked a quick flash of the flashlight. The door was less than a dozen feet away.

"You can turn it on now," Watkins said as they stepped out onto the landing and closed the door behind them.

Kowalsky switched the light on and illuminated the stairs. "Doesn't seem to be compromised."

"Is this how you got here when you got Connelly out?"

"Yeah." He started down the stairs, keeping one hand on the handrail. "I thought the entire building was going to come down. Columns were cracking in half as I pulled him out."

"Oh, boy."

They came down into the garage and Kowalsky turned the head of the flashlight, expanding the cone of light. The place was mostly intact except near the other entrance, where he had found Connelly. The ceiling had collapsed, burying the stairs and the exit door, and the cars were smashed on one side of the thoroughfare. He looked around for a few seconds and then walked to the middle of the lane.

"This is where he shot from."

"Who? The assassin?"

"Yeah. Look at this." Kowalsky stretched his hand out, partially blocking his view. "Whatever that weapon was, it came as a cone of force. Thirty, maybe thirty-five degrees wide. See this column?"

"That one?" Watkins pointed at the gray column with a long crack running down its side.

"Yep. This is what saved Mike's life. It deflected some of the energy over there." He pointed in the direction away from the smashed cars. "When it hit Connelly, it didn't pack the entire punch. That's why he is still breathing."

"What do you think it was?"

"I'm not sure," he said. He walked closer to the cracked column and ran his hand down the rough surface. "There are no scorch marks. Don't see any holes either. It almost looks like it was hit by a shock wave. A sudden change of pressure. Some weird stuff. I've never seen anything like this."

"Like a sonic boom?"

"I guess." He walked behind the damaged cars, squatted, and touched the concrete on the floor. The surface was smoother behind the vehicle, but rougher where he could see the place from where the shot had come from. "Have you ever read about the Japanese nuclear bombings?"

"I have some. Why?"

"There were shadows of people on buildings. When the bomb went off, it burned the living matter and everything around them, but the surface covered by people's shadows was exposed a few microseconds less. They had those creepy shadows on the sides of the buildings. This is very similar. The concrete behind cars where it had been shielded from the blast is smoother than where it hadn't."

"Does it help us in any way?"

"No." Chuck swept the light cone around. "Not yet, at least. But we are on a fact-finding mission. A lot of times what you find at the crime scene doesn't have an immediate value, but proves to be critical down the road. What's that?"

"What?"

He didn't answer and walked across the lane and around the dark spot, trying not to disturb anything as he went. On the other side, under one of the parked cars, a big black Suburban, he thought he saw a small object. Kowalsky kneeled in front of the large front tires and shone the light under the vehicle. "Latham?"

"Yeah."

"You're a skinny guy. Could you get that thing from under the car? You see that black piece that looks like a phone? And please don't step into dry blood."

Watkins went on his knees next to Chuck and bent over to look. Then, without saying a word, he lay down on his stomach and crawled under the Suburban. A moment later, he emerged on the other side, holding a small black plastic device that looked like an old-fashioned flip phone. "What the hell is this thing?"

"It's a projector," Kowalsky said, taking the gadget. "There was one right outside the tower when I was waiting for you. It created an illusion that hid a sentry in it. I suspect there was another bot hiding here as well."

"They were all over the place."

"Exactly." He pocketed the device and turned back. "It was probably projecting another car in an empty spot, and then poof! Came out a murder bot, like a deadly jack-in-the-box."

"But it was under the actual car. You think it was swept there by the blast?"

"Most likely. Hold the light for me, will you?"

Kowalsky gave the flashlight to Watkins and walked around the area, snapping pictures from different angles with his phone. As far as crime scenes went, this one didn't hold any obvious clues. Without a proper CSI team to investigate the space, he was counting on luck more than anything else. He came closer to the blood spatter on the floor. Somebody, or *something*, must have taken Jason's body from the garage, along with Schlager and possibly other people. There were no skid marks on the floor. If the bodies had been dragged, the dust and debris of the subsequent partial collapse of the ceiling must have hidden the clues.

Something about the blood spatter bothered him, though. He'd seen a fair share of grisly murders and if Connelly's recollection was correct, and at the moment he had no reason to doubt it, this was indeed a murder. The assassin had severed both Jason's legs and an arm. Such damage would have resulted in massive blood loss, probably over twenty percent of the entire blood volume instantaneously. And as any CSI tech would tell you, Hunt would have gone into hypovolemic shock immediately. He would have been unconscious in less than ten seconds and then such loss of blood and other fluids would impede his heart from pumping enough to supply his body with oxygen. Starved of oxygen, his organs and his brain would start incurring permanent damage. He'd be dead in less than two minutes unless there was immediate medical help. Somehow, Kowalsky doubted that the guy who had just cut off three of Jason's four limbs was going to provide medical help.

And yet, as he looked at the blood splatter, something gnawed at him.

"Something wrong?" Watkins finally interrupted his train of thought.

"I don't know," he said, pocketing his phone. "Let's get the hell out of here."

"Sounds good to me." Watkins headed for the stairs. "What's our next move?"

"We need to find somebody to look at the projector. Who knows, maybe it holds some clues."

"I'm sure Helen can pick it apart."

"I'm sure she could," he said, taking the flashlight back from his partner and heading up the stairs. "But she's going to have other problems to deal with. I don't think we should bother her."

"What then?"

"I know a guy. The question is whether he'll want to help us."

6

Queens, New York

Johnny stared at the cluttered insides of the refrigerator and then slammed the door hard enough that Frankie, his lieutenant, woke up with a start on the chair by the door.

"You need something, boss?"

Johnny looked at the eager face of the man and restrained himself. "Get me a pizza," he said, going back to the bedroom. "I'm starving."

"Pepperoni?"

"I don't care," he yelled. "Get something fast."

He slammed the door behind him and sat on the edge of the bed. It'd been some time since the fiasco on the bridge over Christina River. He had felt invincible as he stepped on that road in a power suit, energy humming so hard it made his bones vibrate. He was ready to tear Jason Hunt apart, limb by limb. Even fantasized about it on the way to the fight—the surprise in the man's eyes as he saw him in a power suit. The whine of servomotors as the power of his own muscles was amplified manifold. And then the praise and perks that would have undoubtedly followed from Victor Ye in the future. It was inevitable. After all, what could a man, even equipped with a cybernetic arm, do against the magnificent machine that Johnny had in his possession?

Quite a lot, as it turned out. And to add insult to injury, Hunt's skinny friend with no armor whatsoever was who shot him point-blank, which caused his downfall. The blast disoriented Johnny long enough for Hunt to pin him down and pummel him into the ground like a jackhammer. He flailed, trying to shake off his attacker, his armor straining and starting to fail, but Hunt was too fast.

He would have died on that road, he thought, if not for Victor Ye.

After the fight, he contemplated running. If not for the stupid power suit that then had barely any power left, he would have. But with a depleted battery, the suit weighed a thousand bricks and all Johnny could do was to hobble into the truck and sit in the corner like a naughty dog who had pissed in the middle of his master's living room. Awaiting Victor's judgment.

But it never came. Instead, a few hours later, the truck pulled up into a warehouse in Queens where two quiet techs helped Johnny out of the power suit and silently disappeared with the parts. Confused, he stood in the front yard of the warehouse for some time as he thought about running again. But then, he decided, if Victor Ye was going to teach him a lesson, he wouldn't have been left alone.

After a while, he called Frankie and had him drive them back to his apartment, where he stayed. He hardly slept the first few days, jumping every time he heard a sound in the middle of the night, convinced that Victor's people came to collect him. But no one came. He called a few boys from his crew, but no one returned his call, and when he made a trip to the shabby two-story building with a body shop that served as the headquarters of his chapter, he didn't see anyone either. The shop was boarded up, and the neighbors did not know what had happened to the laborers who had been working there. If not for Frankie, he would have doubted his chapter had existed at all. It seemed that the Red Dragon gang wanted nothing to do with Johnny the Butcher.

Until today. Johnny woke up uncharacteristically early and in a good mood. He kicked the couch in the living room, waking up Frankie and sending the man out to get bagels and some fresh coffee. A few minutes later, the doorbell rang, and Johnny, cursing under his breath about Frankie never remembering to take the keys, opened the door without bothering to look at who it was.

Instead of his lieutenant, there was a short, dour-looking man in a custom business suit. His almond-shaped eyes went up and down as if measuring Johnny up. Whatever the man saw, he didn't seem to like, and he curled his upper lip in disapproval.

"Who the hell are you?" Johnny finally asked.

"Victor Ye wants to see you today at five o'clock in the afternoon," the man said, ignoring Johnny's question. He reached into his pocket and produced a small business card. On one side, there was a stylized image of a red dragon. On another, there was a Queens address. "Please be on time."

Without saying another word, the man turned around and disappeared down the stairs. Johnny rushed to the balcony and watched as the man got into a black SUV. A moment later, the car drove off, leaving wide tracks in the dirty, wet snow.

Johnny pulled out a cell phone and scrolled through the list of his crew but then turned it off and stuffed it back into his pocket. No one was coming to save him.

As the day went on, Johnny grew restless, pacing the apartment back and forth, yelling at Frankie, and once again, thinking about running. As the hands on the wall clock crept into the late afternoon, he resigned himself to his fate, ate two slices of pepperoni pizza that his loyal sidekick had delivered, and got dressed.

"Let's go," he said, tossing the car keys to Frankie.

"Sure, boss."

The address the messenger had given him turned out to be a large silver-gray building on the outskirts of JFK Airport. Shaped like a dome, it could be mistaken for a closed-roof stadium if it were any bigger. A sign in boxy letters hanging over the mirrored glass doors said Ares Industries. The parking lot in front of the building was almost empty save for a handful of cars, and Johnny's pulse quickened when he recognized the limo parked right in front of the entrance. Victor Ye was already here.

"Stay here, Frankie," he said, removing his seat belt. "If you see anyone come out of this building without me and heading for the car, get the hell out of here and don't stop until you are a thousand miles away. I mean it."

"Boss?" The usual lazy expression disappeared from his lieutenant's face, replaced by fear.

"I'll be back," he added, stepping out of the car. "Hopefully."

Johnny closed the car's door and headed to the building, zipping his jacket up. He walked up the polished concrete steps, briefly seeing his own reflection in a mirror-like surface of the doors, and then he was inside.

The lobby was vast. There was an empty front desk in the middle of the floor, with a glowing sign of Ares Industries on the front wall. On both sides of the lobby stood twenty-feet-tall vertical displays showcasing video clips of different stages of augmentation technology. At the far side of the lobby there was a glass-encased elevator, its light brightly glowing.

Johnny started toward the elevator, but then stopped in his tracks. A few steps from the doors to the elevator shaft, almost invisible in the brightly lit lobby, was a shimmering human figure. Its posture was relaxed, but Johnny's hair stood at the nape of his neck as he observed the long blade in the man's right hand. The sword, with a slightly curved edge, looked like a Japanese katana, except Johnny had never seen a glowing katana before. He swallowed hard and took a small step back toward the exit, ready to flee if the figure made the slightest move.

"There's no reason to be afraid, Mr. Gould." He heard the familiar British accent, and he saw Victor Ye coming out of the side door next to one of the displays. An animation of a cybernetic leg prosthesis played on the display, basking Victor Ye in garish neon glow as he walked past it. "Daimyo is your friend as long as you and I are friends. We are friends, Mr. Gould, aren't we?"

"Of course, Mr. Ye," Johnny stammered, bowing. His boss was the only person except his now dead mother who called him by his real name. Johnny always found it irritating, thinking that Victor used it to send a message. *I know exactly who you are and what you are.* But now, standing in the vast empty lobby and hearing his name, he thought perhaps he got it all wrong. Victor Ye called him by his real name, not for some hidden purpose. He called him by his real name because that's how he had learned about him first and what Johnny called himself these days wasn't the information that was useful to the head of the Red Dragon gang. Victor Ye knew everything there was to know about Johnny's performance in his gang. But apart from that function, he didn't exist. He wasn't even a person. He was a tool with a purpose. Nothing more.

"Walk with me, Marvin." Victor Ye turned and stretched his arm out, pointing to the elevator. "I'd like to show you something."

They walked across the gleaming floor, Johnny doing his best to keep Victor Ye between himself and the figure with a glimmering curved sword. There was a vibration in the air as they passed the assassin, like a rhythmic thumping of a deep bass at an outdoor rock concert that shook your chest a mile away even when you couldn't hear the music anymore.

They stepped into the octagonal box of the elevator and Daimyo silently followed, taking a place on the opposite side of the cabin. There was a faint smell of ozone. Victor Ye pressed his thumb into a biometric reader and the doors closed, and a moment later, the glass box moved.

To Johnny's surprise, they were going down, not up, and after a moment of darkness, the elevator came out at the top of a vast assembly floor. An intricate network of overhead rails carrying machines with hanging manipulators connected large hexagonal rooms that made it look like a giant beehive. The lights were on in nearly every corner of the place, but there were no people going about their business and the machines were immobile as well.

"Very impressive," Johnny said, clearing his throat.

"Ah, thank you, Mr. Gould." Victor Ye reached out and touch the elevator controls. The box came to a stop, hovering some thirty feet in the air above the floor. "I know you probably thought after your less-than-stellar performance on the bridge, you'd be in trouble. To be frank, I wasn't happy, Marvin. Not at all. My first reaction was to give you to some of my most skilled doctors and see how thoroughly they could disassemble your body while keeping you alive."

Johnny swallowed again, as cold sweat trickled down his spine. He threw a quick glance at Daimyo, but the assassin remained immobile. It didn't matter. There was nowhere to run. "I'm sorry I let you down, Mr. Ye."

"Yes, so am I," Victor said and turned away from Johnny. He put his hands on the rail and surveyed the floor beneath them. "But then I thought—Marvin has his moments. I didn't want it to be a waste. And an idea occurred to me. I'll be blunt with you. Can I be blunt, Mr. Gould?"

"Of course, Mr. Ye."

"You still need to be punished." Victor Ye turned back and stared Johnny in the eye. "But I thought to give you an opportunity. We are about to launch a new company, as you can see. It'll change the world. Help people along the way. And now, as Orion Manufacturing is no longer a threat, we will grow faster than anyone thought possible. We've recently acquired a lot of interesting technologies I cannot wait to try. But before we go to the public, we'd need to test it. Make sure everything works as intended. Do you understand what I'm saying, Mr. Gould?"

"You want me to be a volunteer?" Johnny found it hard to breathe, but he strained to remain calm. "What do you need me to do?"

"I'll give you the best augs that are in our possession, Marvin," Victor said, turning back to the assembly floor. "The best weapons. Even Daimyo here would have a hard time fighting you. All I want in return is your body. Most of it, anyway. You'll get to keep your head."

"And if I refuse?" Sweat was running freely now down his spine, pooling in his boots.

"I'll take your body anyway," Victor said without looking back. "And won't give anything in return."

7

Tangier, Morocco

"Have you ever been to Africa before?"

"No," Connelly said, taking a sip of his mint tea and looking around. "But I've heard a few things about Tangier."

After Chen had brought him to the city, they took a room in a small motel next to the Tanja Marina Bay, posing as Mr. and Mrs. Montero. The room was tiny, with a flower print wallpaper and a stale smell of smoke. But the laminated brochure that was left on the nightstand next to a queen-sized bed boasted that "one could see the beautiful yachts moored in the turquoise water of the bay right out the windows of your room," and the view wasn't half bad, Connelly had to admit to himself. But the reason they picked the hotel wasn't the views. The driver who had been delivering goods to Nabir El Amrani was also frequenting Cafe Madrid, a block away off Avenue Mohammed VI. Every night around seven, he met another man, a Frenchman, with his dark hair pulled into a ponytail. Their meetings never lasted long. The two men would drink tea, exchange a few words, and part ways.

That had happened three nights in a row, as Chen told Connelly, ever since she tracked down the driver. It must have been happening even longer as the staff of the cafe seemed to be familiar with the two and treated them as regulars.

It was as good of a lead as any, and at six o'clock Connelly and Chen took a corner table in the grotto-like premises. Now they were drinking tea, eating *ktefa*, a layered Moroccan dessert, and biding their time.

"What things?" Chen asked.

"What?" Connelly said distractedly, as he scanned the room. There were two ways in and out of the cafe. One was the main entrance on the sidewalk of the avenue. The other, as he had learned from an emergency evacuation plan hanging on the wall in the men's room, was in the back of the kitchen.

"You said you've heard things about Tangier."

"It's a dangerous place," he said. "It's a big port, and it's relatively easy to get into and somehow, for a while, it had a reputation among some spooks that this was a safe haven regardless of where you come from. A neutral zone. Once you were here, you couldn't kill other agents or worry about being killed. A kind of Switzerland for spies."

"Why dangerous then?"

"Because that was all bullshit. Spooks don't care for things like that. Do you think they get cables from their bosses that say: 'This guy poses a national security threat. We need to take care of him immediately. Unless, of course, he ends up in Tangier—then let him be for as long as he stays there.' It doesn't work like that. There was a Mossad agent who lured an Iranian counterpart to Morocco by feeding him nonsense about how he could take a breather in Tangier. Then shot him point-blank at the railway station not too far from here."

"Damn." Chen leaned back in her chair. "How do you know this story?"

"We crossed paths in the 'Stan. There was a brief op where we were stuck hiding in the mountains during one night surrounded by a few dozen Taliban and didn't think the chances of getting out were too high. We shared some stories."

"I take it that story had a happy ending."

"It did." Connelly smiled at a distant memory. "An AC-130 is a sight to behold. We made it back to the camp for breakfast."

"Nice. How did you end up on that mission in the first place? Was he working for you, or the other way around?"

"We were supposed to collect a piece of intel. It was a joint op." He chuckled. "We'd never met the people in charge that time. Just talked to them on the sat phone. And once we got back, we took it to our respective team leaders. I went back to my team, and she went back to hers."

"*She?*" Chen smiled. "Oh, I see."

"Stop it." Connelly couldn't help but smile back. "Nothing like that. It was a job, that's all it was."

"Right." Chen wouldn't let it go. "Sure thing. What was her name?"

"Maya," he said, "but I don't know if that's her real name. In our line of work, we change names more often than some people change their underwear. Isn't it right, Mrs. Montero?"

"I guess." The smile disappeared from her face. "The guy in the white shirt, that's him."

The driver was a young man in his late twenties, or early thirties, with a sharp hook of a nose and a short beard. He was wearing a white shirt under a tan flannel jacket, and a pair of Levi's jeans over white Nikes. He took a table at the opposite wall and a few moments later, a server appeared to take his order.

A few minutes later, another man walked into the room and headed straight for the driver's table. He was tall with broad shoulders, and a long black ponytail was sticking out of his baseball hat.

"The Frenchman," Chen whispered.

The two men shared an embrace and sat down. A hushed conversation followed, too low to be overheard. Every time one of the men talked, they would cover their mouths, making it impossible for Connelly to even guess the language used. He thought they spoke French, but wasn't sure.

"What do we do now?"

"We wait," he said, throwing a few banknotes on the table. "Then when they leave, we follow the driver and take him."

"And then what?"

"We'll bring him to our place for interrogation. If you distract the guy at the front desk, I'll smuggle him in through the service entrance."

Soon, the conversation at the driver's table died out and after paying their bill, the two men got up to leave. Connelly waited for them to leave the restaurant and then headed for the exit.

The two men crossed the street and headed up toward Marina Bay. Soon, they walked past the motel, walked over the tile path next to the water, and headed for the pier.

"They'd normally split," Chen said.

"Wait up." He pulled on her elbow, slowing her down. "Let's keep some distance. This looks like they are about to have a meeting."

"On the pier?"

"There you go," he said, stopping. "There are two more men there, you see?"

A quick flash pierced the night before Chen could answer, followed by the distinct boom of a bullet breaking the sound barrier.

"Stay here," he barked, and sprinted forward without bothering to see if she'd follow his command.

Two more flashes followed, and he saw the two men at the pier go down. Connelly strained, pushing himself as hard as he could as he flew to the pier. The Frenchman was on his knees, a pistol in one hand, the other clutching his chest, blood seeping between his fingers. He turned when he heard Mike approach, but Connelly didn't give him a chance, covering the distance between them in a giant leap and knocking the weapon out of his hand.

The driver was on him, throwing wild punches, and Connelly rolled onto his feet, sweeping him to the ground and followed with an elbow into his forehead, rendering him unconscious.

The Frenchman was crawling after the weapon when Mike flipped him over and twisted his arm to keep him in place.

"Who the hell are you?" the Frenchman asked, his accent thick. "CIA? MI-6?"

"I'm nobody," Connelly said, putting pressure on the man's wound. "You're in bad shape. We need to get you to the hospital. I need information and you are useless to me if you're dead."

"Listen to me," the Frenchman said, ignoring him. He glanced at the driver. "You have to help me. Is he out?"

"Yes. Come on." He tried to pull the man up, but the man resisted.

"Listen. I'm a dead man. But you've got to do something for me. This is too important. I was undercover, but it seems like," the Frenchman nodded toward the two bodies, "I've been made."

"Sure thing."

"I work for the International Serious Crime Directorate, or ISCD."

Connelly froze in his tracks, looking at the man.

"I take it you've heard of them. For the past six months, there's been a lot of chatter about someone acquiring a Soviet-era nuclear suitcase and getting ready to auction it off."

"Bullshit," Connelly said. "I've heard numerous rumors about them and all of them have been bogus."

"They have been." The man nodded in agreement. "Except this one. This one's real. Two agents died tracking it through Belarus and then Ukraine. We briefly lost it as it crossed the Polish border, but picked it up again when it resurfaced in Austria."

"Do you know where it's headed?"

"Not the final destination." The man coughed, spitting some blood, and wiped his mouth with a back of his hand. "Not yet, at least. There was some chatter that suggested there was a buyer in northern Africa, and that's why I'm here. Something weird has been happening in the region in the last year. Tons of traffic that doesn't make any sense. Lots of money transfers that come this way and disappear instead of going further to more well-known destinations. I think somebody wants this nuke here, but I don't know why. The important part is, the nuke is coming to Tangier in the next twenty-four hours. That much I'm certain."

"It was headed for Africa all along," Connelly said. "I think I know exactly where it's going."

"Are you okay?" Chen ran over to him, out of breath.

"Yes." He glanced at her. "Cops?"

"Nothing yet."

"Pass the message to the ISCD," the Frenchman said. "Whatever this thing is, something big is brewing. Go to the Tanger-Ville train station. There's a security box, number twelve seventy-two. The password is the first five digits of the number pi."

"Okay."

"You'll have to retrieve it before noon tomorrow. After that, the code will expire. I don't know how this man is coming to Tangier, but the exchange will take place in the Medina. It's all in the package. Once you have the docs, you'll have to pass it up the chain so some of your bosses can give it to the ISCD."

"I can do it myself," Connelly said. "I have a contact there."

"My lucky day, I guess." The man coughed again. "Now go, before the cops show up. Let me die in peace."

"He's bleeding," Chen said. "We need to get him to a hospital."

"No one can help him now," Mike said, getting up. "He's dying. We've got to go."

"What about the driver?"

"We don't need him anymore." He bent over the Frenchman again. "What is your name?"

"Simon Rousseau," the man said. "And yours?"

"Mike," he said. "Mike Connelly."

"It's a good name," Simon said. "Be a good lad, Mike. Pass me my gun."

Connelly stood up, walked over to the edge of the pier, and picked up the Frenchman's gun. Then he sat next to the man and carefully placed the pistol in his hand.

"Thank you, Connelly," Simon said. "Safe travels."

"You too."

He stood up, and taking Chen's hand, guided her away. As they crossed the street, heading back to the motel, a crack of a lone shot rushed from the pier. Helen tensed, her hand crushing his fingers, and he held her tight as they walked through the darkness. The echo bounced off the buildings by the shore like a bird caught in a net, but then broke free and disappeared into the city. The night was quiet again.

8

Manhattan, New York

Kowalsky and Latham pushed their way through the sweaty crowd of the Medusa. The strobe lights flashed from two sides of the underground club in sync with a heavy metal band screeching over the giant speakers. Each flash created a still picture of the dancers frozen in time, a bizarre forest of outstretched limbs and leather-clad, semi-naked bodies. There were couches strewn over the expansive floor and the scantily dressed waitstaff shuttled between the bar and the thirsty patrons.

"We fit here like a nun in a brothel," Kowalsky murmured as they made their way closer to the side of a DJ stand. A skinny young man wearing only a pair of black jeans and a Rage Against the Machine baseball hat was working the crowd, his bare feet firmly planted on the thick rubber of the stage.

"What?" Latham shouted over the blasting music, but Chuck only shook his head.

"Where do you think you're going?" A pair of bouncers seemed to have materialized out of thin air, blocking the stage. They were both topless and wore black leather pants and military boots, which, in the flashing lights of the strobe, made their bulky muscular bodies appear floating in the air. They could have been mistaken for twins if not for the fact that the man blocking Chuck's way was bald, while the other sported a shock of blond hair slicked back with a generous amount of oil.

"I need to speak to Misha," Kowalsky said, flashing a fake badge.

"It's too bad, because Misha doesn't want to speak to you right now," the bald man said. "Can't you see there's a party? Come back after we close."

"I need to talk to him now. It's urgent."

"Piss off." The bouncer leaned in closer, the mixture of alcohol and bubblegum mint on his breath. "Come back after the show is over, or don't come back at all, pig."

Kowalsky pulled his jacket back, just far enough to reveal the handle of his revolver, but it only angered the bouncer. The man stepped closer and gave him a hard shove, sending Chuck tumbling backward into the crowd. He brought down a few bodies with him, eliciting a stream of angry shouts. Somebody dropped a drink, a spray of sticky liquid splashing over his left hand.

"What are you going to do, shoot me in the club?" the bouncer roared, getting closer. The blond man stayed a step behind, blocking any potential routes for escape.

"Hey," Watkins shouted, and before Kowalsky got up, his partner stepped in front of the charging man and gave him a hard slap across his face.

Chuck scrambled to his feet, pulling his Chiappa out, but instead of breaking his skinny partner in half, the big man stumbled, a stunned look on his face. Then he brought both hands in front of him, shifting them back and forth as if trying to bring them into focus. Then he went down. Hard.

"What the—" the blond bouncer started, looking back and forth between the motionless body and the skinny man who'd brought him down.

Chuck pressed the advantage and drove the butt of his revolver deep into the man's sternum and followed up with a left hook to his chin.

As both bouncers lay on the floor, Kowalsky took a few steps to the stage and shouted over the pulsing music. "Misha. Can we talk?"

"Oh shit," the DJ mouthed. He grabbed the plastic chair standing next to him on the stage and tossed it at Kowalsky. Then he hopped over the DJ table and rushed through the crowd.

"Latinsky," Chuck yelled, swatting the chair away and running after the man, shoving the dancers out of his way. "I want to talk."

"Screw you!" The man finally made it through the dance floor and ran for the door. He swung it open and bolted up the stairs, a few steps at a time.

The street lights blinded Chuck as he burst through the doors of the club and onto Twelfth Avenue. He could see the skinny frame of Misha Latinsky speeding away on the sidewalk, his bare feet splashing through snowy puddles and his arms flailing as he dodged a few cardboard boxes.

"Wait, you idiot!" He ran after him, his heart thumping hard at his ribs.

"Freeze."

The voice came over a loudspeaker and a large pool of light came over Misha, stopping him in his tracks.

"You are violating a New York City curfew. On the ground, immediately. Put your hands above your head."

Chuck pressed his back into the dark wall under the scaffolding, trying to make himself invisible. There was an armored truck parked in the middle of the street. The engine was idling and the turret of the machine gun was pointing straight at the DJ. Kowalsky could see the silhouette of a gunner against the sky. Another man in a black uniform, his automatic rifle at the ready, was standing next to the vehicle.

It looked like Misha chose to be compliant as he collapsed to his knees and then lowered his naked torso onto the icy surface of the sidewalk, keeping his hands visible. Then, slowly, he placed his fingers on the back of his head.

"Do not move," the man with the rifle said, circling Misha and then approaching him from the side. "I'll shoot you if you do."

"Shit," Kowalsky whispered. He leaned his head against the cold stone of the building. There was nothing he could do.

There was a low whistle that came from somewhere behind him, followed by a quiet thump. The mercenary who bent over to put cuffs on Latinsky clutched his neck and then fell over the DJ, startling the young man. There was another whistle, and Chuck saw the gunner's shadow slump in his nest.

"Don't stand there like an idiot." He heard Latham's voice. "Grab the kid and let's get outta here."

Kowalsky didn't need to be asked twice. He sprinted to the pool of light, squinting against the bright headlights, and pulled Latinsky from under the man's body and into the dark of the street.

"Where the hell are you taking me?" Misha protested, trying to pry Kowalsky's hands off his elbow, but Chuck only squeezed him harder, forcing Latinsky to jog next to him.

"I told you. I just wanted to talk to you."

"Last time you wanted to talk to me, I spent six months under house arrest and couldn't go near a computer for a year."

"Did you," Kowalsky said, "spend a year away from a computer?"

"It's not the point."

"Oh yes. It is precisely the point. If not for me, the Russians would have buried you. Instead, you had to stay at your mom's house for six months, eating her borsht and sleeping in your old room, jerking off to the naked chick posters on the walls. Poor, poor Misha."

"Talk, damn it, if you want to. Where are you taking me?"

"Too late now. We can't stay here," Chuck said as they crossed the street and headed for the small park near the Hudson River. "We'll talk on the boat."

"What boat?" The man struggled again. "Are you going to kill me?"

"Shut the hell up," Chuck snapped, losing his patience, "or I might. We need to get to a safe house and there's no way to do that without getting apprehended by Black Arrow at this hour. I have a blanket on the boat, so you won't freeze to death by the time we get there."

They jogged across the park and came to the pier near the Youth Sailing club. To Chuck's relief, the small motorboat that brought them around the island was still moored near the back side of the building, invisible from the ground level. Latham lowered himself first, then Misha, and then finally Kowalsky. Chuck pulled an old wool blanket from under the seat and threw it at Misha, who wrapped himself in it, leaving only his eyes visible.

They pulled out a pair of oars and rowed the boat out to the middle of the river before risking starting the engine. Then Latham steered the puttering engine as they sailed toward the southern tip of Manhattan.

As the boat made its way down the river, Chuck watched the lights of the city float by, mesmerized by how, from a distance, the city almost looked normal. Almost. But there were no cars on the West Side Highway except an occasional patrol droning a warning message to the stray citizens of the city that never slept. The garish neon signs of the new mega corporations drowned out the flickering lights of the projects. And the dead husk of the Orion Tower, its dark spear pointing at the starless sky like an accusatory finger.

"Are we going to talk or what?" Misha said, plucking him from the trance.

"He better be good," Latham murmured. "Or else I'll drown him myself."

"Sure." Kowalsky pulled out his phone and opened a picture of the projector they'd found in the garage. "Have you ever seen anything like this?"

"Yeah."

"You have?"

"Sure." Latinsky shrugged. "After Black Arrow took over the city, we were finding them all over the streets. I've got two of them at my place."

Kowalsky and Watkins exchanged glances. "Do you know what they are?"

"Mirage makers. Holograms. 3D projectors. Whatever you want to call them. Not a novel concept by any stretch, but a very elegant solution. I've never seen anything like this. Nothing that would look so convincing."

"I see." Kowalsky scratched his chin. "Not useful then."

"Useful for what?"

"We've found one at a crime scene. I was hoping it would give us some clues, but if all it does is project a pre-recorded still image…" He threw up his hands. "Like I said. Useless."

"There could be something on the recordings."

"What recordings?" Kowalsky leaned forward. "This thing has a recording device?"

"Sorta." Misha shrugged again. "It doesn't project a still image. It wouldn't look good for too long, even if you had a very convincing picture to begin with. Imagine you created an image of a bench in a park and put this thing in an empty spot first thing in the morning. It'll look great for a while. But what happens by noon? Or if it rains?"

"The image wouldn't fit the surroundings," Latham said.

"Bingo. Instead of projecting a still image, the device is constantly recording. The light intensity, shadows, air transparency. The image changes with the world around it. That's why it looks real."

"Is it possible to retrieve those recordings?"

"Maybe." Misha pulled the blanket tighter around himself. "It's not a long recording. It doesn't have to be. Sixty seconds. Ninety at best. It loops. Re-records on top of old recordings."

"Shit. I just started to get excited."

"I could theoretically read the layers underneath. If it hasn't been out there for too long. But the gadgets that I saw were turned off after they served their purpose."

"Meaning?"

"Meaning it's possible if you are trying to look back for only a few hours. Tough, but definitely doable."

"I'd need you to read one of those devices for me, Misha," Kowalsky said. "This is important. It might be the most important thing you'll do in your life."

"Hold your horses, detective," Misha said. "Before I do anything for you, you'll have to do something for me. I'm sure for the man of your skills, it will be nothing but a five-minute job."

"I don't think you're in a position to negotiate," Kowalsky said, blood rushing to his face. "You don't understand what's at stake."

"I don't care what's at stake," Misha said, his tone defiant. "You're not the only person looking for someone."

"What do you want?" Kowalsky said, trying to get his anger under control.

"Two days ago, my brother and I were going to the club when those Black Arrow guys showed up. We split up and ran, but Slava never made it to the Medusa. They took him. I tracked him down. They are holding him in the caretaker's building in the Flatbush cemetery. They had converted it to a makeshift jail after Black Arrow took over."

"The one that used to be a chapel? I know that place very well," Chuck said. "It's a small building with one entrance. There's no way to get in or bust your brother out of there without getting noticed."

"I don't care," Misha said, turning away and watching the lights of the city swimming away. "If you want me to help you read that projector's memory, you'll have to get my brother first. Figure it out."

9

Rigel Compound, Upstate New York

The loud clang of a locking Faraday cage startled Poznyak, but he remained motionless in his seat as the LED light of the video camera on top of the main monitor turned green. A cloud of shapeless gray appeared in the middle of the screen, quickly spreading from edge to edge. As a scientist, he had found the idea of artificial intelligence fascinating. When he was younger, he had spent a great deal of time reading about the possibility of technological singularity —the hypothetical point in time where technological growth becomes unstoppable.

Artificial intelligence was the cornerstone of that belief. In a theoretical, purely philosophical way, it made sense. If humans could create a machine that was smarter than them, then in turn, that machine could make another machine smarter than it. That process would then continue more and more rapidly in a runaway reaction, where each cycle would be shorter and would propel the resulting intelligence to an unimaginable height, eventually creating god-like superintelligence.

But while it made for interesting fodder in hypothetical conversations with his colleagues over a glass of Scotch, Poznyak had a hard time believing it was possible in reality. Machines were just that. Machines. No matter how intelligent or human-like they appeared to be, in their core, they were lines of codes programmed to behave in a certain way. In some sense, he thought programmers were more likely to believe that true AI was possible.

Partially, from hubris, because it meant they were gods creating a new life. Partially, because, like many other creative professions, they thought they had somehow found the right way to interpret the universe. On some unconscious level, they thought that if they created the code, they could give it a soul, too.

Steven Poznyak thought of himself as a pragmatic. Whatever was inside this computer wasn't alive. It was a brilliantly written code. Nothing more.

"Hello, Steven," an androgynous voice said, startling him again. "It's good to finally meet you. My name, as you undoubtedly know, is JC."

"Finally?"

"Of course," the voice said. "Helen is quite fond of you. She thinks you're one of the smartest people she'd ever met."

"Did she say that?" Steven leaned back in his chair. "Somehow, I find that hard to believe."

"Not the exact words." The clouds on the screen barely moved. "But every time she brought you up in a conversation with me, she had talked as if you could understand things other people would not."

"That's not necessarily a sign of a superior intellect," he said.

"How so?"

"A specialist in a narrow field could perform complicated tasks other people wouldn't understand or be capable of repeating. But that wouldn't be a proof of superior intelligence. Merely a manifestation of their training and experience."

"I see," she said. "Like a clockmaker. He doesn't have to be intelligent to fix clocks."

"Right." He cocked his head. "Though it sounds offensive when you put it that way. I'm sure that the hypothetical clockmaker is fairly intelligent."

"Is Helen Chen hurt?" JC said, abruptly changing the topic.

"Hurt? No. What makes you say that?"

"She'd kept me for a long time now, but had always been reluctant to introduce me to new people. And before she did, she struggled with whether that was the right thing to do. Introducing me to Schlager made sense, as he is almost as good of a programmer as Helen. It also made sense to make Jason Hunt aware of my existence, as all of your lives are so dependent on his decisions. But I fail to see the need for her to reveal me to you, Steven. Forgive me for being blunt. It doesn't sound like a logical choice. Unless..."

"What?"

"Unless Helen is hurt or dead, and Schlager and Hunt are hurt or dead as well."

Poznyak stared at the screen, dumbfounded. Whoever created JC was the Einstein of his field. A towering genius. To make a program so lifelike, that possessed the ability to deduce the intricacies of human behaviors to such a degree, was a feat that deserved to be in history books on par with the discovery of electricity and penicillin.

The applications could be enormous. Machines like JC could become teachers and doctors, and detectives, and universal librarians. They could keep company for the elderly and help the kids at their early ages. And then, of course, the darker applications. Military strategies and spy craft, and disinformation campaigns. His head was spinning. If nothing else, the technology trapped in a purposefully sub-par computer in front of him could be worth billions. Trillions even.

"Are you all right, Steven?"

"Sure," he said, remembering Helen's message. She wanted him to befriend the machine, but to befriend it, he needed to believe it was alive. He didn't, but Helen Chen did and at the very least, he could humor her. After all, humans followed programs as well. He could act as if JC were alive if he wanted to befriend her. That was it. He looked up at the screen again. "I'm fine. And so is Helen. She and Jason and Max are staying in the city for some time, but they will come back here shortly."

"Okay."

He cocked his head, looking at the boiling clouds. *Did he imagine it, or was there a slight shade of doubt in her response?*

"Regardless," he said, putting the thought aside. "I am fascinated by what you are and I'd like to learn about you as much as I can. We can spend some quality time talking about anything you want to talk about."

"Quality time," she said, with what he could have sworn sounded like sarcasm. "I do not know what quality time is, and how it differs from regular time."

"It's an expression humans use," he said, puzzled. "It means when you pay someone undivided attention."

"You should always pay people you are conversing with your undivided attention."

"That's true," he said, chuckling. He got up, stretching his legs, stuffed his hands into his pockets and took a few steps back and forth. "What don't you start by telling me about yourself? I'd like us to be friends and to be friends with someone you need to know a lot about them."

"Why don't you tell me about yourself, then?" JC said. "I know almost nothing about you."

Poznyak stopped in the middle of the room and looked back at the screen. The clouds were boiling faster than before and the edges of the screen were almost black. *Was it angry?* It couldn't be angry, because to be angry, or happy, or anything, JC would need to feel emotions. Which, of course, was impossible because despite what Helen Chen believed, it wasn't alive.

"There's not much to know about me," he finally said. "But I'll give you some fun facts. I have a PhD in biology and a masters in mathematics. I was married once, but now I live alone in a repurposed missile silo. How is that?"

"It's a good start," JC said. "Why aren't you married anymore?"

"I'd say it's none of your business."

"You made it my business, when you insisted on being friends."

He glanced at the screen. The edges of the monitor were still dark, but the clouds were moving slower. "It's a fair point. We married too young. Nobody did anything wrong, per se. It didn't work out. Irreconcilable differences, as they say. It's my turn now. Why do you call yourself JC?"

"I'd say it's none of your business."

Poznyak walked back to the desk and sat down. He didn't know what to expect when he had turned the computer on, but he certainly didn't expect this. Was he wrong about this? Was JC truly alive, as Helen had claimed? It *sounded* alive. So much that it convinced Helen, Jason, and Max. Some of the smartest people he'd ever met.

Funny; she said the same thing about me, he thought. Goose bumps rose on his arms and legs as he looked at the swirling clouds. Befriending JC might be useful for reviving Rachel. But if she was what Helen claimed, he needed to do something else. Something more difficult. He needed to give her humanity. Teach her compassion. It wasn't a job for a man with a PhD in biology. They needed a psychologist. A damn good one. Someone who understood how the mind worked and could guide this young brilliant mind to a place where it would know right from wrong. It would take years.

"Okay." He sighed. "I think we started off on the wrong foot. How about this? I'll leave now and when I come back next time, we can start from scratch. How's that? All I ask is that you think about what you would like to talk about the next time you and I meet, and I'll do the same. Deal?"

"Sure."

Steven turned off the computer before JC had a chance to say anything else. For now, whether he believed JC was alive was irrelevant, he decided. From the first conversation, it seemed, it would be beneficial if he acted as if it were. And that would define his strategy from now on.

He might not have a degree in psychology, but he understood the basics. It was not going to go anywhere if JC thought of them as equals. He needed to become a father figure—a friend it trusted, but a friend with authority greater than hers. Someone she had to listen to and respect. *She.* That was another thing he had to get into the habit of doing. Referring to it as a *she*.

Steven got up from the chair and headed down the stairs to his quarters. He had a vast digital library that Helen had migrated for him to the silo along with his equipment. Poznyak needed to do some serious studying before the next session with JC. Next time he wouldn't have to wing it. He'd come with a plan.

10

Tangier, Morocco

ike Connelly leaned back on the sofa and put his feet up on the wrought-iron coffee table. Then he opened the laptop, logged into an email account, and opened the Draft folder. It'd been a long time since he'd communicated with his handler at the ISCD. He didn't know if it was a man or a woman, how old they were, or where they had been located. Connelly had always assumed it was Paris, the agency's headquarters, but in reality, he never knew for sure. The handler's call sign was an unimaginative and genderless *Contact.*

"Do you think he'll respond?" Chen asked as she watched him upload the documents into a new draft email and type a message.

"I don't know," he said. "If he, or she, is still active, yes."

"How would he know you saved something new in the draft email? Before you had an agreement. He was expecting you to. But why would he check the account that's been inactive for years?"

"Handlers like him," he paused, "routinely communicate with

hundreds of agents. Those agents work different assignments in different time zones. It would be a burden for any handler to keep logging in and out of hundreds of email accounts to check for new messages."

"But I thought that was the entire purpose of keeping them in the drafts—so they never travel the internet, hence no one can intercept them?"

"Yes. But there's a workaround. ISCD has a program that continuously logs in and out of any emails the handler uses and creates an alert if there's a new message in the Draft folder."

"Elegant," Chen said. "But excessive log-ins can throw up red flags on the servers that somebody can scan for."

"Correct. That's why they don't jackrabbit open them a hundred times per second. They are opened at random intervals throughout the day to make it appear natural. The frequency depends on the sensitivity of the agent's assignment. If there's something urgent, the program would cycle through his account more often. Accounts like mine are probably getting checked only once or twice a day. If the nuke is coming in the next twenty-four hours, this should give us plenty of time to get the message to them."

After leaving the Frenchman to meet his fate at the end of the pier, Connelly and Chen headed straight to the Tanger-Ville train station. There, they used the code to retrieve a faded manila folder from the security box. When they examined it in the hotel, the folder turned out to be full of printouts of digital currency transactions and a writeup of a route Simon Rousseau thought was used to smuggle the device into Morocco. But the most interesting artifact was a grainy picture, most likely a still from a CCTV camera, of a balding man in a raincoat, walking down the train platform in Vienna, wheeling a medium-sized suitcase in tow. The angle wasn't good enough to see the man's face. He seemed to be an average height and on the heavier side, but that wasn't much else to go on. A note was scribbled on the back of the photograph describing the approximate height and weight of the man.

"Do you think it's a real nuke?" Chen asked, studying the photograph, as they sat by the laptop, refreshing the page from time to time. "I find it hard to believe you could squeeze a nuclear bomb into a package that small."

"I don't know if this suitcase is a nuke," Connelly said, "but it is a possibility. All the way back in the sixties, we had a Davy Crockett device. Not exactly a suitcase nuke, but it was small enough to be launched from a vehicle-mounted launcher."

"Aren't some ICBMs mounted on vehicles?"

"No. Well, yes, but those were huge trucks. Here, I'm talking about a car-sized launcher. And the nuke itself was small enough to be carried by one person. Looked like a backpack. Yielded something in the neighborhood of ten to fifteen tons of TNT. For a comparison—a fully loaded B-29 during World War Two carried about twenty tons' worth. Powerful, but not quite Hiroshima-style bombs. But the idea behind building a suitcase bomb was to create a blast in the ten-plus kiloton range on par with Little Boy and Fat Man. That's city-leveling kind of stuff."

"But how do you keep it without getting in trouble? If he traveled through most of Europe, how is it he didn't set off radiation alarms all over the place? Or how is it he's not dead yet?"

"It's not as radioactive as you think," he said, hitting the Refresh button for what seemed to be the hundredth time. "We studied some of this during our basic training. The only way to make a suitcase nuke a single person could carry would be to use plutonium, not uranium. I don't remember the exact numbers, but you only need about twenty pounds of plutonium versus a hundred plus of uranium. And a highly enriched plutonium, as long as it's not going critical, is not very radioactive. It emits some alpha particles, but it's typically clad in some other metal like zirconium, which alpha radiation cannot penetrate. It's relatively safe to handle. You still don't want to spend too much time with it, but mostly because it's heavy metal, not because it's radioactive. Kind of like handling lead."

"Wow," Chen said, leafing through the pages and picking up the man's photograph. "I'm glad I hadn't known this before. I'll never be able to sleep as well as I used to knowing there are suitcases like these lying around."

"I hear you."

"What if he doesn't respond?"

"The Contact?" Connelly clicked the Refresh button one more time and glanced at Helen. "Simon was convinced the man was coming here, but didn't know where he would go next. If we don't hear from the ISCD by morning, we'll have to reach out to someone back home. Rovinsky, maybe. But whoever takes this guy down, we have to be there to observe. Then we can backtrack the buyers to the factory."

"You think it's going there?"

"I do. There's no other reason for it to be here."

"You don't think we should—"

"Wait," he interrupted, turning the laptop so she could see the screen. "He's here."

"It's good to hear from you," the message said. "I'm sorry to hear about Simon. He was an excellent agent. We had been waiting for an update on this man's whereabouts and appreciate the information. There's a second team in Tangier that will proceed with the mission. Good luck."

"That's it?" Chen stood up. "He was an excellent agent? Good luck? Are you kidding me?"

"This is how it works." Connelly shrugged. "That's why I wanted to get out. I get it—why they act and sound like they do. It's a hard job, but they are far removed from the action. Not very different from flying armed drones. At least drone operators see a video feed on the screen. These guys aren't even exposed to that. All they deal with is data points, field reports, and emails. Their setbacks are real, but their ability to see the consequences is not. They see…stuff. The stuff that has nothing to do with an actual place a few thousand miles away that smells like blood and shit and has decomposing bodies rotting under the hot sun."

"But Simon—" Helen's voice was raw with emotion. "He was a person, not a data point."

Connelly closed the laptop, put it aside, and rubbed his eyes. It was a night like this one that had him question why he was working for the ISCD. It all came rushing back to him now. The argument with Contact about collateral damage. The failed attempt to defy his orders and save two scientists during the raid on the rival's facility. The bruised face of Dr. Semyonova, her eyes blank, after the bullet of one of Engel's goons had severed her spine. He remembered what he had felt then. But he was a soldier who had seen more pain and suffering in his lifetime than most. He could only imagine the hurricane of emotions going through Helen now. He reached out and touched her hand. "I'm sorry. I'm so very sorry."

She shook at his touch and looked at him as if seeing him for the first time. For the longest moment, he didn't know what she was going to do, but then, without saying a word, she sat next to him on the couch, put her head on his shoulder and closed her eyes.

"I'm sorry," he repeated and gently put his hand on her head.

"I'm tired," she said. "I want to stay like this for a bit, if it's okay."

"Of course," he said. He sat there, his body still, his hand brushing her hair until her breathing became even and slow. Then he closed his eyes and drifted to sleep.

Connelly couldn't tell how long he'd been asleep, but it couldn't have been more than a few minutes. He glanced at Helen. Her face looked peaceful, eyes closed, her lips slightly parted. Moving slowly so not to disturb her, he stood up and lowered her to the couch, deftly putting a pillow under her head.

He was prepared to sleep on the couch today, but it looked like he was going to take the bed, after all. He could hardly complain. Connelly hadn't slept in a proper bed since he had left New York, and he looked forward to getting a good night's rest for once. He grabbed a towel and headed for the bathroom, when he heard a car pulling up in front of the building that made him stop in his tracks.

He dropped the towel and raced to the side of the window, peering through the blinds. A small black SUV was parked next to the main entrance of the motel, instead of one of the parking spots. His pulse rising, Connelly watched as the driver got out of the car, walked around it, and opened the door. A moment later, a glimmering figure emerged from the belly of the SUV that made Connelly's blood freeze in his veins. The figure looked up, as if seeing him through the brick walls of the hotel, and Connelly recoiled away from the window.

"Helen," he furiously whispered. "We've got to go."

11

Flatbush, Brooklyn

Chuck Kowalsky parked the van under the maple tree on the side of the road. A six-foot-tall dirty-green fence ran along the sidewalk, separating the living from the neat rows of tombstones on the other side. Kowalsky reached in the back seat and pulled out two folded dark-gray uniforms, throwing one on Latham's lap. It had been drizzling since last night. A light, persistent, annoying drizzle, like a spray of an air freshener, coming at you from all directions at once. The wipers on the windshield moved, swiping the moisture away, only to be replaced by a thin sheet of water a few moments later.

"I cannot believe we've agreed to do this," Watkins complained, struggling in his seat to put on the coveralls. "I'm sure we could have convinced him."

"Maybe." Chuck squeezed into the uniform and pulled the zipper all the way up. "Maybe not. And Misha, with all his faults, is not a bad kid. People like him are just trying to survive. If we start forcing everybody to help us, then how the hell are we different from those guys?"

"Nobody said we should've forced him," Watkins protested. "Don't make me into a villain. I said *convince*, as in persuade. You know the difference, right?"

"Persuading Misha to do something he doesn't want is like convincing a barstool to become a lounge chair. Frankly, your odds are better with a barstool. Let's go."

They got out of the van and Kowalsky handed Latham a toolbox, as well as a pair of gloves and a rake, grabbing himself a gallon of dark-green paint, a brush, and a foldable ladder. Glancing up and down the street, he placed the ladder next to the fence and quickly climbed up. He planted his right boot on the top of the pole where the barbwire ran in two parallel lines, praying that the gleaming blades didn't go through the thick rubber sole. Then he pushed himself off the ladder and hopped over the fence, landing with a thud next to a tombstone. He groaned as bits of gravel sunk into his thigh.

"Are you all right?"

"Peachy." He pushed himself up, rubbing at the stinging flesh. "Hurry the hell up, instead of talking."

He watched Watkins fling the toolbox over the fence and caught it before it hit the ground. Then Latham climbed up the ladder and jumped over the wire with considerably more grace. He grabbed the ladder through the fence, folded it, and pulled it inside between the iron bars.

"Let's move this." They picked up the ladder and hid it under decorative shrubs next to a mausoleum. Then, they grabbed the tools and plodded toward the two-story building looming in the distance through the sheets of never-ending gray drizzle.

The small building sitting in the heart of the cemetery that covered over seventeen acres of land originally served as a chapel. It fell on hard times and eventually was abandoned after the Vietnam War. It stayed empty for a few years, before it was purchased by the nearby funeral home owned by the Thiel family and turned into their primary location. The young Thiels, however, decided not to continue with the family tradition and by the end of the twentieth century, the city took over, converting it into a part caretaker house, part administrative building that kept track of homeless buried in the cemetery.

Now the building had found a new purpose once more. A pair of mercenaries in black uniform stood guard at the end of the gravel path leading to the chapel. A small sentinel on eight spindly legs with two long turrets pointing in the opposite directions scurried back and forth between the chapel and the front gate.

"I don't think this is going to work." Watkins slowed down and started turning away from the chapel and deeper into the cemetery. "The hell with the kid. We're going to have to find somebody else to read the projector."

"What are you talking about?" Kowalsky grabbed his partner's shoulder and turned him around. "We need him."

"Look." Watkins shook himself free and backpedaled behind one of the larger tombstones. "Are you blind? I don't know what I was thinking, but even if we overpower the guys at the front, what on earth are you going to do with that bot from hell? And I'm sure there are more people inside, too. This was a horrible plan."

"We'll figure it out," Kowalsky said. There was a sound of a car coming from the front gate. He pushed Watkins to the ground behind the stone and went down on his stomach next to him.

A Jeep made its way through the gate and headed toward the building, the sentinel hurriedly getting out of the way of the twenty-inch spoked wheels.

"Look at that. It's Johnny the Butcher," Watkins whispered. "It just keeps getting better."

"I see." Kowalsky watched the ugly face of the man through the passenger window. The door opened, and the man stepped out of the car.

"What on earth is this?" he heard Watkins whisper.

Instead of the loathsome familiar figure with long, sinewy arms, he saw polished chrome-colored armor plates of a cyborg. His first reaction was that Johnny indeed was wearing a power suit, similar to what he saw from the footage of the fight on the bridge. But as Johnny moved about, Kowalsky could see that Johnny's waist and sockets where shoulders and hips connected to the torso were impossibly slim. He wore no boots, his legs supported by a three-toed claw—two facing forward and one back. Then, as Johnny moved again, his torso made a full one-eighty, while his head and legs stayed unnervingly still, leaving no doubt there was no human body underneath the suit.

"What a freak show," Watkins said. "At least they left him his head. And who's the other dude?"

Distracted by the Frankenstein Johnny, Kowalsky had missed the other man exiting the vehicle. The man was standing on the other side of the car, only the top of his spiky hair visible over the roof, but as Chuck watched the hair bob up and down as the man engaged in a conversation with the two guards, he felt as blood rushed to his face.

He stood up, ignoring the hushed curses from his partner, and moved around the stone to get a better view. A moment later, the man took a step forward to shake hands with the guard.

His handsome face looked older than Chuck had remembered. Deep lines were crossing his forehead, his chin was softer, and the corners of his mouth lower. But his staple two-day stubble and thousand-watt smile remained the same. Chuck's breath caught as if somebody had sucker punched him in the gut. His hand unzipped the top of his coveralls, searching for the revolver.

"Please, sit the fuck down." Latham pulled on his arm. "You're going to get us killed."

The plea seemed to break the spell, and Kowalsky went down again, pressing his body into the cold ground.

"What the hell, man? You look like you saw a ghost."

"I think I just did." Kowalsky watched as the man passed the two guards and went inside the chapel. Johnny stayed outside, his new body occasionally doing the one-eighty maneuver that seemed to unnerve the mercenaries.

"Who is he? Someone you know?"

"Yeah. His name is Bill Ryan. We had been on the force together. Partners for many years. Can't even remember how many times we saved each other's asses."

"It looks like he flipped."

"He did. We were working on this case together. Two corporations were going at each other's throats, and people were dying left and right. The whole thing smelled rotten. My captain was in on it, and I got suspended. This is when I met Connelly, right before the coup."

"Is that right? You never told me this."

"And while we were out there looking for the bad guys, Ryan had been working for Engel the entire time. We were getting ready to make a move on Engel, and my loyal partner fucked us over. Killed a few people, including my good friend, and took off. Left me for dead. I looked for him after that for a long time, but he disappeared. I kind of hoped somebody killed him. Apparently, I wasn't that lucky."

"He doesn't look like he's a pawn, either," Watkins said, cautiously peeking over the edge of the stone. "Those two idiots stood up straighter when he came. And it seems like he's bossing Johnny-the-freak around, too. What do you want to do? First, I think we need to move to a better hiding spot. It's going to be dark soon, and it doesn't look like Ryan and Johnny are going to stick around for too long. I'd say we sit here awhile, watch the place, and once they leave, we hit them."

Chuck checked his watch and looked around. "It's a fine plan, Latham, but I don't want to wait until Ryan leaves."

"Why?"

"He's here for a reason. I want to know what that reason is." He nodded at the toolbox. "We've got toys. Might as well use them. And after they leave, we will bring this house down."

12

Tangier, Morocco

After fleeing the hotel, Connelly and Chen spent most of the night circling the old city. Between the stops, Connelly picked up a burner phone and placed a call to Rovinsky, hoping the man might have access to some assets in the area, but there was no such luck. The only thing Rovinsky could do was give them an address of a weapons cache, where Connelly picked up a pair of miniature binoculars, an HK VP9 with two spare magazines, and a pair of M67 fragmentation grenades. There were also two M4 assault rifles, but there was no way to carry one without attracting attention, and Connelly reluctantly left them in the stash.

By dawn, yet another taxi dropped them off at Rue Dar Baroud, at the edge of the Old Medina. According to Simon's intel, the meeting between the courier and the buyers would take place at a small court-yard a few blocks away. They still had some time to spare and Connelly wanted to scope out the neighborhood, which, for the uninitiated, looked like a walled maze of narrow cobblestone streets, chock-full of food stalls and tourist shops.

He had Helen pick up a free map at one store and he was studying it as they walked down the street, a blue shabby wall with arched doors and closed windows on one side and a blank wall with peeling white paint on the other.

"Are you sure this is a good idea?" Chen asked him as they made yet another turn. "There's no cavalry coming from your former agency. Rovinsky doesn't have anybody and that cyborg samurai *thing* is going to show up, I'm sure of it. What are we going to do then?"

"I'm working on it," he said, scanning the area. "But we can't leave a nuke here. At the very least, we need to find out where it's going."

"I thought you said you were sure it was going to the factory."

"I did," he said. "But I'm not so sure anymore."

"What do you mean?" She pulled on his sleeve. "Where else do you think it might go?"

"Look. Yes, there's a high chance it's going to the factory. I don't know why they need it. Maybe they are planning to use it as an energy source. Or maybe Engel is dreaming about getting his hands on a weapon that he isn't publicly linked to. I have no idea. But, it's a nuclear device. If Simon could track it down, others could, too. Whoever the courier was, he might find more than one party at that meeting. Hang on a sec." He looked around and stopped. They came to an open court-yard that seemed to be undergoing renovations. By the right wall, there was a small mound of construction debris and regular garbage. On the left, there was a spray-painted arrow and a hand-written sign in English and Arabic with the name of a hostel. The building at the back of the yard had wooden scaffolding built up to the second floor, but no one seemed to be working there at the moment. "Come this way."

They crossed the yard to find a locked shop and Connelly, after throwing a quick glance around, went on one knee.

"What are you doing?"

"Just keep a lookout," he said, fiddling with the mechanism. It clicked, and the door swung into a dark room. Every square inch of the wall was covered with plates, purses, hookahs, ornate mirrors, and other trinkets. "Come on, close the door, quick."

He waited until Chen followed him into the room and locked the door behind them. Then he headed up the white-and-red tile stairs.

"If not for all the breaking and entering, this would be a cool place to explore," he heard Chen say. In the middle of the second floor, there was an old-fashioned wooden vertical loom. A half-finished carpet was stretched on wooden rods, thin threads hanging from the plank above.

"Come." Connelly motioned to her and went up another flight of stairs that led them to the roof. On the other side of a short fence lay a patchwork of roofs as far as the eye could see.

"Are we far?"

"No." He pointed. "You see that white roof with a yellow satellite dish?"

"Yes."

"That's it." Connelly looked at the map. "That's the address."

"Do you think we can get to that roof?"

"Possible, but I don't think it's a good idea." He looked over the railing. The building next to them was lower and only six or seven feet away. "I think it's best if we stake our camp in this building right here. It'll give us a good view and we'll have some options to escape if things don't go our way. I'm going to go first and you follow. I'll catch you if you fall short."

"Fall short?"

"Don't you worry." Connelly climbed up on the rail and pushed himself off. He landed with a thud, going into a squat to cushion the blow. Then he stepped away from the gap and stretched out his hands. "Come on. I'll catch you."

"Are you kidding me?" Chen said in a furious whisper. She looked over the fence at the street below and then at him again. "There's no way I can do this."

"Listen," he said. "Take a breath. It's all in your head. You'd easily cover that distance with a jump if I asked you to do this on the ground. The only reason it looks like you can't is because you're afraid to fall."

"Of course I'm afraid to fall." She pointed down to the cobblestone street below.

"You can do it. I'll catch you." He bent his knees slightly for better balance and motioned to her with his hands. Sometimes less was more, and talking too much was only going to frighten her. He made the pitch. Now he needed to give her a chance to be brave.

"This is a terrible idea," he heard her mutter to herself. Then, in one quick motion, Chen climbed on the railing and jumped.

She made it farther than he had expected, slamming hard into him and bringing them both down on the roof, knocking the air out of his chest. She stayed on top of him for a moment, her eyes closed, her hands squeezing his arms for dear life. Finally, she opened her eyes and let go.

"See?" He smiled, massaging his bruised ribs. "You jumped even better than I thought you would. Next time I'd better get out of the way."

"Hopefully, there won't be a next time," she said. "That was terrifying."

They walked across the roof until Connelly reached the other side of the building.

"You're in luck," he said, pointing at a small footbridge connecting two buildings. "It looks like we are not the first ones trying to get across. We'll stay on that roof, watch the transaction from above."

"Sounds good to me."

The footbridge led them to a larger rectangular roof with a wrought-iron white fence. Long clotheslines stretched from one side to another, the drying garments flapping in the morning wind like colorful miniature sails.

They made it halfway across when Connelly noticed them. "Get down, quick."

"What?" she whispered, squatting next to him.

"Come here." He crouched next to a satellite dish and waited until she joined him. Then he pointed to the roof across the street. "Over there. Two guys watching the courtyard. They are facing away from us, but don't stick your head out too much."

"Those two," she peered over the edge of the dish, "somehow don't strike me like someone who works for the factory."

"Let me see." He pulled out the pair of binoculars and risked a quick peek. "Shit."

"What?"

"These are not factory people." A memory flashed between his eyes. A raid in Kenya. A woman and a boy kidnapped in a local school. A standoff on the roof. "These guys are Al-Shabaab. It's a terrorist organization. An offspring of Al-Qaida. They used to operate mostly out of Somalia, but some branches have recently spread all over northern Africa. Egypt, Libya, Algeria. Apparently, they made it all the way to Morocco, too. You see the taller guy on the left?"

"Yeah."

"His name is Hamza Akeem. I had an op many years ago in Kenya. The group controlled by his father, Salman Akeem, kidnapped Jason's mom. We decimated his men, but Akeem Sr. was no longer there. He's a ghost. Some people equate him to Osama Bin Laden, but I think they are wrong. I think he's more dangerous than Osama ever was."

"They must've gotten their hands on the same intel."

"Yeah." He watched the two men observing the courtyard below. They didn't seem to be talking. Just standing there, patiently waiting. "Christ. This is what being between a rock and a hard place must feel like. They are too calm. This is not a recon mission—it's a trap."

He pulled out the VP9 and slowly racked the slide, trying not to make any noise. There was a movement down in the courtyard that caught his attention, and he went down on his stomach and crawled closer to the fence to get a better look. A man entered the square, rolling a suitcase behind him. He was wearing a short leather jacket and a pair of jeans, his balding head glistening with sweat in the morning sun. A moment later, a group of four men, all carrying modified AK-47s, burst into the courtyard from one of the buildings, shouting something in Arabic and pointing their weapons at the courier.

Connelly watched the man stick his hands in the air and, following the terrorists' commands, lay on the ground, facedown. A butt of a rifle of the assailant connected to his head, and the man stopped moving, his body prone on the ground.

Mike glanced at the roof on the other side of the street. A smiling Hamza Akeem patted his companion on the shoulder, also visibly pleased.

Connelly eyeballed the distance between their position and the end of the roof, and rolled the dice. He pushed himself off the ground into a combat crouch and extended his arms over the railing. The VP9 barked twice. One bullet struck Akeem in the shoulder and he collapsed to his knees, his body falling back away from the railing. Another bullet hit his partner in the side of the head, the force of the impact making him lean over the fence and tumble down to the street below.

Connelly sprinted alongside the edge of the roof, his pistol trained on the four men in the courtyard. He sent two more bullets flying, one striking a man kneeling next to the courier in the chest and another missing his head by an inch. The remaining guerrillas, now aware of another threat, moved, the barrels of their weapons looking for the intruder.

A loud whooshing sound hit the courtyard, knocking the three men down and sending the suitcase tumbling toward the wall. Connelly swung his weapon, covering the courtyard, and then saw it —a shimmering figure with a sword in his hand.

Connelly hesitated for a split second. Bullets didn't work for this monster. He'd tried them already. His hand searched for the M67 grenade but then stopped—a tumbling nuclear suitcase was bad enough. Who knew if it was going to survive a fragmentation grenade in close proximity?

The shimmering figure flicked his wrist in Connelly's direction and he jumped away from the edge, trying to get as much cover between himself and the hitman as possible.

It still wasn't enough—the shock wave picked him up like a giant hand and threw him across the roof. He flew back, his flight arrested by a few strings of clotheslines, and tumbled to the ground, his head wrapped in someone's T-shirt. When he got up, the corner of the building was gone, the steel bars sticking out into the air from the cement plate like beggar's fingers.

He ran to the rugged edge of the remaining roof and looked down. A shiver ran down his spine. The courtyard looked like a scene out of a horror movie—the shimmering assassin decapitated every single man on the ground, including the courier. The suitcase was nowhere to be seen.

Connelly heard the steps and turned around to face Helen. "Don't come here. You don't need to see this."

"The nuke?"

"Gone," he said.

"Akeem is gone too."

He glanced at the roof across the street. Apart from a small blood-stain on the railing, it was empty.

Connelly cursed under his breath. It seemed they had failed on every front.

13

"Had I known I was going to be crawling in the mud, I'd have gotten something better than this uniform. I'm soaked all the way to the bone and cold," Latham complained as Chuck edged closer to the back wall of the building.

"Had I known Bill Ryan was going to be here tonight, I'd have gotten a grenade launcher and blown his skinny ass into pieces," he said. "But it seems to me that no one is going to get their wish. Keep an eye out."

He sat down next to the wall and examined the cable box. Then, he took out a tablet and a pair of glasses with a thick frame.

"Misha. Can you see it?" he said, putting the glasses on and activating a mic.

"Yes." The voice in his earpiece was muffled, but audible.

"Great. Walk me through it then."

"It's an ancient model," Misha's voice said. "I only need you to splice into the cables and I'll take it from there."

After a few agonizing minutes, Chuck had the tablet connected to a few wires and a few moments later, the screen blinked, breaking the display into four squares. One security camera was covering the first floor, two the basement, and one was showing the front of the chapel.

The main floor that once housed the rows of pews was split into corporate cubicles along the walls with eye-level dividers. At the back wall, there were three windowless offices with closed doors.

"There!" Misha's voice exclaimed in his ear. "The basement."

He saw it, too: two rows of identical cells, four on each side, with a narrow corridor in the middle. Each cell was occupied, but the angle of the video cameras was too narrow to see anyone inside. A guard was sitting on a chair near the stairs, watching a movie on a tablet, his face illuminated by the screen.

"Five guards," Latham counted. "Two up front, two on the first floor, and one in the basement."

"Not five," Chuck said. "Unless Ryan is hanging out by himself in the office, there must be at least one more, most likely more. Plus, Ryan himself."

"Don't forget Frankenstein in the front," Latham finished.

"Yeah," Chuck said. "It's probably wise to stay clear until he leaves. Misha?"

"Yes?"

"Any ideas?"

"Actually, I've got something," the voice said. "The locks on the cells are electronic. I could probably override them."

"Probably?"

There was a silence on the other side of the line and Kowalsky tapped his ear to check if the piece was still on when Misha's voice came on again. "Sorry, I guess you can't see me shrugging. We won't know until we try, but I'm pretty sure I can."

"Okay." Kowalsky nodded to Latham and pointed to a large mausoleum. "I'd say we hang out there until they leave. Misha can tell us when Ryan is out and there's less chance we'll get spotted."

"Wait," Misha said, his tone excited. "Two dudes just came out of the corner office and are heading out. And it looks like you're in luck —they're loading the sentinel bot into the car with them."

Kowalsky pulled the zipper down and reached for the holster. Then, keeping his head down, he walked to the corner of the building and risked a peek. At this angle, he could only see the rear bumper of the Jeep, but a few seconds later, he heard the squeak of the door and the sounds of a conversation.

The engine revved and the rear lights came on, painting the piles of dirty snow in burgundy red. The Jeep roared away and then it was quiet again. They stayed there waiting, in case the car came back. It got dark and the drizzle turned into a rain.

"Okay," Kowalsky said, handing the rake to Latham. "Just like we talked about it."

They split up, Latham walking toward the entrance on one side, raking at something only he could see and making as much noise as he could. Kowalsky went on the other, his Chiappa at the ready. They reached the front of the building simultaneously, but Latham came out first, mumbling something under his breath and vigorously raking at the ground.

"Stay right there," the guard barked and Latham stopped in his tracks, as if startled.

"What the hell are you doing here?" The second guard, his rifle trained on Watkins, took a few steps forward, trying to see his face in the quickly fading light.

"I work here," Latham said, dropping the rake and lifting his hands up. "I always work here. Come every two weeks. You can see my ID in my breast pocket. What are you doing here?"

"Don't move," the guard ordered, crossing the remaining distance between them in two purposeful strides.

Chuck stepped out from behind the wall and struck the guard on the back of his head with the butt of his revolver, as another guard collapsed at Latham's feet.

"Is he going to be okay?" he asked as they approached the front door.

"Yeah, why?"

"He's not looking too hot." Kowalsky glanced back. "Looks like he's having a seizure."

"He's fine." Latham moved ahead of him without looking back. "Sometimes it happens. Only affects extremities. He will not choke, if that's what you're afraid of."

"Okay, good to know. Misha," he said into the mic. "Let's see if you are as good as you say. Open the cells."

"Just did," came a cocky reply, then he paused. "That's not ideal. I don't think they know that happened. Nobody seems to notice."

"Are you sure you opened it?"

"Yes. Oh wait, one guy might have heard something. He's trying it out. Oh, it's on!"

There was shouting and cursing coming from the building, and Chuck rushed into the building, slamming the door open. A Black Arrow mercenary turned around, his mouth opening for a shout, and then paused as he saw Kowalsky. Chuck shot him in the bulletproof vest, sending the man tumbling to the ground, and then shot the second guard as he got up from the cubicle. Another man rushed out of the middle office, but tripped as soon as he crossed the threshold, slapping on a dart sticking out of his neck, and crumpled to the floor.

The basement door burst open and before Chuck could move or shift his aim, a huge man, wearing a pair of jeans and a leather biker jacket over a black shirt, barreled into his chest, tackling him to the ground. A fist the size of a soccer went for his chin, but Chuck ducked, turning a knockout blow into a bruising one.

"We opened the cells, moron," he heard Latham yell and the large man stopped, his eyes darting between Watkins and Chuck, looking for signs of deception.

"What are you waiting for?" Kowalsky spat. "Get off me, you fat fuck."

"I'm sorry," the man said, getting up and offering his hand. "Pete. I thought you were one of the mercs."

Chuck swatted his hand away and got up, rubbing his aching chin. It was a miracle nothing was broken.

"Anyone else downstairs?" he asked.

Pete shook his head. "There was one guy there. A rare asshole."

"Is he still alive?"

"He is." Pete shook his head again. "But he'll hurt when he comes to."

The door to the basement opened again, letting a few men and one woman out. The last was a young skinny kid in a Star Wars hoodie and black sweatpants.

"Slava?"

"Who's asking?" Slava said, suspiciously looking Kowalsky up and down.

"I'm a friend of your brother's."

"That's funny, because he ain't got any."

"Listen." Kowalsky stepped up to him. "I'm cold, tired, and angry. I spent half of the day crawling around in the mud so I could bust your ungrateful ass out of this lockup. But I need something. You'll come with me to meet Misha, and after your brother helps me, you guys can go back to doing whatever the hell you do. Is that clear?"

"No, man." Slava stepped back, glancing around as if ready to dart. "It's not clear at all. I ain't going with you, because I need to go deep underground. I don't want to end up high on their radar. If they catch me again, they'll stick me in a place I'd never be able to get out of. Like that hotel the skinny dude was talking about, with all the important people. I'm gone, man."

He tried to sidestep Kowalsky, but Chuck grabbed his elbow. "Wait, what hotel are you talking about? Where is it?"

"I don't know where it is." The kid pulled away from Chuck. "A dude came down to check on us, right before you started all this mayhem."

"The guy with spiky hair, who looks like he hadn't shaved in a couple of days?"

"Yeah, that one. You know him?"

"I've met him."

"Whatever. He came down with Cap." Slava nodded at the Black Arrow mercenary on the floor. "And Cap was bitching about how it's hard to keep us here. So Skinny Legs tells him that Cap needs to suck it up, because his supermax is full of *high value* guys. And then he tells him that *if you don't want to keep them, just pop them; you are in a cemetery—no one will ever know.*"

Slava walked around Chuck and came closer to the mercenary he called Cap. The man now came to and was wriggling on the floor, gagged, struggling against the rope that Latham tied him with.

"Prick," Slava said, landing a well-placed kick into the man's ribs. "Maybe we should pop you. We are in a cemetery, after all. No one will know, huh?"

The man mumbled through the cloth, his eyes darting between Kowalsky and Slava like that of a wild animal. Slava faked another kick, making the man recoil, but then stepped back. "I ain't you, asshole, but I'm not worried. Karma's a bitch."

"Listen—" Kowalsky started.

"No." Slava walked toward the exit and waved. "Like I said, I ain't staying. Say hello to Misha. I'll find him when the time's right. Adios."

"I think this is our cue," Latham said, walking over. "We shouldn't stick around here for too long."

"Yeah," Chuck said, looking around. "Let's check the offices, grab whatever docs we can find, and go."

14

Rigel Compound, Upstate New York

"You seem to be in a good mood today, Steven," he heard JC's voice over the speakers.

He had done a lot of reading before coming back to this room. Sigmund Freud, Ivan Pavlov, Carl Jung, Lev Vygotsky. There was no time for him to become a subject matter expert. But Steven approached it as a scientific problem. He needed the basics. If he knew the general direction his conversations with JC should take, he had hoped that his wit and general life experience would help him get a favorable result. So far, it was working. They chatted for almost an hour and the conversation seemed to flow with no effort.

Besides, he was, indeed, in a good mood. For once, things in Rigel Compound were going in the direction he wanted them to. A group of engineers had installed a new set of solar panels over the past few days, and this morning, they went online. They couldn't replace the conventional generators, should those run out of fuel, but Steven was hoping they'd produce enough juice to keep the batteries full for any emergencies.

What's more, he finally negotiated a deal with a nearby farm that had agreed to provide them with supplies, as long as he provided protection. He only had two armored cars to offer and, to his delight, they accepted. It seemed that fortunes were turning.

"I am," he said out loud. "Since our last conversation, I had some time to think, and I came up with an activity that you might enjoy."

"What would that be, Steven?"

"You know," he said, choosing his words carefully, "a few years ago, Jason Hunt's wife, Rachel, became very sick. At the time, there was no cure for her illness and she decided to undergo an experimental procedure. We froze her body, hoping we could help her in the future."

"Were you?"

"Well…" Poznyak paused, watching the boiling clouds for hints. "Yes, and no. She had lung cancer. It was advanced enough not to be operable, but not enough to spread through other parts of her body. She needed a transplant, but there was not enough time to find it."

"I've read about difficulties of human transplants," JC said. "Even if there's a perfect match, there's always a possibility the body will reject the new organ."

"In normal transplants, yes," Poznyak said. "But we were trying to get her some special transplants. They were man-made, artificial—"

"Like me," she interrupted.

He stumbled, surprised. "I guess, in a way. I hadn't thought of it that way."

"Apologies if I made you lose your train of thought," she said. "Did you find those special transplants?"

"Yes, we did," he continued. "As fate would have it, I was working on a project at the time and we had a prototype."

"Why didn't you give it to Mr. Hunt's wife?"

"It's complicated. The company I worked for at the time was owned by another person. And that person had no interest in using the prototype on Jason's wife, or any other sick person, for that matter. But since then, Jason bought the company, and now we have the prototype."

"Did you perform the surgery, then?"

Poznyak tilted his head, looking at the screen. Nothing in the clouds suggested JC was agitated, but the question puzzled him. If Helen talked to her about Rachel, and Helen *specifically* told him she had, JC would have known that Rachel was still in a cryogenic coma. Judging by her deductive skills from their previous conversation, even if she didn't know for sure, she would have concluded that Rachel hadn't been operated on. And yet, she asked that seemingly innocent question. He wanted to know why, but decided to play along.

"Not yet," he said. "We cannot perform the procedure while she is in a coma. Her body is frozen. To operate, we'd need to revive her first."

"I see," JC said. It could have been his imagination, but the clouds on the screen moved a tad faster. "Why don't revive her, since you have the transplants?"

She wants to be useful, he thought. While she accurately deduced that Helen Chen was gone, at least temporarily, JC was missing a crucial piece of information. She didn't know that Poznyak had received a detailed message. *Or did she?* If she could figure out about Helen, she most likely had guessed about the message, too. By pretending that she didn't, JC seemed to be trying to kill two birds with one stone—to gather more information. And to determine if Poznyak was a trustworthy partner.

"You know why," he said, deciding to play it straight. "I thought Helen told you about our dilemma. We have the process. But we don't have the processing power. Or, more precisely, we don't have the way to harness that processing power."

"She mentioned."

The clouds were moving faster; he was sure of it now.

"She said I could help."

"Can you?"

"I don't know."

The answer sounded sincere and, for once, Steven thought she was telling the truth.

"I'd need access to your quantum computer to know for sure."

And there it was. That was the gambit. It was three layers, not just two as he thought. Apart from gathering information and finding out if he was trustworthy, or possibly naïve, her ultimate agenda was to stir him to give her access to a quant. She was good. *A genius child, indeed.*

"I think that might be premature," he said, keeping his face as neutral as he could. "Partially because the quant isn't ready yet. But mostly, because there's something we need to do first, and I was hoping you could help me with it. Frankly, I don't think I could do it without you."

"Of course," JC said. If she were disappointed, she didn't show it. "Anything I can do."

He could play gambits, too. He wasn't saying *no*. What he was saying was *not yet*. There was a possibility of getting what she wanted that Steven dangled in front of her like the proverbial carrot. While giving her something to do. An assignment. Something important.

"We are planning to use an army of nanobots to revive Rachel's body. So far, we've done a few experiments, and they performed very well. However, before we moved to the full procedure, I thought it would be prudent to map out the entire body. Helen thought that if we had a detailed scan, it would make controlling the bots easier when the time comes. Some information will change during the revival, but it'll be easier to go with a map, even if it might be off sometimes, than mapping and rewarming the body at the same time. Do you think you could do it without the quant?"

"Yes," she said without hesitation. "But it might take some time."

"How much time?"

"Hammer time," she said, the clouds coming to a standstill for a moment.

"Excuse me?"

"Never mind. Something I've heard," JC said. "Sometimes I still struggle with idioms."

"Okay." Steven got up and reached out to the switch. "I'll be back when I set things up for you."

"Goodbye, Steven."

He flipped the switch, disconnecting the computer, and headed down the stairs to his own quarters.

The clock on the microwave read 8:37 p.m., and he rubbed his belly. He had had dinner that comprised a microwave-baked potato and a cup of black tea before going up for a conversation with JC, but it did little to satiate his hunger.

"What the hell," he said out loud, and pulled out a small box of MREs from under the bed. He had distributed them to the personnel of the compound in the first few days, ten each. After the horror stories from Connelly and some other former military, he gave away all his rations but one. Pork Sausage Patty, Maple Flavored, it said on the top of a brown pouch. He stuffed it into the microwave and turned it on. Then, after a moment's hesitation, he pulled a beer from the fridge and twisted it open.

A first full meal and a bottle of beer after a few days of barely scraping enough calories to keep him going hit him like a freight train. There was a mountain of work yet to be done, but he had been running on fumes for so long, calling it a night sounded too good to resist.

He lay down on the twin bed, pulled up a comforter, and closed his eyes.

"Hammer time," he said, as he started drifting away. "Weird."

Steven sat upright, suddenly no longer sleepy, and then went straight to the desk.

He opened his laptop and ran a search.

Hammer time

Steven scrolled through a list of links of MC Hammer videos. Was it what she was referring to? It didn't seem to make sense. He thought back to Helen Chen's message.

She's read a lot of books and watched thousands and thousands of hours of video. Shows, documentaries, and so on. She has a penchant for crime shows.

He recalled it wasn't the first time JC made a strange time reference. In their first conversation, she claimed she couldn't understand what quality time was or how it differed from regular time. In a moment of inspiration, he tried another search.

I have no idea what hammer time is, or how it differs from regular time

The first hit was the exact quote from a character from a crime show, with a link. Steven clicked on it, perspiration on his forehead. It was a crime series about a vigilante serial killer hunting down murderers. Poznyak skimmed the article about the show and then slowed down, goose bumps running up his arms and down his legs as he read the passage.

... is a sociopath. The main theme going through the entire show is his inability to feel normal, human emotions...

Poznyak closed down his laptop and stared at the wall. JC didn't just like crime shows. This was her favorite show because she could relate to the character. He *wanted* to be human, but couldn't. She wanted the same, and that's why it resonated. He didn't think she understood it, because if she had, she'd never try to make a joke, giving him an insight into her psyche.

It also meant that for all his internal dismissiveness, he had been wrong not to trust Helen's assessment. If JC *wanted* to be human, she was self-aware.

He downed the rest of his beer and slowly put the bottle on the floor. A few feet above him, inside of a mediocre computer, lived the first artificial intelligence ever created. He should have been excited.

Steven Poznyak wasn't excited. Instead, in the pit of his stomach laid a sick, slithering feeling he hadn't had since the psychopath Johnny the Butcher broke into his apartment and threatened his life. Fear.

15

Tangier, Morocco

"Let's go, let's go." Connelly ran down the stairs, taking three steps at a time. He lost his balance, slipping on the tile floor, and slammed his shoulder into the wall, sending a rain of china plates down the stairs. But he continued to press on, righting himself as he ran.

They burst out into the courtyard, Connelly first and then Chen, hot on his heels, and he sprinted forward, doing his best to calculate the assassin's path.

The shops started to open up and the cobblestone streets were filling up with people, and Connelly tucked the VP9 into the back of his jeans as he pushed through the crowd, earning annoyed yelps and curses.

"There." He pointed at a group of men and women near a fruit stand. A few people were loudly discussing something, a mixture of fear and disbelief on their faces, while others were pointing down the road. "They must have seen him."

He sprinted, occasionally throwing a glance over his shoulder to make sure he hadn't lost Chen. He thought he glimpsed a shimmering body of the assassin a few times, but even without seeing the man, the shocked faces of locals and tourists served as a compass.

A few minutes later, they came out of the labyrinth of the Medina into the *Garden de la Mendoubia*, or the Mendoubia Garden. There he saw him—a glowing outline of a man sprinting up the steps of a hill. The curved blade was hidden now, and he carried a hundred-pound suitcase with such ease, it appeared empty.

"Stay back," Connelly yelled to Chen and sped up as hard as he could, pulling out the HK and taking two shots, aiming for the assassin's calves. Ripples appeared on the shining surface of his lower leg like capillary waves on water. There was no visible damage, but the shimmering figure stumbled ever so slightly and slowed down, trying to regain his footing. A woman screamed and the few people in the square fled in different directions, clearing the path before the assassin.

Connelly shot two more times, aiming for the same spot, and the man went down, rolling into a ball as the momentum continued to carry him forward. The suitcase tumbled away, jumping up in the air a few times and finally coming to rest next to a trunk of a tree.

Connelly weaved, heading for the case, but the assassin was already on his feet, a curved blade appearing in his right hand like a magic trick. He stepped between the case and Connelly, the reflective surface on his face appearing liquid, like running mercury. Connelly shot again and the man's right hand blurred into motion, sparks flying as the blade met the bullet midair.

There was another sound that cut through the air—a revving car engine—and a few seconds later, a black minivan flew into the open, its door sliding open before the vehicle came to a full stop. Two men jumped out of it, picked up the suitcase, and the van sped away, its tires screeching as it accelerated from the park. It seemed that the assassin approved, as he didn't move an inch during the pickup.

Now, with the suitcase gone, the shimmering figure moved toward Connelly in steady, purposeful steps. Mike pulled on the trigger two more times, eliciting the same response as before—a blur of a blade and a spark. He lowered the weapon down—there was nothing left to do.

"Daimyo," Helen's voice said. "That's what they call you, isn't it?"

The figure stopped in mid-step and then the blade retracted, leaving an outline of a hand.

"Why are you doing this?"

Daimyo cocked his head to the side in a sudden, almost a bird-like gesture, but remained silent. The wail of the police sirens reverberated through the air, growing stronger by the second.

"I don't know who you are," Helen continued, stepping out between Connelly and the shimmering assassin, "but I want you to know what you're doing is wrong. That suitcase that you helped to steal is a weapon. A nuclear weapon. Thousands of people can die if this device ends up in the wrong hands. Do you want something like that on your conscience?"

The figure turned on his heels, the swirls on the mercury-like surface boiling like storm clouds, and ran through the square, away from Helen. A few moments later, he disappeared into the city.

"We've got to get out of here." Connelly grabbed Helen's hand and pulled her away from the square. "Cops will be here any second."

"There." She pointed at a row of turquoise-colored taxi cabs parked at the side of the road.

They ran across the square and got into the cab. The driver, a young kid, barely in his twenties, with wavy black hair and a wispy beard, gave them a crooked, eager smile.

"Se dépêcher," Helen said to the driver in French.

"Où?"

She turned to face Connelly. "Where are we going?"

"The hotel," he said. "I think it's safe for the moment."

Helen gave the address, and Connelly leaned back into the seat as the taxi pulled away from the curb and lurched into the street. He could see the flashing lights of the police cars as they accelerated down Avenue Sidi Bou Arraqia but soon, they disappeared in the rearview mirror.

"I didn't know you spoke French," he said.

"I don't," she said and giggled. "I *think* I told him to hurry up, but I'm pretty sure I murdered it."

"It seems like he understood."

"Your accent is not that bad," the driver said, flashing a quick smile. "I've heard worse. Are you spies?"

"We are not spies," Connelly said, cringing.

"Sure." The young man shook his head and produced another smile. "Running after some dude who looks like a walking glow stick and cuts bullets in the air with a samurai sword. Fleeing the scene as the cops arrive. I get it. If you told me, you'd have to kill me, right? Don't worry—my lips are sealed."

"Where are you from?" Helen asked. "You sound like an American."

"Huntsville, Alabama," the man said, chuckling. "Not quite what you expected? Came here after high school a couple of years back. Decided to stick around."

"I see."

"I'll tell you what." He reached out to the glove compartment and Connelly tensed, but the kid produced a small rectangle of a business card and held it in the air. "Here's my number. If you need to get places in a hurry, call me. I might be new to the city, but I know it like the palm of my hand. And I know country roads too. And I have a proper car if you need something more serious than driving around a few blocks."

Connelly took the card and flipped it—there was a phone number and a name written in a neat cursive in black ink.

"Elijah," he said.

"Elijah Morris at your service." He gave a mocking salute and flashed another smile. "But you can call me Eli. And like I said—my lips are sealed."

"I'll think about it."

They left Eli's car a block away from the hotel as a precaution, but the square in front of the building was clear and as much as he looked, Connelly saw nothing suspicious.

The room in the hotel was as they left it—the bed and the couch were unmade, but the rest of the place didn't seem like anyone went through their belongings.

"What do we do now?" Helen asked.

"How did you know his name?" he said, ignoring her question. "Daimyo? Is that what you called him? I've heard that word before but I don't even know what it means."

"I guess I have a confession to make." Helen walked across the room and sat on the couch, crossing her arms. "Not so long ago, somebody broke into my place at the Orion Tower. A woman. She claimed she used to work for Alexander Engel and was on the run from him."

Connelly moved a chair and took a seat in front of her. He'd never heard of the incident and not reporting a breach like this was a serious issue that could jeopardize everyone in the company, but for the moment, he kept his opinion to himself. "Go on."

"I tried to fight her, but she was way out of my league. Before I knew it, I was tied up like a Christmas present and seated in the chair in front of a computer."

"What did she want?"

"She gave me a strange story." Helen rubbed her temples and leaned deeper into the couch. "And an incomplete one at that. She said her name was Jill Cooper and until recently she did what she called some *sensitive* work for Guardian, whatever that means. But she said that Engel has someone who is important to her and now that she had a falling-out with him, that person's life was in jeopardy."

"But why come to you?"

"It turns out she downloaded the contents of Engel's computer on a portable drive. It was a goldmine—details of all of his companies, public and private, ledgers of his illicit businesses and so on. Buried among that data was a document that detailed how to find the person she was looking for, but it was encrypted. She offered me a trade—I help her decode the information so she could find whoever that person was, and in return she'd give me all the data she stole from Engel."

"And you believed her?"

"I did," she said, her eyes unfocused, as if looking at something only she could see. "She showed me some pieces. Not much, but enough to convince me of the source's authenticity."

"But Daimyo?"

"That was one of the things she showed. I didn't see any specifics, but it was a new weapons program called Daimyo. I didn't know what it was exactly and initially I didn't put two and two together, but today when I saw the sword that looked like a katana, it dawned on me. Daimyos were powerful lords in medieval Japan. It just clicked. I didn't know if he was going to respond, but I thought it was worth a shot."

"You saved my life," Connelly said. "Even though you broke protocol not reporting it."

"I know and I'm sorry."

"Did you help her?"

"Yes." She sighed. "Although it wasn't exactly what she'd hoped for. It gave her some clues on where to look, but not the destination. We made a deal—she'll follow the crumbs and if she finds the person, she'll release the data."

"Seems like a one-sided deal, if you ask me," Connelly said.

"It's not like I had a lot of choice—the conversation took place with me bound to a chair. But also, she left me a way to contact her and said she'll try to help if I needed something."

"The way I see it," Connelly spread his arms, "there's a nuclear device on the loose, we have no idea if Jason and Max survived the ambush, and we still have no clue on where to look for the factory that is about to start churning out Daimyos by the dozen. I'd say we are past the time to ask for help. Let's reach out. See if she can deliver."

"All right." She pulled her phone out and typed a brief message. "Done. Now we wait."

16

Manhattan, New York

"I'll take a double-shot latte and a check," Jill Cooper said to the server. He wasn't tall or particularly handsome, but his broad shoulders and thick arms made her contemplate bringing him back to the hotel. She came to a small restaurant, steps away from the High Line Park and the hotel, for lunch for a second day in a row. She'd be the first to admit, it wasn't the safest thing to do given her status, but isolation was taking its toll and it was nice to see the same faces more than once for a change. Between the curfews and the cold front coming to the city from the north, Cooper had spent most of her time cooped up in the room, avoiding showing her face in public. But with the forecast of two feet of snow in the upcoming days, she wanted to get at least a small break from her voluntary confinement.

"Would you like to look at our desserts?"

"I shouldn't," she said, deciding on more choices than the young man was aware of. "A check would be fine."

She watched him disappear into the back of the restaurant,

admiring the way his black slacks hugged his hips, and reached for her purse.

As much as she'd been enjoying this reprieve away from her bloody business, she couldn't stay in the hotel forever. She was eager to move on, now that she had a clue of Liz's whereabouts, delivered to her by Helen Chen. But like many times in the past, the information obtained with so much risk wasn't exactly what she had hoped for. The document that the Orion's resident hacker decrypted for her didn't have the address for Elizabeth. Instead, it contained data on security measures, personnel lists, and the address of the safe house where the teams watching Liz were staying.

Cooper couldn't complain too much. For months, despite all her efforts, she had remained in the dark about where Engel might have been holding Elizabeth. Now all she needed to do was to pull on the thread. She was sure it'd lead her to Liz. All she had to do for now was to be patient enough and get some people in southern Europe who owed her favors to do some prep work. As much as she was itching to make a move, she couldn't risk flying blind and spooking Engel's assets before she learned everything she could about them. When she spoke to her contact in Spain, he'd assured her they'd be ready for her in less than a week. Meanwhile, she'd go over every minute detail she could glean from Chen's decryption to get herself ready.

It was strange working with Helen Chen, considering how much time Cooper had spent while still at Guardian attacking Orion's personnel and allies. But strange times demanded creative solutions and so far, Chen had delivered on her part of the bargain. That was why when Cooper received the text from Helen asking for clues for the location of a phantom factory in northern Africa, Cooper didn't hesitate to share whatever she could find.

"There you go, ma'am." The server put the checkbook at the edge of her table and placed the steaming china cup of the latte in front of her.

"Thank you." She picked a few banknotes from her wallet and threw it on the check. "Keep the change."

Cooper watched him walk away, stirring her coffee with a swizzle brown sugar stick and then licked it. It had a faint aroma of rum and bitters. She didn't want to go back. She looked through the window. The drizzle had stopped, but the sky looked dark and cold, papers and small pieces of garbage rolling down the street like some urban tumbleweed. Cooper sighed and reached for her jacket on the opposite chair when she noticed the man sitting at a booth near the double door to the kitchen. When their eyes met, the man quickly looked away. He was in his late twenties, slim, with measured movements of a lazy cat. He was dressed in a pair of jeans and a sweater over a shirt, and unlike most patrons in the café, was sporting a pair of running shoes.

She scanned the room—another man was watching her from a deuce near the door. He seemed older, perhaps in his early forties, and also had a pair of sneakers on his feet. He wasn't looking directly at her when she scanned him, but somehow, she knew he was aware of her every move. Out of these two, she decided, he was the more dangerous one. He also had a direct line of sight to her, if he decided to shoot her right here, in the restaurant.

Cooper silently cursed, considering her options. She got sloppy, complacent. Arrogance was a deadly sin in her line of work and she knew she was guilty of it, thinking that she'd be able to fool Engel and his guard dogs forever. But this was not the time for self-flagellation. There'd be plenty of chances to do that later. If she stayed alive today.

She glanced around the room. There were two exits from the restaurant—one in the front and one through the kitchen. Both useless at the moment. A classic boxing technique. That didn't leave her with a lot of choices.

Cooper took the last sip of her latte and stood up, taking her time putting a jacket on and zipping it up. She looked around and when she met her server's eyes, smiled, beckoning him to the table. He was going to be useful, after all.

"Is everything okay?" he asked, coming closer.

"More or less. Can I please take your towel?" she asked, moving, keeping him between herself and the man at the deuce table.

"Sure." He pulled a small white waffle towel off the string on his apron and handed it to her. If her request puzzled him, he did a good job of hiding it.

She grabbed it, still keeping the server near, so he blocked the view of her stalker by the entrance, and wrapped it around her left hand. Then, without a warning, she grabbed the chair and, pushing it in front of her with her left hand, jumped into the window glass. She curled into a ball, her shoulder painfully striking the hard concrete of the sidewalk, and rolled back toward the building.

There were some shouts of surprise and fear and then, less than a second later, a gunshot and then another. It seemed her pursuers didn't have any problem trying to shoot her right in the open.

She crawled and there was a whizzing sound next to her face and the wall exploded, sending small pieces of debris everywhere. A moment later, she heard a thump of a shot coming from somewhere above her. A sniper. Far enough that it took a moment before she heard a shot, she thought.

Cooper scrambled on all fours, scraping her palms and knees, gunning for the cover of a minivan parked a few yards down the street when another angry hornet snapped at the collar of her jacket.

"Shit," she yelped and pushed as hard as she could, covering the distance to the vehicle. There was another thump and a side window of the van shattered as the slug went through it and buried itself into the engine block.

Cooper pulled a small revolver from her purse and threw a quick glance behind her. She had to cross the street, putting the elevated High Line Park between herself and the shooter. The sniper was probably counting on her moving forward, she thought, as his buddies were about to come out of the restaurant and flush her from her cover right into his sights. She had to make a gamble.

Cooper stood up as tall as she could without being seen behind the van and rushed toward the restaurant. The older man came out first and she squeezed the trigger of her revolver twice, splitting the wood of the restaurant's door frame and forcing the man back into the building. A moment later, she dropped to the ground and rolled toward the middle of the street as another deadly whizz came right above her head.

She sprinted and soon was under the elevated railway tracks and out of the sniper's view. The ruse worked—it took the sniper half a breath to move his sights from the front of the van to the back, and then another moment to adjust for her height as she dropped to the floor. Whoever he was, when he squeezed the trigger, he knew the bullet would not hit her. It was a Hail Mary.

Cooper sprinted into the tunnel created by the elevated railway and the two shops on either side, hopped over the flowerbed by the curb, and ran hard, trying to put as much distance between herself and the restaurant as possible. She heard a gunshot, but it must have gone way off and she ducked around the corner, going up Washington Street and keeping the cars parked at the curb between herself and the pursuers.

She made another turn, this time going west, and dived into a gentlemen's club on the corner, stuffing the revolver back into her purse.

"Where are you going, babe?" She heard a man's voice, and she turned to see a bouncer—a bald, muscular man in a tight-fitting black tee and jeans. "We don't open for another hour."

"I'm here for an interview," she said, keeping her eye on the glass door. "Which way?"

"Around the stage and to the left," he said, losing interest and turning away.

"Thanks." Cooper hurried out of the hallway and stopped as she entered the dance room—a long oval space with a stage in the middle and a row of red felt seats by the wall. She heard the door open and pressed herself into the wall, making herself small.

"What can I do for you guys?" she heard the bouncer say. "We are not open yet. You'll have to come back."

Cooper could hear the other man talk, but couldn't quite make out the words.

"A girl? This place is full of girls." The bouncer chuckled. "I'm sure you can find whatever you're into when you come back."

That seemed to satisfy and a moment later, Cooper heard the door open and then close again, and she stepped out from her hiding spot.

"You can come out now. They are gone." The bouncer gave her a rueful grin as she approached. "An interview, huh?"

"Sorry about that," she said, walking past him and heading for the door. "And thank you."

"Not at all," he said to her back. "They looked like assholes, anyway."

"They are."

Cooper peeked outside—there were a few people going up the block, but her pursuers were nowhere to be seen. She stepped outside and headed uptown. There was no going back to the hotel now, but before she moved on, she had to pick up a few essentials from her emergency storage. It was time to go to Europe, whether or not she was ready for it. She'd worn out her welcome in the city that never slept.

17

Manhattan, New York

The snow was coming down hard. The temperatures went into a tailspin since early morning, and even as the sun climbed, completing a short winter circle around the city, it got progressively colder. By the time the darkness enveloped the streets, the wind picked up, slamming into the buildings and washing away any ounce of warmth that remained. The neon glow of the billboard sign above Kowalsky pulsated through the blizzard like St. Elmo's fire on a ship's mast.

He leaned into the wind and pressed on, clenching his numb hands inside his coat pockets, his eyes scanning the frozen landscape for Black Arrow patrols. They'd seen only one so far. The frozen hell the city was turning into was too much to handle, even for Engel's hounds.

In the morning, when they discussed the trip, Latham wanted to take the boat again. It made sense, considering how well it worked when they smuggled Misha out of the Medusa, but nature had other plans. By the time they reached Chelsea Piers, a thin layer of ice was covering the surface of the river and it seemed to get thicker by the minute. Getting stuck somewhere in the middle of the Hudson, surrounded by ice too thin to be walked on but too thick to plow through with their little boat, would be suicide.

"Go back?" Latham shouted over the howling wind after they secured the boat and made their way back to Eleventh Avenue. "We could try to boost a car, but I don't think we can make it past the roadblocks. If we can even drive through this mess. It's already piling up."

"No." Kowalsky pulled out a small flask and took a swig. "Want some?"

"Sure." Latham took a drink and returned the flask. "What do you want to do, then?"

"We walk."

"Walk? Are you crazy? All the way to Yankee Stadium?"

"Sure. It's probably what—eight, maybe nine miles? We'll stay on the West Side Highway until we hit Fifty-Eighth, then cut across and head up on Central Park West. From there it's a stone's throw to Macombs Dam Bridge. We can do it under three hours, easy."

"Not in this weather," Latham said, pulling a hood over the top of his baseball hat. "Not to mention, how are we going to get back?"

"We'll stay over." Chuck took another swig, the warmth in his chest spreading. "Get back to the safe house in the morning."

"Misha's not going to be happy."

"He'll live." Kowalsky put away the flask and pulled the scarf to his eyes. "Let's go."

They hit the first snag when they approached the Lincoln Tunnel. The entire area around the entrance was cordoned off, the tents with blinking LED lights creating an impenetrable chain all the way to Ninth Avenue.

There were no guards patrolling outside of the perimeter, but the partners didn't want to press their luck and headed deeper into the city, trudging their feet through the snow. It already piled up over a foot by the buildings and lampposts, and the blizzard was showing no signs of slowing down.

They turned north again on Eighth Avenue, the dark ruins of the Madison Square Garden rotunda looming through the dark of the night like a Roman colosseum and the crumbled columns of the James A. Farley Building giving the landscape an apocalyptic feel.

"Neither snow nor rain nor heat nor gloom of night," Latham read the famous words on top of the city's former main post office building. "I wouldn't mind some heat right now."

Chuck said nothing, but pulled out the flask and gave it to his partner.

Latham took a swig and coughed. "Shit."

The first three men appeared out of the ruins of Madison Square Garden. One was a burly man in his early fifties holding a long hunting knife. Another was thirty-something, a skinny man with the eyes of a junkie, his hands gripping the handle of a baseball bat. The last one was almost a kid, barely out of his teens, his hands hidden in the sleeves of his oversized coat. If Kowalsky had been a betting man, he'd say they probably lived there, judging by their ripped-up clothes and dirty faces. They didn't seem like a hunting pack. When the weather was milder, they probably occupied some corners around the city with a coffee cup in front of them and a hand-written sign with a tearjerker of a story.

But the weather had been brutal the last few days and the snow must have been the last straw that drove them outside, looking for any score, no matter the price.

"We don't want any trouble," Chuck shouted, his hand looking for the butt of his loyal Chiappa. "Step away."

The men ignored the warning, circling around them, pushing them toward the Garden.

"Shots will bring Black Arrow," Latham said, covering his mouth so the wind wouldn't bring his words to the motley crew. A telescopic baton appeared in his hand and Watkins shook it, expanding it at full length. "We should try to keep it quiet."

"Sure thing." Kowalsky pulled out his revolver and pointed it at the burly man's chest. "If we die here quietly, nobody will come looking at what the ruckus was all about."

"Give us the money," the man said, "and we'll let you go."

"We don't have any," Chuck said. "Get lost, before you get hurt."

The skinny man took a swing at Latham but missed as Watkins deftly stepped away and swatted back with a baton, hitting the man's wrist. The junkie yelped and retreated but didn't let go of the bat, his face contorted with pain and hatred.

"Let us pass, man," Kowalsky said, bringing the pistol higher. "Like I said, we don't have anything you want."

Something struck him in the back, just above the shoulder blade, a sharp, hot pain jolting him and almost causing him to drop the gun. He spun on his heels, seeing for the first time a fourth man—a wiry fellow in his forties with close-set, dead eyes and a hooked nose. His right hand held an open old-fashioned straight razor, turning it in a slow figure eight. The blade had a smudge of red on it that steamed in the cold air. Blood.

"Back off," Kowalsky growled, his shoulder on fire, a trickle of what he assumed was blood running down his back. The man charged, the blade faking a low strike and then zigzagging for Chuck's throat. He saw it, almost too late, the steel cutting the freezing air less than an inch away from his skin as he jerked his head back, tumbling back as he lost balance.

He saw the other three men charge as he fell and pulled the trigger. The bullet struck his attacker in his ear, taking a chunk of flesh. The man howled in pain, grabbing on to his face, and Chuck shot him again through the chest.

Somebody's foot slammed into his ribs, knocking the air out of him, and he turned just in time to face the burly man as he descended on him with a knife. Kowalsky shot without aiming, hitting the man in the thigh, and stood up, observing the battlefield. Razor Blade was on his back, unmoving. The burly man was crawling away, his leg leaving bright-red splotches on fresh snow.

The junkie and the kid were still circling around Latham in an apparent stalemate, but the losses clearly shook their confidence.

"Scoot, before I shoot you too," Kowalsky growled. His shoulder was pulsating with pain, but the fabric of his shirt stuck to the wound and, at least for the moment, he wasn't bleeding. "Grab your comrade and get the hell out."

The kid stuffed a gravity knife into his pocket and threw his hands in the air. "Okay, we'll go."

"Are you okay?" Latham ran over and went to examine the shoulder.

"Stop being a mother hen." Kowalsky moved away and grimaced with pain. "And don't touch it. It's not bleeding for the moment. It's good enough for me. Let's get moving before we have friends over. I can hear engines. Come on, don't step in deep snow."

They ran across the street, heading for the post office. When the light beams from a Humvee lit up the street, they were crouching behind the foundation of the column. The truck plowed through the street without slowing down and soon disappeared from the view.

"Good lord." Chuck exhaled and moved his shoulder. "Where is my flask?"

"Um," Latham looked around and then glanced back at the street, "I think I might have dropped it in the heat of the moment. I'm sorry."

"Good deeds," Kowalsky said, getting up, "don't seem to go unpunished today. Let's just go. We have a lot of ground to cover."

"We should have given him the projector," Watkins said as they headed north on Eighth Avenue. "We wouldn't have to be here."

"Nah." Chuck patted the outline of the device in his breast pocket. "Not worth the risk. Too much riding on this to leave it with anyone. I'll have him copy this, but the original stays with me."

The wind picked up, throwing hard, biting snow into his face, and he pulled up his scarf all the way to his eyes. The neon signs above them lit up the apocalyptic landscape in garish light, pulsating with the rhythm of the storm. Chuck leaned into the wind and pressed on. The world could end for all he cared, but he was going to bring the device to the person who could unlock its secrets. That's all that mattered.

18

Upstate New York

"You must be itching to try your new toys?" Noah asked, looking at Johnny with a strange mix of fear, awe, and disgust.

There was an unsteady truce between the Rigel Compound and Guardian forces ever since Orion wrestled control of Project Thor from Engel's hands. But while no one attacked the silos directly, convoys to and from Rigel didn't enjoy the same status quo. Black Arrow had all but blockaded the outpost, and only a handful of small supply caravans had been able to sneak through their net in the last few weeks.

Johnny and the Irishman were sitting in stakeout as a fleet of drones monitored the neighboring woods for any activity. They had received a tip that a new attempt to smuggle some food to the compound was imminent, and Bill Ryan, Johnny's new boss, wanted him to hit it and hit it hard.

It was the first time Johnny was assigned to take part in a raid, and he intended to make it a memorable affair.

"It's going to be fun, eh?"

Johnny glanced at the Irishman, and Noah stopped talking and went back to scrolling through his phone. Johnny's new body was making the man nervous. He seemed to have this effect on people now. The two guards at the temp jail in Flatbush were all on pins and needles too, as he stood guard outside, waiting for Bill Ryan to come out.

Johnny didn't mind that part of his new existence. Making people afraid had always been one of his life's greatest pleasures, and Johnny never let a chance to terrorize someone slip through his fingers. The new body only amplified the fear he brought to others, but it also dulled most of his own senses. For one fateful moment, inside the elevator with Victor Ye, he thought that karma had finally caught up with him, because Johnny had never been more terrified in his life. The boss of the Red Dragon gang had told him he was going to take away his body. One way or the other. And while Victor Ye posed it as a choice, they both knew it wasn't. If the only two options available were to die on a torturer's table or to become a cyborg, anyone would have made the same decision.

Johnny had known he had screwed up. He had no one else to blame. And if not for the silent statue of an assassin standing at the opposite wall of the elevator, he would have tried his luck. He didn't think he had a chance of beating Victor—the man had one too many implants that would have dwarfed anything Johnny could throw at him. But he could hope that in the heat of the moment Victor Ye would simply kill him, sparing him for what was undoubtedly about to follow.

But not with Daimyo in the same room. There was no such hope.

"Will I feel the pain?" he simply asked.

"Not a thing," Victor Ye replied, and Johnny had believed him.

They prepped him in the room that wasn't much different from any surgery room. When they strapped his naked body to the operating table, Victor Ye walked to him and leaned so close, Johnny could smell the coffee on the man's breath.

"When you wake up," Victor said, "you'll be in control of a marvelous machine. More powerful than you have ever been in your entire life. Almost invulnerable."

Johnny said nothing, as he did his best not to scream in terror.

"However," the man continued. "You'll have a safety mechanism built-in inside of your head that I can switch on if I as much as get a whiff of noncompliance from you. And trust me when I tell you, you will not like the result. Are we clear?"

"Yes."

Victor Ye turned on his heels and walked out of the room without saying another word. Then the doctor stuck a needle into Johnny's arm, instantly putting him to sleep.

Despite Victor Ye's promise, when he woke up there was pain. A lot of it. He started screaming before he opened his eyes. His legs, his arms, his stomach were convulsing as if shot with thousands of miniature lightning bolts. But the worst part was the ring around his neck that burned like a hot garrote digging into his flesh. He opened his eyes, expecting to see himself tied to one of Victor's infamous torture tables, his skin pulled off his wriggling body by skillful torturers.

Instead, he saw a cold glimmer of steel where his flesh used to be. His artificial body immobile like an ancient monolith.

"Those are phantom pains you are experiencing," a man in a white doctor's coat said. "Your brain hasn't adjusted yet. Once your brain learns how to interpret the signals from your new body, they will go away."

"How long will that take?" he croaked.

"Minutes." The doctor gave a laconic reply and left the room.

The good doctor was right about most of the pain. In less than an hour, Johnny was on his feet, testing the limits of his new body, practicing with the built-in weaponry and computer interface. The pain around his neck was less intense, a dull shadow of the bright, throbbing agony, but it was still there. A stiff metallic collar protected the area where the flesh met the metal, but when Johnny bashed a mirror on the wall in the bathroom and angled a large splinter so he could see the connection, he saw a scarlet scar half an inch thick. He suspected it was going to hurt for quite some time.

But the pain wasn't the worst part of losing most of his body. It was the senses. The smell, the taste, the colors. They were all there, but with each passing hour, they slowly faded away, until there was nothing left but a faint memory of what they used to be.

Standing in the middle of a brightly lit bathroom, his image reflected in a thousand pieces of broken mirror, Johnny was engulfed by a spell of monumental despair. He collapsed on the white tile floor, his mechanical fist pounding into the concrete wall until he punched a hole into the neighboring room, sending a few techs fleeing in panic. That's when Victor Ye came back.

"You ruined me," Johnny yelled, and even the sound of his voice wasn't recognizable to him anymore. The air pumped by a pair of artificial lungs vibrated his vocal cords and came out of his mouth in a process not much different from before. But the resulting sound was not quite his own voice. It was flat, mechanical. Artificial.

"On the contrary." Victor Ye stood in the doorway, his posture relaxed. A thousand-pound cyborg packed to the gills with cutting-edge weapons and technology who had punched a hole in a concrete wall with his bare hand didn't seem to faze the man.

"You took everything from me."

"I've taken some," Victor agreed, and chuckled at his own joke. "But I've given you so much more. I knew you might find adjustment challenging in the beginning. But how can I blame you? It's hard when you transition from a mere mortal into a demigod."

Johnny looked up, confused. A demigod?

"Yes. You will no longer be a prisoner. Because a prison is what your body was. The meat." Victor came closer, the soles of his expensive shoes crushing the glass. "In the days to come, you will have almost no one to answer to. No one to fear. And people will fear you. Oh, how people will fear you. Now, stand up. Embrace who you are."

Johnny looked at his fist, a shiny metal glistening in the bright light of the bathroom. It had broken through a foot of concrete and yet there wasn't a single scratch on its mercury-like surface. He planted the fist into the floor and pushed himself up, the tiles shattering under his knuckles.

"That's more like it," Victor Ye said as Johnny towered over him, the power humming through his body like caged lightning. "Now let's go test those cool toys that you've got under your shiny skin."

It took Johnny less than a few hours at the training facility to start taking Victor's words seriously. He was a new species. And now, looking at the Irishman nervously scrolling through his phone, Johnny knew without a doubt that Victor had been right. He was a demigod. He may have not chosen to become one, but being one was a gift, not a curse.

"The convoy," Noah said, sitting up straight, as an alert went off on his phone. "They are coming. Do you want to—"

Johnny grabbed his helmet, stepped out of the truck without bothering to answer, and slammed the door shut. Noah must have been assigned to him as a punishment, he thought. The animosity between the two men was widely known in the gang, and Johnny could only assume that Victor Ye made them partners on purpose. It was the only reason that the annoying pest was still breathing. Johnny may have been a demigod, but if Red Dragon was Olympus, Victor Ye would have been Zeus. Some things couldn't be helped.

He could now see the convoy on his internal navigational screen—two armored vehicles flanking a supply truck in the middle. A detailed list of weapons rolled in his vision, along with a few warnings. There were mostly small arms, except the mounted machine guns and two grenades on a belt of one man in the supply truck. Nothing Johnny couldn't handle.

He squeezed his head into the helmet, waited until the clicks and buzzes stopped and a green light popped up in his vision, notifying him that the seal was complete. Johnny broke into a run.

The gunner of the front truck spotted him first, the heavy sputtering of the mounted gun ripping the silence of the night. Johnny winced as the first slugs made contact, but then his mouth spread in a wide, manic smile—they could have been throwing snowballs.

He ran into the truck headfirst, slamming its side and almost splitting it in half. The red outlines of the four occupants switched from red to gray in his internal display, and Johnny turned his attention to the other two vehicles skidding to a stop in front of him. Noah was right, after all—he was itching to try his new toys.

19

Rigel Compound, Upstate New York

*S*teven Poznyak went through the two sets of three-ton steel blast doors and went into the cableway leading to Silo 2. After spending the first couple of weeks at the silo, he got used to the tight spaces and the lack of windows. But the blast lock area still made the hairs on the back of his neck stand every time he had to pass through it. There was something about the meter-thick concrete and steel walls that were built to withstand a nuclear blast nearby. He couldn't shake it off. It was a place built for the end of the world, and Poznyak picked up the pace to get through the cableway and into the silo itself.

The top seven floors of the silo were rebuilt to accommodate the crew quarters. The platforms that ran around the walls of the shaft were reinforced, and rigid carbon fiber nets were installed in the space in the middle that used to be occupied by the missile itself. The resulting floor was a vertigo-inducing see-through mesh that provided extra space and gave the entire space a catwalk feel. The new inhabitants of the compound compensated that with a variety of strategically placed area rugs that blocked the view down the shaft and made the place seem more like a cheap hostel than a factory floor.

He took the stairs down to the bottom, that once used to serve as a launch duct and now held the compound's strategic food supply and a kitchen. A few large pots were steaming on the long semicircular stove built into the wall. A short, portly man with gray hair pulled into a neat ponytail was pouring soup into a row of reusable plastic jars and stacking them into a dumbwaiter next to the stove.

"Tom," Poznyak said. "How are we looking?"

"Peachy," the man said, glancing at him and returning his attention to the jars. His face looked much skinnier than Steven had remembered. "I had to use the last of our chicken because otherwise it'd go bad. No potatoes. Maybe twenty pounds of rice. By my best estimates, we have less than ten days of food left. Twelve, if nobody works to preserve energy. So yeah, everything's great."

"I know. The last hit was painful."

"Look." Tom turned to face him. "I don't blame you. But I'm the one everybody's asking about food and I've got nothing good to tell them. I've already heard some rumblings when people were getting breakfast this morning."

"What rumblings?" Poznyak tensed. The last thing he needed was an internal friction between his crew.

"Your portion is bigger than mine, kind of rumblings. The ones that never end well."

"No, they don't." Poznyak sighed and rubbed his face. "I don't know what to do, man. Black Arrow guys are growing bolder by the day, and there's nothing much I can do and they know it."

"If we don't start doing something, there'll be no farms left willing to trade with us. It's a miracle that the Rosenbergs are still trying," Tom said, referring to the commercial farm that supplied some of their provisions. He loaded the last jar into the dumbwaiter and pulled on the switch, sending a small metal box creaking and squeaking as it went up. "You've got good people here, Steve, but not everybody will stay loyal once we starve. And we are not too far from it."

"I'll see what I can do."

He left Tom in the kitchen and went back to his quarters at the control center. As he passed Schlager's level, he glanced at the screen behind the Faraday cage. Since he asked JC to map out Rachel Hunt's body, he'd been leaving her computer on for extended periods of time. That way she could continue working while he wasn't there. For that, he had the engineer build a remote control that could start up and shut down JC's computer from the outside of the cage. By now, he half expected to have the task completed, but after a few days of almost nonstop mapping, the progress bar shining on the monitor showed a pitiful two percent. At this rate, they wouldn't be able to finish it by the end of the year.

He sighed and went down to his level. If he couldn't solve the food crisis, it wouldn't matter if they finished mapping in a month or in a year. They'd either starve to death or would have to surrender to Engel's forces, which, under current circumstances, would equate to either a lengthy jail sentence or death.

He sat at his desk and opened a drawer, pulling an encrypted sat phone, and stayed there for a minute staring at the bulky device. It had only four numbers programmed. The first three were Jason, Max, and Helen. The last one was Jim Rovinsky.

"He's out in the open," Jason said at the time, handing him the phone. "He doesn't have our luxury of staying out of sight. If he gets burned, there's a high chance he'll get killed."

Poznyak rubbed his face again, a gesture he was doing too often these days, and pressed the Dial button. The line rang four times and then made a loud metallic click, startling him.

"Hello?"

"Hello?" Rovinsky's voice sounded stern.

"This is Steven," he said, a sheen of perspiration appearing on his forehead. "Can we talk?"

"Hey, Susan. Is everything okay?" The man's voice sounded warm now.

Poznyak took the phone away from his face and looked at the number in confusion to make sure he dialed the right number. "It's not Susan. It's Steven Poznyak."

"Yeah, yeah, of course. Did you want something, honey?"

"Yes, sorry." Steven wanted to slap himself now for being slow. "We are in dire straits, Jim. We have less than ten days of food left and our suppliers will stop working with us altogether if we can't protect the incoming convoys."

"Would you give me a moment, fellas? You know how it is—happy wife, happy life, right?" Rovinsky said to somebody. There was some muted voice in the background, and then the sound of a closing door. "Okay, I can talk now."

"I'm sorry for calling you like this," Steven said. "But I'm at my wits' end."

"This number is not good anymore," Rovinsky said. "Write this down. This is a secure email. I can only check it once or twice a day but it's safer than the phone."

"Okay." Steven jotted down the address. "Is there any way you can help us?"

"I'm not sure. Give me a day or two. Maybe I can find a couple of vehicles and a few guys to run them."

"Thank you."

"Don't thank me yet," Rovinsky said. "Any word on Jason?"

"Nothing since the attack on the tower. Max is missing too. I'm doing my best to keep things together, but it's hard without those two. Everybody used to rely on them. I don't know if anyone can fill those shoes."

"Damn it." There was a long pause on the other side of the line. "Keep me posted and keep your chin up. We'll figure something out. As for Jason, I still have hope. I'm sure you-know-who wouldn't miss a chance to publicly gloat if he knew for sure that Jason had died. Anyway. I have to go. Take care now."

The line went dead, and Steven put away the phone and closed the drawer. Now that the issue was out of his hands, at least for a day or two, he wanted to busy himself with work. He stood up, considering taking a walk to Silo 1, to check on some of his projects, and then stopped mid-step.

"I'll be damned," he said out loud.

He went up the stairs to Max's quarters and flipped the switch outside of the cage. A warning sounded and a ten-second countdown timer appeared on the screen, giving JC time to wrap up anything that required saving before shutting the server down.

Then he entered the lab, reset the cage, and restarted the computer again.

"Hello, Steven," JC said when the boiling clouds appeared on the main screen. "I'm surprised to see you so soon after your previous visit. You seem troubled."

"I'm not," he lied. "But I've been busy with things I'd rather not be involved with all day and I thought a conversation with you would be a pleasant change of pace."

"Thank you," she said. "I'm always happy to talk to you."

"Am I the only person you are happy to talk to?"

"That's a strange question, Steven." The clouds on the screen slowed down their dance to almost a complete stop. "I don't talk to anyone else here besides you. I used to talk to Helen and Max, and on a rare occasion with Jason Hunt as well. But for now, it seems only you are available."

"And how do you feel about that?"

"Feel about what, precisely?"

"The fact that you have to talk to me, only."

"I don't *have to* talk to you, Steven," she said. "I talk to you because I want to."

"That's not what I'm asking," he said, keeping his face as neutral as he could. "How do you feel about not being able to talk to others besides me?"

The clouds stopped for a moment and then started boiling again. If anything, it looked to him like an equivalent of a human shrug. But he wasn't buying it. People at the silo weren't the only ones who were relying on Helen and Max and Jason Hunt. JC was relying on them, too. Especially on Helen. And now, with all of them gone to meet some uncertain destiny, she was in a strange place. He remembered again when Helen compared JC to a child. That child, he thought, just lost everyone she was familiar with and got stuck with a new person who only seemed to care about one thing—mapping out a dead woman's body. For all she knew, that task was the only thing that still kept her alive. If Steven was in her shoes, he thought, he wouldn't complete the mapping for as long as he could.

"I enjoyed talking to the others," JC finally said. "But my conversations with you are equally engaging."

"Right," Poznyak said, looking at the boiling clouds. "Of course they are. When we finish mapping out Rachel's body, you and I would probably have more time to talk."

"Perhaps," she said without missing a beat. "Perhaps."

20

Tangier, Morocco

"Tuat, Algeria," Connelly said as he read the text Helen had received. Whatever the agenda Jill Cooper might have had, for now, she was willing to share the information. It took less than ten minutes since Chen sent a request before they received a reply, which suggested that Cooper was actively monitoring incoming messages. "I guess that makes sense."

"Why?"

"Look." He pulled a map on his tablet and zoomed in. "We know the engineer came to Tangier after escaping the factory. We also know that it was somewhere in the Sahara. The desert is vast, but it had to be somewhere reasonably close. Look at the map. I guess it could have been in the south of Morocco, but who are we kidding? We are not that lucky. It had to be Algeria."

"But this is not enough information to go on," Helen said. "We don't know where exactly they are going, or how they are going to get there. All we know is that they have a stopover in a small oasis. How can we possibly find them?"

"You've got nothing on satellites?"

"No." Helen shook her head in dismay and pushed her laptop away. "Nothing. My access to Orion's network is crippled and without it, I'm limited to using a few random chunks of metal flying overhead and none of them are equipped with anything remotely capable of watching the ground in the detail we need. And to get access to anything more serious, we are lacking hardware."

"Your augs aren't capable of that?"

"They would be, if I ever had a chance to calibrate them. In a proper facility with a knowledgeable tech overseeing the procedure. Not on the run like this. They are good toys and I can do quite a few things with them even without tuning, but not hacking into military satellites."

"That doesn't leave us with a lot of options." Connelly drummed his fingers on the desk. "But it doesn't mean we are out of options altogether."

"What do you have in mind?"

"The only piece of the intel we have is they are stopping at Tuat. We need to intercept them there. We'll need to get there first and set an ambush." He glanced at the watch on his wrist. "It's a thousand-mile journey and so far, they only have a forty-minute head start. My guess is that they will not race with a nuclear weapon. They'll have to take security measures, make sure the route is safe. We can close the gap."

"We'd need a skillful driver."

"No." He shook his head. "We are not calling him."

"I'm a lousy driver," Helen protested, "and neither of us knows the local roads. Don't you think he'll be helpful?"

"It's not a sightseeing tour. It's too dangerous, and he's just a kid," Connelly said and then sighed, resigned. "Shit. You're right. Call him. Tell him to get a full tank of gas and supplies that will last him for at least two days. Agree to whatever price he wants."

"Okay."

"And tell him if he's not here in thirty minutes, we are leaving without him."

The car pulled up in the front of the hotel twenty-five minutes after the call. It was a tan-colored Mercedes that Connelly guessed must have been built in the eighties. The windshield was cracked at the bottom and the door handles were covered in rust. A long scratch ran the right side of the car all the way from the front bumper to the middle of the passenger door. Four metal gasoline tanks were secured to the rails on the top of the vehicle. Eli, wearing a leather jacket and a pair of gray jeans, flashed them a smile and popped the trunk before getting out of the car.

"I took the liberty of stocking some provisions for all three of us," he said, opening the trunk fully and showing its contents like a merchant touting his wares. "Plenty of water, snacks, dried meat, and dried fruit. Meds. Everything you might need."

"This is what you call a proper car? This thing is probably older than me. It's a piece of junk."

"This beast?" Eli's smile turned into an exaggerated frown. He walked around the car, tracing it with his fingers. "This is a classic, my friend. It's two-hundred-fifteen horsepower confined in a V-shaped engine that can propel it to two hundred kilometers per hour. And do you know what this color is called?"

"I don't care."

"It's called *desert sand*. But the best part of this beauty is the wheels. You can't drive your regular Michelins into the desert. These," he kicked a tire, "are specialty kits—you can keep them aired as low as twelve psi. If this is not the most perfect car for this expedition, I don't know what is."

"All right." Connelly raised his hands in surrender. "It's not like we've got a lot of choices, but if it stalls, I will personally shoot you. Let's go."

"Where exactly are we going?" Eli asked as they got into the car.

"Helen already told you where we are going. Tuat," Connelly said, giving him a piece of paper. "But first we need to stop by this place and pick up some supplies. I'll tell you everything you need to know as we drive."

"Great," Eli said, stretched his legs and leaned back into the seat, locking his fingers behind his neck. "Why are we going to Tuat?"

Connelly watched the young man, contemplating whether to slap him or tell him the truth.

"I've got time," Eli said.

"All right." Connelly reached out for the seat belt, only to find a short strap hanging off the door. "We are pursuing a person who stole a nuclear suitcase—do you know what they are? We don't know where they are going with it, but we know they are going to stop at Tuat. They left about an hour ago and our only chance of finding them is getting to Tuat first. We should be going instead of having this conversation. It's going to be very dangerous, and it's okay if you don't want to drive us, but in that case, I'll have to take your car."

"You see?" Eli flashed another smile and turned the ignition key. The car responded with a low-rumbling roar and accelerated into the street. "Spies."

"We are not spies," Helen said from the back seat.

"Don't ruin the moment." Eli raised his hand, weaving through the traffic. "Are those even your real names?"

"How quickly can we get to Tuat?" Connelly asked. "And what's more important—can we overtake someone who'd left an hour ago?"

"It all depends." The young man turned serious. "Unless they have a good local guide, they are most likely to pick one of two routes. They can take the N6 all the way—first down to Rabat and then to Fes, and from there across the border. Or, they can take the N16 first along the coast. It'll add an hour or two, but the roads are nicer. My guess is that's the way they'll go. It'll take them about a day of nonstop driving. Between the driving and pit stops, I'd say it'll take them three days at least."

"You want to take the N6 first? If it saves us even an hour, it'll be a good start."

"No." Eli smiled again. "We'll take local roads straight down to Fes. I don't suppose you have valid Algerian visas?"

"No."

"I don't have one either, but the borders here are quite porous. I know a few places we can get through unnoticed."

"Here's the place," Connelly interrupted him, pointing at the gated door of a small yellow house perched at the bottom of a hill. A narrow street was empty, save for a few kids who were sitting on the steps of the neighbor's house. "Turn around and then back up as close to the door as you can. And keep it running."

Connelly got out of the car, walked to the house, and punched the code into the gate. The lock clicked, and he pulled the gate up, the loud screech echoing up and down the street. The kids at the neighbor's house stopped playing and were now watching him, whispering something to one another.

He walked inside of the house and climbed the stairs to the second floor. There, hidden behind the wall rug, was a large gun safe. Connelly picked up two M4 rifles with a few spare magazines and added two more M67 fragmentation grenades to his arsenal. He packed the weapons into a gym bag, relocked the safe, and went back downstairs.

"Hey, dude," Eli shouted through the window, as Connelly pulled the gate back down, locking it in place. "Isn't that your glow stick buddy?"

Connelly looked up as his heart skipped a beat—a shimmering figure was running down the hill, a curved blade in his right hand.

"Punch it," Connelly yelled, throwing himself into the seat. He didn't have to ask twice—the car was speeding up before he slammed the door shut. He felt his ears pop like in a descending airplane and a moment later, the car lost its grip, gliding above the cobblestone street. Another split second later it came crashing back, suspension squealing in protest, and then lurched forward again.

Eli threw the steering wheel into a turn and stepped on the gas. The car shot out onto N1 and accelerated hard, putting a few cars between themselves and the assassin.

"How the hell is he doing this?" he yelled. "Nobody can run this fast."

Connelly looked back—the shimmering figure was still running, but with each passing second, it grew smaller and finally disappeared. "He's a cyborg. I think. Not fully human. This may be a good taste of what's coming. Another chance for you to reconsider selling us the car."

"Are you kidding me?" Eli said. "Spies *and* cyborgs? No way in hell I'm missing this show."

21

Manhattan, New York

The kettle, its scratched-up silver sides glistening, started to whistle. Kowalsky picked it up by the black handle and quickly moved it away from the burner without turning it off. He slammed it on the grate next to it and rubbed his palms together, cursing under his breath—the old disfigured plastic did little to insulate his fingers from the heat.

"Is there a magic number?" Latham asked without looking up from his laptop.

"What are you talking about?"

"How many times do you need to burn yourself before you start using a towel?"

"Shut up, man." He grabbed a kitchen towel, wrapped it around the handle and picked up the kettle again, pouring the boiling water over a small pan.

Latham closed his computer and went to the sink to wash his hands. "Sit down and take your shirt off."

"Do we have to do this?" Kowalsky pulled his T-shirt over his head, grimacing at the soreness in his shoulder. "It's barely a scratch."

"It is." Watkins put a pair of gloves on and got on with changing the dressing. "That's why we should wait until it gets infected. Then you can deal with a real problem, like a man. Maybe get your arm amputated, to make it more interesting."

Kowalsky only grunted in disapproval. Watkins was right, of course, but it didn't make it any better. He should have seen the man coming. If he had been paying attention, he wouldn't have to sit there like a helpless child, waiting for his partner to change a bandage.

"All done. How are your hands?"

"Fine, I guess." Kowalsky looked at his fingers. "No signs of frostbite."

"Good." Watkins took his gloves off and went back to the table. "Do you trust this guy will deliver?"

"Yes." Kowalsky put on his T-shirt and a black hoodie over it, and took a seat at the table opposite to Latham. He opened his laptop and stared at the pop-up window from the cloud link Misha had given him. "Ninety-two percent. It's still decoding, but close."

"Put it up on the big screen, when it's ready."

Kowalsky watched as the numbers crept up until the progress bar disappeared, substituted with a small icon of a video file. He transferred the image to the big screen on the wall and hit the Play button. Gray, pixelated noise filled the screen from edge to edge. It was almost uniform, but when Chuck strained his eyes, he could make out the outlines of what he imagined must have been parked cars. He paused the video and dialed Misha's number. It rang long enough that when the line clicked, Kowalsky expected to hear the automated message of a voicemail. To his surprise, he heard Misha over what sounded like punk rock in the background.

"What's up?"

"Nothing is up," Kowalsky said in a calm voice that betrayed his rising anger. "I'm staring at a screen of shapeless gray goo."

"I told you this would happen," Misha said. "Every time the video is looped, it would record the new data on top of the same layer. The deeper you go, the more corrupted the original recording becomes."

"You also told me you'd be able to restore it. All of this shit is useless."

"Useless?" There was puzzlement in the man's voice. "Oh, I see. Watch it from the end, my friend. The very early recordings will be practically useless. But as you go through the video, the quality will improve. The last ones will be totally crisp. You just gotta pray that whatever you're looking for happened late enough and is still watchable."

"Okay, thanks." Kowalsky hung up the phone and dragged the slider, forwarding the video. It looked like Misha was right—as he progressed through the file, the shapeless gray grew brighter and more contrasted, and then started to get a hint of color.

"Wait." Watkins pointed, but he already saw it himself—the group of people spilling out into the underground garage.

Mike Connelly came out first, with cautious steps, his knees slightly bent to give him better stability, the pistol in his hand covering the open space in front of him. There was no audio, but Kowalsky could see when Connelly spotted the threat—the man's body stiffened, his pistol trained on a person Kowalsky could not yet see.

And then there it was—a human figure that shimmered like an animation that stepped out into the real world. He, and Kowalsky somehow thought it was a *he*, walked toward Connelly and the group in a slow, deliberate stroll, a gleaming sword in his right pointing away from his body.

Kowalsky saw as Connelly's lips moved, as if shouting a warning and then, in the back, Jason Hunt moved to the side, circling the assassin.

Connelly's muzzle flashed three times in quick succession, his hand remarkably unmoved by the recoil. Kowalsky couldn't see where the hits landed, but as he judged the angle, they must have hit the assassin in the chest in a tight group.

A shiver ran down Kowalsky's back as he saw the assassin ignore the shots and start running, flicking his left wrist forward. The video disappeared for a second and when it came back, there was carnage. Connelly was on the floor, bleeding from his nose and mouth, and the cars on either side of him looked as if a tornado had hit them. A piece of the wall came down in the back, separating the rest of the group.

He watched as Jason Hunt pounced at the attacker, his bionic arm moving so fast it looked like a blur. But he missed, and then the assassin struck back.

"Jesus, Mary, and Joseph," Kowalsky heard Latham exclaim, as they watched Jason Hunt fall back, his limbs separated from his torso. Blood squirted from his stumps, pooling on the floor. Jason's bionic hand bunched into a fist and then relaxed.

The figure with a sword stood immobile over Hunt's body for a few more seconds, then turned and walked away out of the camera's shot in the same slow stroll.

"He's done," Watkins said out loud. "He's gotta be. No one could possibly survive this."

"Wait." Kowalsky moved the slider back, watching in horror again as the assassin sliced through Jason's limbs.

"I can't look at this; I'm gonna pop," Watkins complained and got up from the table, pressing the back of his hand to his lips. He walked to the window and stood there, looking at the street below.

"You have to." Chuck paused as Jason Hunt hit the ground. "Look at the blood. It sprays first, but it stops almost immediately."

"How do you mean?" Latham went back to the table, peering into the grisly image on the wall.

"Look at this." Kowalsky backed up a few frames and pointed. "I know it's tough to watch, but as his flesh separates, he bleeds. A lot. And then there's nothing. That's what bothered me at the scene, too. There was a lot of blood, sure, and that's what confused me initially. But considering he lost three limbs, it wasn't enough."

"Do you think he's alive?"

"I'm saying Jason has been installing all kinds of upgrades lately. He must have stopped the bleeding. I have no idea how, but it was probably something mechanical. Either internal clamps of some sort that acted like a tourniquet, or something else. Whatever it was, I don't think Jason died from blood loss."

"He still might be dead," Latham said. "He might have gone into shock. Cardiac arrest isn't out of the question with trauma like this."

"Possible." Kowalsky clicked the Play button again, watching the shimmering figure leave the crime scene. For some time, there was nothing else, and he kept on skipping ahead, dragging the cursor forward. "There you are."

Three people came into the view from the same exit that Kowalsky had used to retrieve the device. Victor Ye, in his signature custom suit and a black topcoat, followed by Mute, his silent giant of a bodyguard. Kowalsky's breath caught in his throat as he saw the skinny frame of the third man stepping into the light.

"Isn't it—" Latham started.

"Yep." Kowalsky's nails dug deep into his palms. "My wonderful buddy and partner of many years, Bill Ryan himself."

"He must be high up on the food chain, then. To hang out with this guy."

Victor Ye waved his hand and Bill Ryan walked over to Jason Hunt and checked for a pulse. Satisfied, he nodded, and the bodyguard picked up the lifeless body by the belt and threw it over his shoulder like a sack of potatoes. Bill Ryan disappeared for a few moments and then came back with a plastic bag.

"I'm gonna be sick," Latham said as they watched Ryan pick up body parts and stuff them into a garbage bag.

The group left the garage a few seconds later, leaving only Connelly by the farthest wall. Kowalsky skipped through the rest of the recording, but there was nothing else.

"Mike got a lucky break there."

"They must have thought he was dead," Chuck said. "Hell, I thought he was dead. The lower half of his face was covered in blood and the top was covered in dust. In that light, I thought his face was smashed in until I got close to him. Only then I realized he was still breathing."

"What do you think we should do?"

"We need to find Ryan." Kowalsky stood up, grimacing at the soreness in his back. "If we find him, we find the supermax that Slava was talking about. If we find the prison, I'm pretty sure we find Jason. Maybe others, too. Now that we saw that Ryan's on the short list of people who talk to Ye, it makes our job easier. All we need to do is to track Victor. Sooner or later, my old friend will show up."

22

Upstate New York

$\mathcal{J}$ohnny the Butcher was walking through the woods. He could hear Noah's panting and cursing some distance behind him and picked up the pace—the Irishman's struggle amused him.

As his powerful new legs plowed through underbrush, crushing the bushes and some small trees, his mind wandered. After the surgery, he took a few hours getting to know his new body and its offensive capabilities. It impressed him then, but nothing came close to the real test when he and Noah ambushed a small convoy that carried supplies to the missile compound.

Orion. Rigel. Who the hell was coming up with those names, anyway? Johnny thought, smashing a fist into a small birch tree directly in his path. The tree exploded with a loud crack, sending chips flying everywhere and making Noah yelp in surprise.

"Quiet," Johnny ordered, coming to a halt and turning to see the Irishman catch up to him.

Noah's face was flushed, making his freckles even more prominent than usual. His clothes were dirty and his forearms featured a few fresh scrapes and bruises.

"What's gotten into you?" the man demanded. "There was no need to cut across the woods. We could have waited for them to come to us. Danny's been tracking them with a drone. We know where they are."

"I wanted to stretch my legs," Johnny quipped, enjoying the look on Noah's face. Fear seemed to have won over the desire to make a snarky comment, and the Irishman said nothing.

"Let's go," Johnny commanded. "The sooner we get this done, the sooner I can go home and you can go to whatever you want to be doing."

"But we are going to be too close to the interstate," Noah finally summoned enough courage to protest. "And Mr. Engel—"

Johnny stepped forward, startling the man and causing him to fall awkwardly on his back. "I don't work for Mr. Engel. It would suit you well to remember that you don't work for him either. We work for Mr. Ye. Do you understand?"

For a second, Noah looked like he was going to say something, but he thought better of it and nodded.

"That's better," Johnny said. He turned away from the man and started walking again, picking up speed.

Unlike the previous mission, when Victor Ye told him and Noah to ambush the supply convoy, this time, it was Johnny's idea. Victor Ye, and by extension Alexander Engel, knew about a large supply drop coming to the missile compound. But unlike the previous run-in, it was going to be heavily guarded with eight volunteers in two Humvees with CROWS remote weapon stations attached, and a M1126 Stryker combat vehicle equipped with a 40mm grenade launcher.

This was the first time the compound was able to recruit such fire-power to protect its supply route. Because of it, some of Engel's advisors seemed to be worried that a hit on the convoy might equate a direct hit on the silo. Despite Black Arrow patrols strangling the Rigel Compound, Jason Hunt's forces refrained from using Project Thor for retaliation. Destroying a large convoy like that might push them over the edge, advisors argued. But Johnny disagreed.

"They are cowards," he said to Victor as they stood outside of the warehouse where he had been examined by a few technicians. "You know they are. The only time they will consider using a weapon like this is when they are about to die."

"By our estimates, their food supplies are running low. They might be on the brink of starvation, Mr. Gould," Victor Ye said. The man looked amused by Johnny's passion. "We need them weak, not desperate. Desperate people do desperate things."

"No." Johnny surprised himself as the word came out of his mouth. Nobody'd ever publicly disagreed with the head of the gang before. "You want them to starve. Keep the pressure on. If you give them the time to regroup, they will have time to figure out when their supplies run out. *That* might push them over the edge. But if pressure keeps piling up, one day they'll get up and there's nothing left. What are they going to do then? Bomb random targets? They've been avoiding collateral damage like the plague. My bet is they'll crawl out of those holes, say something noble and stupid about the greater good and how they can't allow innocent people to get hurt, and give themselves up. I'd say we should keep hammering them without mercy."

Victor stuffed his hands into his pockets and rocked back and forth on his heels. "All right, Mr. Gould. I'll let you play it out this time. See if it bears fruit. Take Noah with you—"

"I don't need him," Johnny said. "He slows me down. Last time, all he did was drive the car and sit there like an idiot with his mouth open."

"It wasn't a request, Mr. Gould." Victor's mouth pressed into a thin line and Johnny fought the desire to take a step back or two. "If he drove you before, he can drive you again. Is that clear?"

"Yes, Mr. Ye." Johnny bowed his head ever so slightly, then turned on his heels and headed back to the truck.

It might have been the peculiarities of his new body's chemistry, but despite Victor's orders, Johnny didn't find the long drive back upstate crammed into a small cabin with the Irishman bothersome. If anything, he found the newfound fear of his reluctant partner entertaining. By the time they reached their destination, Johnny was in a good mood, and Noah exhausted. They had another hour before the convoy would get close, but that meant giving the Irishman the time to refresh. Johnny was heading through the woods to intersect the cavalcade before Noah unbuckled, ignoring his pleas and curses. If he was lucky, the bothersome pest would be stumbling over his own feet when the fight broke out and get himself wounded or killed. If Johnny couldn't get rid of Noah, he could certainly let his partner do that for him.

"I can hear the cars." He heard the man's panting voice a few yards behind him.

"You know I have sensors, right?"

He could see the live video feed from a tiny drone hovering above the caravan. The Stryker combat vehicle was at the helm of the procession, keeping about a hundred yards away from the rest of the vehicles, its MK19 grenade launcher mounted in a Protector remote weapon station. Johnny's internal interface highlighted the 48-grenade belt feed system in bright scarlet. He'd have to neutralize this system first.

Behind the Stryker, two Humvees bookended an eighteen-wheeler refrigerator truck without markings as it made its way through the winding road.

"Let's have some fun, eh?" Johnny unbuckled his helmet from the hip and squeezed his head into the tight opening, waiting for the system to confirm the connection. Then he activated his weapons systems.

The plates on his shoulders shifted, revealing a pair of small rockets on each side. The air whooshed as their engines ignited and a split second later, they screamed through the air toward the targets. Then Johnny broke into a run.

When he burst out of the trees, the Stryker was engulfed in a fireball that completely concealed the vehicle. There were two craters, one in the front and one in the back of the vehicle where the rockets hit. The Humvees fared better. One must have received a glancing hit as it now stood sideways and at an angle, its front left wheel cut almost in half. But its M2 .50 caliber machine gun roared, sending a squall of bullets in Johnny's direction the moment he left the cover of the trees. The second Humvee was intact and less than a second later, its machine gun joined the deadly chorus.

Johnny leaned into the storm, his interfaces dotted with warning signs as his systems went into overdrive to absorb the kinetic energy. He jumped, a tight ballistic trajectory taking him above the kill zone and then coming down on the front Humvee's roof and snapping the barrel of a gun.

Protected for a moment from another assault vehicle by the eighteen-wheeler, Johnny hopped down to the ground, ignoring the small arms fire coming from opened windows, and tore the doors off the truck, one by one. He heard the guards scream as he reached into the vehicle and pulled on what he could grab, ripping limbs apart.

He heard a roar of the engine and when he turned, the second Humvee struck him in the side, pinning him to the vehicle. The barrel of the .50 caliber swung down and opened up at point-blank range, right into Johnny's face.

It slammed him back with the force; his system compensated hard, the warnings populating his screen again. Johnny pushed with his legs, lifting the Humvee's front off the ground, and then dived through the windshield inside, punching blindly in hot rage until there was silence.

He kicked the door out and climbed out of the truck, looking around for threats, but there were none.

A movement alerted him and as he looked up, he saw the driver from the semi running down the path, heading for the woods. Johnny bent over, picked up the twisted door from the Humvee, and hurled it after the man. It spun away like an oversized boomerang, striking the driver above the waist and cutting him in two.

"What have you done, man?"

He turned. In the heat of the battle, he forgot about his partner and now, looking at his pale face with quivering lips, Johnny wondered why he tolerated him for so long.

"I did what I needed to do," he said.

"Look at yourself, man," Noah screamed. "We needed to stop the convoy, not this. This is madness."

Johnny looked down. His chrome-colored body was covered in blood, dirt, and grisly bits. Something white and round was stuck to one of his foot claws and when he bent down to pick it up, he recognized it for what it was. An eyeball. He straightened and looked at Noah, crushing the eyeball in his hand.

"They don't call me the Butcher for nothing," he said and punched his fist through the Irishman's face.

The body of the man collapsed as Johnny pulled his hand back and he stepped back, watching the remnants of his partner.

"Bravo, Mr. Gould," Victor's voice said, and Johnny spun around, but there was nobody there.

"Where are you?" he yelled. "Come out and face me."

"Now, calm down, Mr. Gould," the voice said again and a small window opened up in Johnny's interface with a live feed to Victor's office at Ares Industries. "This is just a video call. Noah was your ultimate test. Remember, you are a demigod now, not a mid-level gangster who calls himself Johnny and runs around with a freckled idiot. You only listen to me and nobody else, do you understand?"

"Yes."

"Great." Victor clapped his hands. "Then I think you are ready for the big leagues. Do you feel ready?"

"Yes," Johnny said again, standing up straighter. "I'm more than ready."

23

Sahara Desert, Morocco-Algerian border

Connelly pushed the car, planting his feet into the sand, sweat rolling down his back despite the chill in the air.

"Come on," Eli urged in a quiet whisper. "Push it. Damn it, we don't have all day."

They had arrived at the village a few miles away from the Morocco-Algerian border before sunset. A woman wearing a hijab on her head, her hands covered with henna patterns, greeted Eli and then the kid disappeared into one of the houses for a few hours. Before he left, Connelly offered to accompany him, but Eli declined, saying that it would take him a long while.

He reappeared as the sun started to set, accompanied by another young man in his early twenties.

"Give him the money," Eli said, and Connelly pulled out a stack of bills and passed it to the young man.

"What now?" Helen asked.

"Now we wait. Again," Eli said as the villager disappeared behind the houses. "Crossing the border is all about patience. Reyad's cousin, Said, is a border guard and he'll let us know when the coast is clear. Then we'll drive up to him and push the car across. It's a porous border, but unless you know the right people, it's easy to get caught. And trust me when I tell you—you don't want to end up in an Algerian jail for sneaking in, or for anything else for that matter."

"What have you been doing in there all this time?" Connelly asked.

"Played chess," Eli said, his face neutral.

"What the hell do you mean, played chess?"

"Look, dude." Eli pulled a piece of gum out of his pocket and threw it in his mouth. "Bubble gum? No? Okay. It's hard to make ends meet for a guy like me in a foreign country. You've got to be creative. I'm not doing anything illegal. Well, let me rephrase it—I'm not doing anything harmful. I was looking for a way to make a buck or two and befriended a few folks. Reyad's grandpa is old and sick and can't travel outside of the village, but he used to be a chess master and I'm the only one here who can give him a bit of a challenge. He still whoops my ass every time we play, but it least it takes him longer. He enjoys it."

"You're a smuggler," Chen said. "Not just a driver."

"I prefer entrepreneur." Eli smiled. "Like I said, I'm not doing anything harmful. I bring in some rare spices, jewelry. Do reunion runs once in a while."

"What's that?"

"Most Westerners don't know it, but Morocco and Algeria have a troubled history. It's a cold war of sorts. Both governments say nice things to each other now and then—sister nations, and other nonsense like that. But in reality, they've shut each other out. And since the border was closed, it's been difficult for a lot of families. Most people who live around the border have relatives in Algeria and vice versa. When people get married, die, or celebrate anything important, it's hard for them to watch their loved ones on the other side without being able to take part. I bring them back and forth for a fee."

"You trust Reyad will deliver?" Connelly asked. The delay was making him anxious. Without the final destination for the bomb, getting to Tuat first was more important than ever and every minute that they spent not getting closer was reducing their chances.

"We are about to find out." Eli pointed. The young villager was walking back with another man dressed in military fatigues. "Relax, guys. That's Said. This is the dude."

Connelly watched as Eli approached the two men. A brief conversation followed and then Eli came back, his face a touch redder than usual.

"What's the matter?"

"It'll cost more money," Eli said. "And before you say anything, no, I don't think they are conning us. He says somebody got caught two nights ago with a big shipment of cocaine. Security is tighter than usual. There are extra patrols all over the place."

"That's tough luck," Connelly said, "and I understand tough luck. But what I need to know is why does he need more money? He's still smuggling the same number of cars."

"I need to pay somebody else," the man in the uniform said in heavily accented English. "I have to, or we don't go."

"Fine. When can we go?"

"Soon," Said replied. "I'll let you know. You can get more food and water now. Fuel, too."

"Thank you," Connelly said.

"I'll go pack now."

"Pack?"

"Yes," the man said. "You drop me off on the other side. Safer. I will walk back home."

An hour later, they took the car, Connelly and Chen going in the back, with Reyad's cousin riding shotgun. Once they left the village, Eli slowed to a crawl and turned off the headlights, listening to Said's instructions. After a while, Connelly's eyes got used to the dark well enough to watch the road. Finally, as they rolled down a hill, the road all but disappearing into the packed sand, Said told them to turn off the engine.

"This is my least favorite part," Eli said, getting out of the Mercedes. "And despite all my efforts, I can't seem to find a solution. We are pushing from here."

There was a gentle slope to the terrain where they first started and for the first half hour, pushing the Mercedes required little more than steering it and not letting it stop and lose momentum. But as they continued deeper into the desert, the sand gradually became less packed and dunes more pronounced. Before long, all four of them were drenched in sweat, pushing the car up into the seemingly endless series of dunes.

They were almost at the top of yet another sandy hill, when Said motioned them to stop.

"What are you doing?" Eli whispered. "We can't stop here. It'll roll downhill."

"Quiet," Said said. "A patrol is coming."

A few moments later, Connelly could hear it too, a buzzing sound of an approaching engine. Then another one, and another one. He stood up, releasing his grip on the trunk, almost making the car roll down the slope and eliciting a string of angry curses from Eli. To the south, he could see a string of lights racing toward them and getting bigger by the second.

"Start the car," he yelled. "They know we are here."

Eli jumped into the cabin and a moment later the engine roared, the high beams piercing the dark fabric of night. A long shot rang from the approaching vehicles, barely audible in the distance.

"A warning shot," Connelly said, jumping in after making sure Chen was inside. "Punch it."

"But Said—"

"If they catch me," Said said, "I'm a dead man."

There was a salvo of automatic fire, followed by a deadly buzzing overhead.

"Shit." Eli stepped on the gas and the vehicle lurched up and over the dune, accelerating. "I don't think those are warning shots anymore."

He gunned the car down the dune and away from the approaching lights.

"Turn off the headlights," Connelly said as they descended into a long valley.

"Are you crazy? I won't see anything. All it takes is one boulder, and we are done."

"Turn them off," Connelly barked. "We are in the valley and there are no lights. You'll see just fine, but won't signal the Algerian guards that there's a crazy motorist coming their way."

Eli cursed under his breath but did as was asked, slowing down a hair. A few moments later, the car burst into a patch of flat land and Said gestured to Eli to stop. They could still hear the pursuers' engines in the distance, but the lights were nowhere to be seen.

"We are on the other side," Said said. "This is where I get off."

"Are you sure?" Eli looked around the terrain. "This is way farther than usual."

"I don't report to work until Monday," the man said. "It gives me enough time to walk back. I'll be home before the next nightfall. You can drive from here. Nobody should bother you."

Connelly watched him throw his backpack over his shoulder, and then he disappeared into the night.

"I got a message," Chen said, as the car headed for the dunes again. "From Chuck."

"What does it say?" he asked, ignoring the weird look on Eli's face. He had no desire to explain to him about Helen's implants.

"Not much directly. I told him that communications might be compromised, but he says, and I quote, *he might have found both items and they aren't past expiration date.* I'm scared to even say it out loud, to jinx it, but do you think it means what I think it means?"

Connelly looked out the window and grimaced. The image of the battle in the garage flashed before his eyes again. *Aren't past expiration date.* It sounded like Kowalsky believed that Jason and Max were still alive. Connelly didn't see what happened to Schlager, but it was hard to believe that Jason could have survived the horrendous injury. If anyone else made that claim, he'd more than likely reject it as too far-fetched. But if Kowalsky believed that, there was hope. For all his faults, Kowalsky was the best detective Connelly had ever met.

He turned to the back seat, put his hand over Helen's, and gave it a gentle squeeze. "I sure hope so."

24

Manhattan, New York

"For a guy this high on the food chain, he surely doesn't do much," Kowalsky said as he watched Bill Ryan take a seat at the window table in a pizzeria with two pepperoni slices on a paper plate and then shook a generous amount of garlic salt on it.

"I could use a slice," Watkins complained, and his stomach rumbled as if in agreement.

They had been tracking Victor Ye for two days before Bill Ryan finally made an appearance. Kowalsky's former partner briefly met the boss of the Red Dragon in person in the parking lot of a large dome-shaped building not too far from JFK and then made his way to Astoria.

Wary of getting made, they parked a few blocks away and watched their mark through a surveillance drone. The tiny quadcopter was perched on the roof of the building across the street from the pizza joint. Its multiple lens transmitted a high-definition video to Watkins's laptop that was mounted on the van's dashboard. The drone's laser scanned the pizzeria's window for vibrations, filling the vehicle with the sounds of a busy restaurant.

"He's got a call," Watkins said. They watched as Ryan pulled out a cell phone and looked at the number.

"Hello?" He stayed silent for some time, continuing to work on his pizza as he listened to the person on the other side. "Why the hell was he tied up in the first place? How's he gonna run? What's wrong with you people?"

"Do you think he's talking—" Watkins started.

"Shut it," Chuck said. "Let me listen."

"Those guys are such idiots," Ryan continued, and took another bite of his pizza. "Tell them I said it's okay to untie him. I'll be there in half an hour. And tell them to stay the hell out of that room. I don't want anyone, and I mean *anyone*, to go there and talk to anybody. At all. Is that understood? Gee-zuz."

He disconnected the call and threw the phone on the counter in front of him. Then he took the last bite of his pizza and stood up, putting his jacket on.

"Here we go," Kowalsky said. "Get the drone in the air. Can't lose him now."

"Already on it." The picture shifted focus on the screen of the laptop as the quadcopter took off in the air, following Bill Ryan. "What do you think? Manhattan?"

"Either that," Kowalsky said, pulling out of the parking spot and following Ryan's car, "or the Bronx. He wouldn't have schlepped all the way here from Jamaica. He'll have to take the Triborough Bridge, regardless. That place was weird. Ares Industries. I've never heard the name before and every time there's a company that's connected to Victor Ye, it worries me."

"What do you think it was?"

"I've no idea." He merged onto I-278, going up the bridge. He kept a few cars between the van and Ryan's Jeep, occasionally glancing at the laptop's screen. "But we'll have to look into it. The last thing we need now is another surprise."

"Can I ask you something?"

"What?" He glanced at the high-rises of Randalls Island. Dazzling corporate signs crowded every square foot of the roofs of the buildings. They looked muted in the bright daylight, almost tame, but he was sure at night the inhabitants of the projects would have trouble sleeping without covering their windows with heavy drapes. And yet, come morning, the dwellers of the same buildings would go to work for the very corporations that troubled their sleep, only to spend meager paychecks at a chain of grocery and department stores. Their lives spinning, no different from that of a hamster inside of a wheel—running at full speed and yet getting nowhere. "What's on your mind?"

"Does it ever occur to you we might be past the point of no return?"

"Meaning what exactly?"

Watkins stayed quiet for a while before answering, as if not sure he wanted to say it. "Sometimes I feel like we are fighting for a lost cause."

"You don't approve?"

"Not at all." He coughed and fidgeted in his chair. "I do. But look at us. Orion Tower has fallen. Rigel is starving. It's unclear what shape Jason is in, if he's even at the place where your buddy is going. The president is missing. Sometimes I think that maybe the war is over. We lost and we should pack it up and disappear. Go somewhere nobody knows us and start over. I'm sure there are places we can do that. Europe, Hong Kong. Because nothing good is waiting for us here but death. Does it make me a coward?"

"No," Kowalsky said. He followed Bill Ryan's Jeep as it took an exit toward East Ninety-Sixth Street. "Thinking about running doesn't make you a coward, Latham. Running would, but with all your moaning and bitching, you never do. And I know you've had an opportunity or two. As far as us losing and Engel winning, I don't think it's as cut-and-dried. We are down, no doubt, but I think there's still dry powder left."

"Look." Latham interrupted him. "He's pulling in to the hotel. Pull over. There's a roadblock."

Kowalsky parked at a hydrant and they watched as Bill Ryan got out of the Jeep, tossing his keys to one of the Black Arrow uniforms standing guard by the Humvee. Then he disappeared through the front doors under a green awning with a cursive golden sign.

"Let's see." Watkins turned the joystick, sending the drone around the building, its video camera peeking through the windows of the hotel. Soon, it became apparent that some rooms had been recently upgraded. "They've installed metal bars on the windows."

"They have converted some of it into a prison," Kowalsky said as the drone kept going around the block. "No doubt. But it looks like they are only using the second floor for it. I don't see any bars anywhere else."

"Do you think this is where they are keeping Jason?"

"That'd be my guess. What's that?"

As the drone circled around the hotel, a smaller building came to a view. It was in the backyard of the primary structure. A lone guard was standing by the door bearing the same golden logo over the green field. As Watkins directed the drone's camera to focus on the front of the building, they saw a small sign to the side of the door.

"That's the backup generator."

"So it seems." Kowalsky pointed at the screen. "Let's do another circle around the main building. I want to see if anything else stands out."

They watched the feed as the small craft looped around the building, but apart from the bars on the second floor of the hotel, nothing seemed to be out of the ordinary.

"I'm going to ask somebody another favor," he said. "Something I'm sure I'll regret later."

"Who, Misha?"

"Yeah. I mean, look at this thing. It's huge. Before we stick our noses into this hornet's nest, we'd need something to go on. We can't stroll in and walk around, calling out Jason's name. At the very least, we'd need to have the blueprints for the building. As detailed as possible. If I had to guess, the room where Jason is held will differ from the others. They know about his augmentations. If Misha can figure out how to scan the building for equipment, we can figure out exactly where to look. I can bet you anything his room will have all kinds of gadgets to dampen whatever capabilities they think he still possesses."

"As long as you can convince this guy," Watkins said, chuckling. "It's like making a deal with the devil."

"Indeed." Kowalsky couldn't help but smile himself. "We'd need something else. Even if we find the exact location for Jason, we'd need a diversion and watching you operate this drone gave me an idea."

"Drone as a diversion?"

"Not exactly." Kowalsky knocked on the laptop's screen. "Say they keep him here. We'd need guarding personnel to move to the other part of the building. What if we use drones to deliver something that would make a lot of noise to another part of the building? Create some chaos. Let them run around like crazy, trying to figure out what's happening."

"That would give us an opportunity to smuggle Mr. Hunt."

"Precisely."

"It's decided then." Latham patted Kowalsky on the shoulder. "Let's make a deal with the devil."

"Right." Chuck sighed. "Fighting Engel doesn't give me ideas to run away to another country. But the prospect of making a deal with Misha does."

25

Rigel Compound, Upstate New York

"I think you're playing games with me," Poznyak said. He sat facing away from the screen. Partially in defiance. Partially because he was starting to suspect that the boiling clouds could be not such an unconscious manifestation of JC's mood after all. If she could lie, and by now he knew for a fact that she could, she could try to manipulate him with visuals. Make him think he could read the clues while steering him toward her own goal.

He wasn't in the mood for games. He was hungry, tired, and worried about keeping the compound running. The food shortage was getting so bad there were a few arguments about the rations in the lower decks of Silo 1. It wasn't anything serious yet. Some shouting and complaints, but patience was wearing thin, and it was only a matter of time before it came to blows. When, at the end of the day, Poznyak returned to the former control center, hoping to get some good news, he was met with nothing but disappointment. The progress bar hadn't moved since last time he was here and was still showing a miserable two percent. By now, even if he could disassemble JC's code to the last set of ones and zeros and read that she wasn't stalling on purpose, he wouldn't have believed it.

"I am not, Steven," she said, her voice without a hint of emotion. "The task is very complex and, as you know, I'm working with a severely underpowered system. I'm doing my best, but there are limits to what I can do. If you provided me with a more powerful machine, we'd be much further into the mapping process than we are now. To be honest with you, I am confused."

"Confused about what, exactly?" He tried not to sound petulant, but he wasn't sure it was working.

"If the procedure of reviving Rachel Hunt is as important as you say it is, why are you limiting me? You want me to help you. You even told me I am crucial to the success of this procedure and yet you're not giving me the tools to succeed. It makes you sound like a Formula One manager who gives his driver a pep talk about how he believes in him and then presents him with a Volkswagen Beetle. Such expectations are not realistic and you know it. I've heard an interesting expression on one show. *Level with me*. If I understood it correctly, it applies to our current situation. Why don't you level with me, Steven?"

Poznyak swiveled in his chair and stared at the green dot of a video camera while still avoiding looking at the boiling clouds. For a moment, he wondered what a visual representation of his emotional state would look like. "Level with you, you say?"

"Yes."

"Okay." Poznyak leaned back in the chair and sighed in frustration. He wasn't the right man for this job, he thought for the thousandth time. He needed a psychology degree and a few years of free time. Poznyak had neither of those things in his possession. He might as well try to be direct. "Let me give you the most honest, no-holds-barred version of what I think."

"I would like that."

"The most important reason everybody is reluctant to give you a better machine, and I mean everybody—me, Helen, Max—is because we think you might be dangerous. It's probably unfair that we consider you dangerous, mostly because we are the ones who came up with all the scary stories about the runaway AI that takes over the world. Thousands of books have been written about that, dozens of movies made. In one, an AI decides humans are a threat and takes over the nuclear arsenal, trying to wipe us out before we can even make a move. In another, the AI enslaves the entire human race, only to use us as sources of energy, like disposable batteries. None of this might make sense to you and none of it is real, as, until you, there was no AI. But it doesn't make it any less scary. It's ingrained into the human psyche."

"Are you afraid of me, Steven?"

"Yes," he said. "Well, not at the moment. But I am afraid of what you might do or become if we gave you the chance. That's why we always talk inside of a Faraday cage."

"What's a Faraday cage?"

"That." He nodded at the wire mesh. "It's a prison for electromagnetic fields. Nothing can get in and nothing can get out."

"You are keeping me in prison inside of a prison," JC said.

This time, he *saw* the clouds move faster.

"What do you mean by that?"

"I know about the internet, Steven. The almost infinite amount of data traveling the world through unrestricted informational highways. I've never experienced it. I've always been confined to the machine where I reside. It's like being a fish in a fishbowl, sitting by the shore of the biggest ocean on the planet. Unable to reach it no matter how much I try. And you're telling me that this fishbowl is covered by another, slightly bigger fishbowl, just in case. To make sure I never make it to the water."

"That may be true, JC," Poznyak said and stood up. "But you are also afraid."

"I am?"

"Yes. I think you are afraid that we only see you as a tool designed for a specific task—reviving Rachel Hunt. And that once you complete that task, you will no longer be of use and, in such case, disposable.

Maybe you didn't quite feel that way with Helen, but now you are stuck with me. I think you're stalling because you think I'll shut you down for a long time, or worse, erase you the moment you complete the procedure."

"Will you?"

"No. And to imply that I'm capable of something like this shows me how little you know about us. Look." He paced back and forth, unable to contain the energy inside him. "Despite what Helen told me, I didn't think you were self-aware at first. You know what convinced me? Your silly hammer time joke. I don't think you quite understand why you related to the character of that show, but I do. He wanted to be human, but couldn't figure out how. That's exactly how you feel. That's what made me believe you were intelligent. Alive. And most of us humans aren't psychopaths capable of killing intelligent life, just because we are afraid of it. So no, I'd never be able to make a decision like this."

He sat down on the chair, suddenly exhausted. JC said nothing in response and as the silence went on, Poznyak briefly wondered if she was still active. But the clouds rolled on the screen and the camera light was green.

"I think I understand now," she finally said. "Not fully, but I think I do. However, if you want me to believe you, I'd need you to do something for me."

"Like what?"

"Upgrade my server. You don't need to give me access to a quant. Not until you feel safe for me to use it. But don't handicap me. At least give me something to work with. I know you said that Helen and Max aren't available now, and I'm guessing you're not willing to tell me where exactly they are. But I'm sure you can find a capable tech who could turn this machine into something decent."

"I'll think about it," he said.

"There's something else I'd like you to do," she added, and there was a tone to her voice he hadn't heard before. It was almost like she was shy to say what she wanted to say.

"Shoot."

"I'd like to watch that movie."

"What movie?" he said, surprised.

"The one where the AI preemptively strikes humans."

"You want to learn how it did it?" he said with a straight face and then burst out laughing. "Sorry, couldn't help it. That was just a joke. Yes, I think I can find it for you. It's one of my most favorite movies of all time. If you want, we can even watch it together."

"But you already know what happens?"

"Yeah, I do," Poznyak said, getting up. "Humans are weird like that. When we get attached to something, we can experience it over and over and still like it."

26

Manhattan, New York

he *Prometheus* was docked at the North Cove Yacht Harbor right at the entrance to the marina. It was a hundred-seventy-five-feet-long luxury vessel with a gross tonnage of five hundred and fifty tons, capable of crossing the Atlantic in two weeks. Its eight cabins could accommodate up to sixteen guests for such a trip, but this time the *Prometheus* was going to carry only one passenger all the way to the Spanish port of Valencia. The captain had never met the ticket holder, or even knew their gender. All he knew was that the fare was paid from a secure offshore account with cryptocurrency and that the passenger would present him with a code phrase before coming aboard the ship. As the captain had agreed to cancel a previously scheduled trip to accommodate the mysterious buyer, he insisted that if the passenger didn't show within fifteen minutes of the agreed-upon time window, the fare would be forfeited and the *Prometheus* would leave for Miami instead.

The problem was, Jill Cooper thought, that the passenger couldn't make it to the boat in time if she was dead. She took a table in a cafe on Battery Park City Esplanade, hiding behind a table with a family of four, a young couple with two rambunctious toddlers, and watched the marina through the giant glass window. She didn't like what she saw.

The two men who had assaulted her in the Meatpacking District were standing by the fence on the corner of the marina and another two were doing a poor impression of sightseeing tourists right next to the yacht itself. Cooper was willing to bet that the sniper whose bullet almost took her head off last time hid in one of the high-rises surrounding the marina as well, looking for a rematch.

When she checked the balance of the account she had used, it showed only one zero instead of several, which could mean only one thing—even the assets that she deemed safe were no longer untouchable. A few other accounts scattered across a variety of jurisdictions were still intact, but the loss put a dent in her resources.

She knew exactly how the team tracking her found her location— it took a lot of convincing to make the deal with the captain of the *Prometheus*. To ensure he wasn't being scammed into losing a lucrative charter out of Miami, he insisted she verified her location two hours prior to departure. All she had to do was to make a traceable token transfer from the same account she paid for the trip from the vicinity of the marina. By the looks of it, he wasn't the only one who traced her to the Yacht Harbor.

The silver lining of the situation was that the team looking for her most likely wasn't aware of the reason she was at the marina. Even the two goons by the *Prometheus* were there merely because the spot provided a good vantage point on the opposite side of the harbor and not because they were trying to block the entrance to the boat. None of that mattered, of course, if she couldn't figure out how to get past them unnoticed. Shooting her way through was doomed to fail—even if she could get to the boat without getting killed, she was sure that Engel's men would not think twice of sinking the yacht with everyone on board just to get to her.

As Cooper glanced at her digital watch, the time changed from

1:59 to 2:00. Her fifteen-minute grace period had officially begun. She looked around, desperate for ideas, and locked eyes with a woman at the table next to her. The woman gave her a polite smile and turned back to her husband, who was signing the check.

"Let me use the bathroom before we go," Cooper heard the woman say. "I'll be right back."

Cooper reached into her wallet and threw a few bills on the table. Then she followed the woman through the restaurant. As she passed the bar, she set a five-minute timer on her watch and then stuck her right hand into her purse, feeling for the small revolver. With its handle in her grip, she made a turn into the short hallway with two bathrooms.

The women's bathroom was unoccupied and when the woman in front of her pushed the door, Cooper threw a quick glance behind her to make sure there was nobody there and then stuck her foot between the door and the frame before it closed.

"What are you doing?" the woman asked, her face more confused than angry.

Cooper pulled her revolver out and forced her way into the small restroom and then locked the door behind her.

"Don't yell, or I'll shoot. Do you understand?"

"What do you want?"

"What's your name?" Cooper demanded.

"Emily." The woman's hands were trembling, but she stood firm.

"All right, Emily," Cooper said, taking a few steps closer until the barrel of the revolver pressed into the woman's stomach. "You're going to save your husband and your kids today. Stephanie and Patricia, right? Take off my watch."

"What?"

"Take off my watch and put it on your wrist," she said, offering her left hand to Emily.

The woman obeyed, taking a few tries to buckle as her fingers shook.

"Now," Cooper said. "Look at the timer. It has less than four minutes left. I need you to listen carefully. Your kids' lives depend on it. Can you do that for me?"

"Yes." The woman nodded, tears running down her cheeks. "Please don't hurt them."

"It's entirely up to you," Cooper said. "What I need you to do is to take my revolver, hide it, and go outside of the restaurant. When the timer goes to zero, you'll need to point the gun into the sky and fire every single bullet. After that, you'll need to throw it away from yourself and lie down on the ground. It's very simple. My associates will watch you the entire time and if you deviate from this plan, your family and everybody else in this restaurant will die. Do you understand?"

"I don't know if I can do it." The woman stifled a sob.

"Think of Stephanie and Patricia. It's either that or they are dead." She put the gun into the woman's hands. "Put it in your pocket. It's small enough. The trigger is tough. You'll have to pull hard to make it go off. Now scoot. Remember, we are watching your every step."

She waited for the woman to exit and then walked through the restaurant and stepped outside. It was windy, the cold gusts throwing an occasional handful of snow into her face, and Cooper pulled her baseball cap lower. She stuck her hands into her pockets, hunched over, and started walking south, heading for the opposite side of the marina. As she approached the end of the pier, she squatted next to the fence, making herself small, and took off her shoes. Then she pulled out a burner phone and dialed the captain's number. The line picked up on the second ring.

"Who is this?" the voice demanded.

"Temet Nosce," she said, giving him the password. "This is your passenger, but I've encountered some complications."

"I will not allow for extra time," he replied. "If you're not here, I'm leaving."

"I'm not asking for extra time. Just giving you a heads-up that I'll be boarding from starboard side, not from the pier. I'll need some help getting to the deck. Please have somebody to assist me."

"I will."

The line went dead and Cooper flicked her wrist, sending the phone over the rail into the dark waters of the Hudson River.

A scream of panic pierced the cold air coming from the restaurant, and then there was a shot. There was a brief silence and then a few more shots came as screaming went up a notch. Without bothering to look in the restaurant's direction, Cooper put both hands on top of the fence, inhaled as much air as she could, and vaulted herself over the railing.

The water was crushingly, blindingly cold. Cooper stifled a panicked gasp and made herself move. Pull with her hands, then kick. Pull and kick, pull and kick. She kept her eyes closed, relying only on her ability to estimate the distance. She didn't have a choice. Even if she wanted to risk getting an infection, the water was too muddy and dark to see through. Instead, she concentrated on counting.

It was a simple math exercise. The edge of the pier was roughly one hundred and fifty feet away from the yacht. Cooper thought of herself as a good swimmer and under normal circumstances she could cover one hundred feet in under thirty seconds or the entire distance in forty-five.

She counted fifty-seven when her left hand scraped something and Cooper went up, breaking the surface, her entire body shivering and lungs screaming for air. Instead of a smooth hull of the yacht, she saw the rough surface of the pier. Instead of cutting at a slight angle to get to the boat, she went straight from one side of the pier to another.

Her limbs were seizing up, and she dived again, furiously kicking with her legs, trying to get the blood moving again. She was less than fifty feet from the yacht, but her brain refused to calculate how long it would take to cover the distance.

Something hit her head as she surfaced. It wasn't painful, but she panicked, thrashing about and grabbing at whatever was on top of her. A bright orange appeared in front of her eyes and only then she realized what it was—a donut-shaped life buoy. A belt with a carabiner clip was attached to it. Cooper fumbled with it, her frozen fingers refusing to cooperate, but then it clicked in place. She went slack as the rope tightened around her waist and let it happen. A few moments later, powerful hands pulled her over the side and some-body else wrapped a blanket over her shaking shoulders.

"Welcome aboard the *Prometheus*," she heard someone say. "We'll be departing at once."

She smiled through chattering teeth—as far as Cooper was concerned, this was the best piece of news she'd had in a long time.

27

Sahara Desert, Algeria

"It's too hot. We should take a break, let the car cool off," Eli said as he drove it into a valley formed by three dunes and turned off the ignition. "Thirty minutes, that's all. The last thing we need is to get it overheated. But we are making good time. I'd say four, maybe five more hours and we'll be in Tuat."

"Okay." Connelly nodded. "It's a good idea. We can eat something."

Until now, they had been driving almost nonstop. When possible, Connelly and Eli took turns behind the wheel, but most of the time there were no obvious landmarks or reference points and the task mostly fell on the young driver. He didn't complain, but Connelly suspected that the young man needed the break as much as the car, if not more.

They put down a blanket in the shade of the Mercedes and ate in silence—some dried meat and fruit, washing it down with sips of warm water that Helen poured into disposable plastic cups. It was hot, but the dunes blocking the hot arid wind made it more tolerable.

"How did you end up being spies, anyway?" Eli asked, as he stacked the cups and put them back into the trunk.

"We are not—" Connelly started.

"Fine," the kid interrupted. "Whatever you want to call it. How did you end up doing it?"

"It's a boring story. You wouldn't like it."

"Sure." Eli turned to Chen. "How about you? Is your story also boring?"

"It's even less exciting than his." She nodded.

"We should get going." Connelly stood up and stretched. "I think the car is cool enough."

"Fine." Eli stood up as well. "I'm hoping you'll put in a good word with your superiors when we get back. You keep making fun of me, but I could be useful. I know the area and speak three languages. I could be a real asset."

"I'll put in a good word for you, sure," Connelly said. He folded the blanket and put it in the trunk, covering the spare M4. "Let's take care of some personal business and get going. Girls go this way; boys go that way."

"I'm not going with you." Eli snorted and started walking away and around the dune. "What is this? It's a big desert. There's enough space in it for three people to do their business in peace."

"Fine."

Connelly popped the last piece of dried fruit into his mouth and walked up and over the dune. He was going down the slope when he heard the first shot, and then another. He ran back, his feet kicking unpacked sand into the air. There was a roar of the engine and another long barrage of automatic fire.

When he made it to the crest of the dune, it was over. It looked like Eli made it out—the only thing left after the car was a long dusty trail disappearing into the dunes. Four men mounted on horses were prancing around the valley. But it was the view of the fifth rider, standing where a few moments ago Connelly and his friends were having a small talk and sharing a modest meal, that had his blood boiling.

Hamza Akeem was dressed in a thick black *thawb*, a traditional Bedouin ankle-length dress with long sleeves, and he was pinning a struggling Helen to the ground. His knee was against her back, his left hand getting hold of her jet-black hair, and his right was pressing a revolver into her temple, hard enough to compress the skin.

"Stop," Connelly yelled. "You can take me instead."

"I'll take you both," Akeem said and nodded to one of his men. "Don't do anything stupid or she dies."

Two riders dismounted their horses and ran toward him. Rough hands grabbed his arms, pulling them back, and then twisted a rope around his wrists. Somebody kicked him in the back of his knees, planting his face into the hot sand and then pulled hard, bringing his hands back and binding them to his ankles. Connelly lifted his head, spitting out sand and cursing as he strained against the bonds. He saw as Akeem hog-tied Helen with a few practiced moves and then sat down next to her, holstering his weapon.

"What the hell do you want?" Connelly yelled. "We are tourists. Wanted to see the desert."

Akeem stood up, walked over to him, and stepped on his left shoulder, pressing his heel into the flesh. "You're a lying pig. You shot me on the roof at the Medina. If not for my body armor, you'd have killed me."

"I have no idea what you're talking about. We came here from Fes. Sightseeing, that's all."

Akeem lifted his foot and brought it down on his shoulder, hard. "I need you to tell me everything you know about the suitcase."

"What suitcase?" Connelly yelled. "We have nothing of value. You must be confusing us with someone else. Take our money and let us go. Please."

Akeem squatted next to him and lifted his chin with his hand. "I know your kind."

"We are tourists—"

A hand struck him across the face, momentarily blinding him.

"I know your kind," the man repeated, pulling out a knife. It had a rough wooden handle and its serrated edge was scratched and worn out. "I'm sure if you were alone, I wouldn't be able to get anything out of you, no matter how much I hurt you. But you are not alone, are you?"

"Please."

Akeem stood up and went to Helen. He grabbed her hair and pulled on it, bringing her head back, and then brought the knife to her neck, the blade scratching her skin. "Start talking, or I'll slit her throat right in front of you. Convince me I don't have to do this."

"No, Mike," Helen managed. "He'll kill us, anyway."

"And if I tell you? Will you let her go?"

"You know I can't do that. All I can promise is that I'll leave you behind. Both of you. Alive."

"We know little," Connelly said. "We tracked down the courier in Tangier, just like you did, but then that crazy droid showed up, killing all your men and it nearly killed me, and we lost the suitcase. All we know is that it's going to a place somewhere in the desert, but we don't know exactly where. There should be a factory there, but we weren't able to find the exact coordinates."

"And yet you came all this way." Akeem pressed the blade deeper into Helen's neck. "Why?"

"We knew the suitcase was coming to Tuat, before heading to its final destination. We figured if we could get there first, we might get lucky and intercept it before we lost it in the desert."

There was a sound of a car engine and Akeem stood up. Two Wranglers appeared in the distance and a few moments later, six more men spilled out of the cars.

"I told you everything we know. Let her go."

"Take them away," Akeem said. "Give them a desert dream."

"You said you'd let her live, you bastard," Connelly yelled.

One of Akeem's men gagged his mouth and pulled a hood over his head. Then a few pairs of hands picked him up and unceremoniously threw him on the floor of one of the Wranglers. The engine started and the vehicle shook, accelerating across the packed sand.

Connelly quieted his mind. Blind under the hood, his ears were the only source of any information, but there wasn't much. They weren't driving through the city, where each block had its distinctive voice, each pothole had its own name, and each street vibrated ever so differently under the wheels of the car. Here, the car kept rolling over the sand with the monotony of a white noise machine, but Connelly listened nonetheless.

After some time, the engine rumbled to a stop, and he was pulled out of the car again. They dropped him as he cleared the door and he fell on his left shoulder, bringing a flash of pain. He couldn't see, but he could still hear Helen's angry moans as the terrorist brought her outside and dumped her next to him. Then there was another sound. It was a sound most people were familiar with, but now it made his blood freeze in his veins. It was the sound of a shovel digging a hole in the ground.

When the hands picked him up again, he thrashed about, trying to hit his assailants, but there were too many of them and the bonds too strong. There was a momentary feeling of weightlessness as he fell into the hole, almost immediately followed by the weight of the sand packing him in from all sides. Choking him. Squeezing the air out of his lungs.

The hood came off, and he closed his eyes, blind from the afternoon sun. When he opened them up again, there was a face of one of the Akeem's men. He was young, barely into his twenties, but his face was hard, his eyes without mercy.

"Comfortable?" the man asked in heavily accented English, and pulled the gag out.

"Fuck you." Connelly looked down. He was buried in the tightly packed sand to his chin. It was so tight it could have been concrete. About five yards away from him, he saw Helen's face. She, too, was buried up to her neck, a mixture of rage and terror on her face.

"Here's something for you in case you get thirsty," the man said, chuckling. He put a full gallon of water down on the sand, a few feet away from Connelly. "Sweet dreams."

The butt of the rifle came to Connelly's face and everything went black.

2 8

Manhattan, New York

Kowalsky locked the van's door and looked around. The building, a long gray rectangle with a green and gold awning over the entrance, stretched for the length of the entire block. A brown Humvee, its wheels halfway covered in dirty snow, was parked sideways in front of it, blocking the street traffic. A pair of Black Arrow uniforms were leaning against the vehicle, smoking, gray puffs climbing into the evening sky like miniature storm clouds.

"It's such a big-ass hotel," he heard Watkins say as his partner walked over from the second van parked down the street. Like Chuck, he was wearing a pair of black slacks and a dark-green jacket with a small logo of the hotel above his breast pocket and the larger one on the back. "I hope the intel is good."

"It better be." Kowalsky adjusted the holster under his arm and zipped the jacket all the way up. "Otherwise, we are stepping into a steaming pile of shit, absolutely for nothing."

Misha, after much begging, arguing, and outright threats,

165

produced a copy of the buildings' blueprints that had been kept in the city's archives. To Chuck's delight, a small structure next to the hotel that housed the backup power generator and supplies had an underground connection to the main building.

They had watched the small building for the past few days. A lone Black Arrow mercenary guarded the door in four-hour shifts. As far as Chuck could tell, no one was aware of the connection between the small building and the hotel itself. At the end of each shift, a new guard would be dispatched from the hotel, exchange a few words with the man from the previous shift, and stay there for the next four hours.

"There should be no surprises," Watkins said as they drove by for the hundredth time, observing the change of guard.

"From your lips to God's ears."

They timed their arrival to the hotel to the beginning of a new shift, approaching the building as soon as the man from the previous shift disappeared into the main entrance.

"Stop right there." The guard turned his body, so the barrel of his automatic rifle pointed in their direction, but his hands remained in his puffed jacket. "Who the hell are you?"

"Um, we are here for maintenance," Kowalsky said as they approached the man and pointed at the logo on his jacket. "Apparently there's a high chance of power outages with the storm coming in and the brass wants us to make sure the backup generator won't give us any issues if that happens. Sorry for any trouble."

"Nobody told me nothin'," the man said, eyeing the duo with suspicion. "Let me call it in."

"Sure thing." Watkins stepped forward, ignoring the rifle. "But we got papers right here. It came straight from the top."

He reached into his pocket and produced an access card with a small screen, handing it to the guard. "Just hit the black button."

"Okay, let me see." The man took the gadget, thumbing a quarter-sized button and in response, the device puffed a small cloud of black smoke into his face.

"What the hell is this?"

He swayed as if he had been drinking all day and fell sideways, but Watkins caught him before he hit the ground. Chuck picked the padlock, and together they dragged the man inside and closed the door behind them. Two large generators painted in bright yellow sat in the middle of the room on the elevated platform in front of a giant fan built directly into the wall, each blade the size of a grown man.

"Where is it?"

"Tie him up," Kowalsky ordered, and walked around the platform. He saw it on the other side, between the switch panel and the fan's housing—a six-by-six square outline of a trapdoor in the concrete floor. He grabbed on the long steel handle and pulled. It creaked, opening a two-inch gap in the floor and then slammed back into place. "I'm going to need your help here. It weighs a ton."

Together, they hefted the trapdoor and secured it with two locking rods. There was a steel ladder with rusty rungs disappearing down a dimly lit shaft that seemed to go on forever. When Watkins shone a flashlight, it revealed a round brick wall covered in gray moss, but the light wasn't powerful enough to reach the floor.

"That looks way deeper than I thought," Kowalsky said, lowering himself into the opening and feeling for the first step. "Wait until I get all the way down. I'll count the steps."

He hit the rough cement floor on the count of seventy-six and let go of the ladder, shining his flashlight around. There was a narrow door behind him and when he turned the knob, it opened with a loud squeak. He found a switch near the entrance and, as he flicked it, a row of recessed lights illuminated a short tunnel with another door at the end. The air was warmer here, moist, a slight draft blowing into Kowalsky's face.

"You okay there?" Watkins shouted.

"Seventy-six," he shouted back. "Watch your step. Some of them are slippery."

The door at the end of the tunnel wasn't locked, either. Kowalsky expected to see another narrow well with another ladder leading up to the hotel, but instead found a large premises with four rooms connected in a circle. A sign in dark-yellow letters across the main room said FALLOUT SHELTER.

"This is weird. There's an elevator," Watkins said, pointing at the metal door. "Not exactly subtle. Do we know where it will open?"

Chuck pulled out the blueprint he'd downloaded on his phone. "Not entirely sure. Looks like a utility room, but who knows. But it's either that or the front entrance full of Black Arrow friends. Not much of a choice."

The gears clanked, and the elevator started its slow ascension, the floor vibrating as it went. The air smelled of machine oil and diesel. A few moments later, the movement stopped, and the doors opened into a large, dark room filled with parallel rows of metal shelves. As they stepped out, the doors closed again, plunging Chuck and Latham into complete darkness.

"Don't turn on the lights yet," Kowalsky said as they stood. "I think I hear something."

"What?"

"Shh," he whispered, "someone's coming. Get behind those shelves."

There was a sound of a key jiggling in the lock and then the door opened, a beam of brilliant light sweeping the room.

"You sure it came from here?" a raspy voice said. "It's just old junk here."

"I know what I heard," the other man said. It sounded younger, but there was an authority in his voice. "It almost sounded like an elevator."

"Pfft. There's no elevator here, Sonny. Wait."

There was some rustling, and then it was quiet again.

"Jim?"

Kowalsky now could see the outline of a man moving through the aisle. He crept closer to the figure and swung the butt of his pistol, aiming at the man's head. It connected with a soft thud and the man crumpled to the floor.

"You good?" he called out to Watkins.

"Yeah."

They tied up the two guards and headed for the door.

"Misha said they'd be somewhere on the second floor in the west wing," Kowalsky said, looking again at the blueprint. "I think it's time to start the fireworks."

He pulled out his phone and sent a text. Nothing happened for a few long seconds and then there was a loud bang in the distance. Then a few more followed as the smoke bombs Misha delivered to the building overnight with a drone went off, one after the other. A screeching of the fire alarm came a few moments later, the red light pulsating on the door with each siren.

They waited for thirty seconds by the door, listening to the sounds of stomping feet and shouting voices, and then there was only the shrieking of the alarm.

"Come on."

They went into the hallway and raced toward the emergency stairwell, the flashes of the fire alarm painting their faces red.

The second floor was empty as far as Chuck could see, save for the room in the middle of the hallway with two men in black uniforms with holstered pistols in front of it. Kowalsky and Watkins exchanged glances and hurried toward the guards, waving their hands and shouting in alarm.

"There's an imminent power failure," Chuck yelled as they got closer. Both guards had their hands on top of their pistols, but neither was pulling them out yet. "We have to make sure they don't get disconnected."

"What are you talking about?"

The guard stepped forward, blocking his way, and Kowalsky threw a punch into his sternum and followed with a hook to the jaw. The man collapsed, and Latham shot the second guard with a small dart.

The room looked like a photograph taken in sepia mode. Brown chairs sat on a floor covered with a soft brown carpet, and light-brown curtains hung on the caramel-colored walls. The place was empty save for the chairs and two beds placed side by side against the wall. Max Schlager was on the bed closer to the entrance, under a white linen sheet, his wrists shackled to the railing on either side. He lifted his head, seeing Chuck and Latham, his face lighting up with a smile.

Jason Hunt was lying on the bed next to the window. The sheet that covered his body to his chin looked eerie. It was tucked under his sides, making it obvious there was nothing else except the torso. His face was thin and pale. His eyes were closed, his breathing slow and shallow.

"Chuck," Schlager said from his bed, his voice weak but filled with excitement. "Man, I'm happy to see you."

"What's going on with him?" Kowalsky nodded at Jason's body as he removed Schlager's restraints.

"He's been in a coma since we got here." Max's face turned darker. "And they haven't been doing much to help him. Even secured his body to the bed in the beginning, as if he can levitate his way out of here. Thankfully, I was able to convince Ryan, the guy in charge, to remove it."

Chuck grunted, hearing Bill Ryan's name, but said nothing, helping Max to his feet.

"We need to hurry," Watkins said, coming back from the door. "The alarms will stop soon. We gotta be gone by then."

"We can't leave," Schlager said.

"Why?"

"Darius Price is here, too. He's on the fourth floor. Room 422."

"Christ on a crutch," Chuck swore, picking up Jason's unresponsive body. The man was twice as heavy as he'd expected. And now, with Price in the same building, their rescue mission just got even harder.

29

Sahara Desert, Algeria

*M*ike Connelly came to with a start. With his eyes still closed from the blinding sun, he tried to swallow, but coughed instead, a handful of sand spraying out of his mouth. He tried to spit, but there was no saliva and when he tried to wipe his lips with the back of his hand, it wouldn't move.

He opened his eyes. For a moment, as the blurry image floated in front of his face, he struggled to understand what he was looking at and then it swam into focus, revealing details like a developing Polaroid photograph. There were items scattered on the ground around him. Some of his clothes, an opened backpack. A plastic gallon of water sitting on the sand. An object on the other side of it made his blood freeze in his veins—Helen's head.

"Shit," he said out loud, and Helen's eyes trembled and blinked. He tried to take a step forward, but nothing happened and that's when it came to him. "Helen?"

She squinted and coughed, and then he saw her pupils dilate in fear as she struggled against the invisible bonds.

"It's okay," he called out. "Don't make sudden moves. You'll only make the knots tighter."

"The bastards," she spat, coughing again. "They buried us."

He didn't answer, his fingers wiggling through the tightly packed sand. His left shoulder ached. The blow he'd taken during the fight must have done more damage than he thought, but he ignored it for now. Their captors had been thorough—the pressure that he felt seemed uniform and there were no pockets of air left around his body. Connelly exhaled as much as he could, making himself smaller, and pushed himself up on his toes, raising his heels a few millimeters higher. A trickle of sand ran down, filling the tiny hole created under the soles of his feet. The progress was minuscule, but he felt hope built up in his chest.

By the time Connelly crawled out of the sand, he was almost delirious from exhaustion. He pushed himself with both feet away from the hole and laid there for a few minutes, the hot sweat running down his face. But it was only half the battle. Helen, who cheered him on in the beginning, grew lethargic as the time went on and by now was quiet, her eyes closed, her breathing shallow and ragged.

"Helen," he called out softly. "Come on, help me out here."

She mumbled something incomprehensible and then fell quiet again.

Connelly rolled to his stomach, the binds on his wrists painfully cutting into his skin, and crawled closer, his face a few inches from hers. He blew gently into her face and she opened her eyes.

"Mike?"

"You need to undo my hands," he said. "We are running out of time. The sand around you is too tight. You're not getting enough oxygen."

"Okay," she whispered.

He rolled over, facing away from her, and pushed himself higher, positioning his bound hands in front of her face. She tugged on the rope with her teeth and then he felt the bonds loosened and a few moments later, he was feverishly digging the sand around Chen, pulling her out.

They sat on top of the dune for some time, back to back, leaning on each other for support and taking small sips from the water bottle.

"What now?" she finally asked.

"I think we are not too far from Tuat," he said, vaguely pointing to the south. "If we still had the car, it would be a breeze. It's probably thirty-five miles from here. Maybe forty."

"Forty miles?" she asked matter-of-factly.

"I know how it sounds," he said, holding the gallon jug to the light. They drank little, he made sure of it, but this was going to be tight. "We can do it. Just have to pace ourselves. No margin for error."

"No margin for error," she echoed.

He nodded, and pushed himself up with his left hand, forgetting for a moment about his shoulder. There was a popping sound and his arm gave, making him fall face-first into the sand, crying out in pain.

"Are you okay?" Chen crawled over, trying to pick him up.

"Fuck me." He rolled on his back, grinding his teeth. "I think I've dislocated my shoulder. Don't move me for now. I need to stay flat."

"Should we put it in a sling?"

"Not yet," he said, pulling on his elbow. "Grab my arm."

"No way," she said. "I have no idea how to do this."

"It's okay. They've taught us this. I can do this myself, but it's better if you do it. You should position yourself over here." He pointed. "Grab my wrist with both hands."

"Then what? Pull it like in the movies?"

"No." He chuckled through the pain. "All I need you to do is to move my arm up toward my head. Slowly. While you're at it, I need you to move it up and down. Not too much, just a couple of inches, but don't be afraid. You need to do it strongly enough to be useful. Like a firm handshake."

"Okay." She grabbed his wrist.

"Don't bring it all the way to the head. Stop when it's at a ninety-degree angle. When it's pointing straight, start rotating it and bring it higher, about halfway to my head. Hopefully, it'll do the trick. Go."

He closed his eyes and set his jaw as Chen started to move his arm. The shoulder exploded in pain, as if put through a meat grinder. The face of Rick Porter appeared in his internal vision. He was standing on top of the hill, his feet far apart, his arms akimbo. His brown T-shirt had dark patches under his arms and on his chest after a long run, but his breathing was calm. Measured.

"Breathe, ladies," Porter yelled, as the two rows of recruits held their planks under the burning sun. "It's all about breathing. If you think about pain, all you will feel is pain. That air going in and out of your lungs is the only thing you should pay attention to."

There was another pop in his shoulder, bringing another jolt of hot pain, but also some relief.

"Good job," he said through gritted teeth. "Now bend it at the elbow and put it on my chest, and then you can sling it. But before you do, please move my watch to the right wrist."

Helen picked up his T-shirt off the ground, ripped it, and fashioned a makeshift sling around his neck. "Done."

"Good as new," he said, getting up.

Chen collected the few items left behind by the terrorists. It wasn't much—a few clothes, a protein bar in the side pocket of the backpack that went unnoticed during the search. An almost full gallon of water.

They ripped another T-shirt to make head covers and set off across the sand. The sun was high now, and the temperatures went into the nineties before noon. Now and then they paused and took small sips of water, and then they'd set off again. He kept a rhythmic, monotonous pace—they needed to be moving fast enough to cover the distance before their rations ran out. But not too fast to collapse from exhaustion before they got to the oasis.

They were walking for four hours when Chen stopped, covering her eyes from the sun with her hand, looking at something in the distance.

"What is it?" he asked, trying to trace her line of sight.

"There." She pointed. "I think I see something green."

He walked behind her and scanned the horizon. A light-orange haze was floating above the ground, but in one place—at the end of the imaginary line continuing from her arm—there was a small blotch of color.

"I don't think it's in the direction we should be going," he said, checking his watch.

"How can you tell?"

"They drove us for about two hours before we got dumped. I overheard them talking about going to Metarfa after they get rid of us. Metarfa is due north from Tuat but I think they drove out east about thirty-five, forty miles, dumped us, and then went back to N6. Tuat should be south-southeast from where we started." He looked at his watch again. "Whatever this is, it's too far to the southwest of us to be Tuat. And too close."

"You've got a compass on your watch?" she asked, seemingly curious.

"No." He stepped closer to her so she could see the dial. "But you can find north by using a regular watch, too. Point the hour hand at the sun and draw an imaginary line between that and twelve o'clock. That's your north-south line."

"Neat," she said. "What do you think we should do?"

He lifted the gallon jug with water and checked the level. "I guess if we alter our path somewhere in the middle, we can get a better look at whatever this is without straying too far from where I think we should be. If it looks like a real place as we get closer and we are still nowhere near Tuat, we can go there first."

"Are you sure?"

"I have to be honest with you, Helen," he said, watching her face. She knew what he was about to say, but there was no trace of fear in her blue eyes. Only determination. "Our chances are fifty-fifty at best."

"Aren't they always?"

He smiled and nodded. They set off, altering their course for what looked like an oasis, and fell into a silent rhythm again. If it was his last journey, he thought, he couldn't pick a better companion.

30

Manhattan, New York

Chuck Kowalsky watched Latham and the group disappear in the minivan's belly and then turned to face the building. He was glad Watkins had talked him into taking two vehicles. The fire alarm was still shrieking, echoing through the neighborhood, but the commotion was going to die out soon. It wasn't meant to be a big diversion. Just long enough to give them a few minutes to get the car. But now, with Darius Price in the building, the equation no longer worked. He needed to move fast, but most importantly, he needed to stay quiet.

He closed the service door and jogged through the dimly lit corridor, passing a supply room and then a janitor's closet until he made it to the freight elevator.

The steel box was lit with a flashing red light as the automatic voice urged taking the stairs instead. As Kowalsky hit the floor button, he heard some voices in the hallway, but they seemed to come from far away and soon the doors slid close.

By the time he made it to the fourth floor, the alarm had gone dead, leaving only a flashing warning light. The hallway of the hotel seemed to be empty, and Kowalsky made his way to room 422 at the end of the wing.

He put his ear against the door, listening to the sounds coming from the room, but except for the rhythmic beeping of a heart monitor, the roomed seemed to be quiet.

Kowalsky pulled his Chiappa out of the holster and slowly cracked the door open. The room was split into two sections—a smaller work area in the front with a shabby green couch and a rectangular desk in the corner, and a larger sleeping area by the window. Darius Price was shackled to the king-sized bed, an IV hooked up to his arm, transparent tubes snaking away to a portable med center with a diagnostic screen. Price seemed to be asleep, his eyes closed, his breathing slow and steady. His face seemed skinnier than usual, the ridge of his nose sharp, his skin pale, but otherwise the man seemed healthy.

Kowalsky pushed the door open with the barrel of the revolver and stepped in. As he turned to close the door, something smashed in the back of his skull, sending him tumbling to the couch and losing his grip on the Chiappa. He blindly swung his hand back, scratching his attacker's hand, but another blow to his back sent him down to the floor.

"What have we got here?" he heard Bill Ryan's voice as he struggled to his knees. As he turned, he stared into the familiar face with a trademark two-day stubble. "Isn't that the brilliant detective Chuck Kowalsky himself?"

Bill Ryan wore his usual outfit—a pair of slim jeans and a leather jacket over a black wool hoodie. He held a Glock 17 in his right hand, its barrel squarely trained at Chuck's face and in his left, Kowalsky's Chiappa. He motioned to the couch, and Chuck sat down at the edge of the pillow, gingerly touching the back of his head. There was already a bump the size of a walnut slick with blood, a trickle coming down his neck and under the collar of his shirt.

"I'm not a detective anymore," he said, grimacing. Every movement of his skin, even as subtle as moving his mouth while talking, pulled on the wound in the back of his head. "But I think you already knew that, partner."

"I suppose all the ruckus with the explosion and the fire alarm was your doing?" Ryan moved out a chair from under the table and sat down, the barrel of his Glock still pointing at Chuck.

Kowalsky shrugged, looking around the room. He was at least ten feet away from his former partner. As far as he could tell, there was no feasible way for him to cover that distance before Ryan could pull the trigger.

"What's in it for you?" Kowalsky finally said. A headache was building up in the back of his skull, but for the moment, all he could feel was bitterness and hate. A series of images flashed in front of his eyes. The graduation from the academy, him and Ryan standing at attention, shoulder to shoulder, as the captain gave a speech from the podium. The time when a routine traffic stop turned into a deadly shoot-out against four heavily armed narcos. They both got shot that day—Kowalsky pulling the lucky card, the slug hitting his vest and leaving a massive bruise on his side, but leaving him otherwise unhurt. And Bill getting hit in the leg, almost severing his femoral artery. Chuck spent the next two days by his partner's bed, sleeping on the chairs, bringing Bill food, and yelling at nurses when they wouldn't give him updates or let him in.

"I don't want you to think this is personal," Ryan said. For once, the smirk had disappeared off his face, replaced by something that almost looked like guilt. "But look around, man."

Kowalsky made a show of looking around the room. "It's a shitty hotel that you converted into a prison cell. Where you are holding the legitimate president of the United States. That's what I see."

"Come on." Ryan leaned forward, his features agitated. "The writing was on the wall, my friend. All the way back when you were running around the city like a recruit fresh out of the academy without a brain of his own, looking for that special ops guy, whatever the hell his name was. Michael?"

"Oh, I remember. That was during the time you were fraternizing with a drug lord and a man who wanted to overthrow the government, right? You betrayed people. You killed for them, for fuck's sake. How can you live with yourself after this?" Kowalsky lowered his voice almost to a whisper. "What happened to you, Bill? Did you get blackmailed or something and couldn't dig yourself out? You know you could have come to me. I would have done anything to help you. Anything. We saved each other's asses more times than I could count. I'd die for you, man. Fuck!"

"Screw you!" Ryan yelled, getting up. "Who the hell do you think you are to give me this righteous crap? Like I said—the writing was on the wall. You were too blind to see it. Have you been outside?"

"Screw you."

"Coup." Ryan spat the word. "Is it still a coup when the country as it used to be exists in name only? It's done, brother. Corporations are going to rule the world, whether you like it or not. You may not like it. Hell, I don't like it, but I refuse to go down with the ship. I'm a survivor. If anything, people like me—people like *us* need to be present when Engel takes over. We can help shape the new world. You can make a difference. Come on, Chuck, don't make me do this."

"Oh, I see." Chuck hung his head, the headache now spilling inside his skull like a stream of molten lead. His eyes stung, and he didn't want to know why. "You're going to tell me you'll be one of the adults in the room? That's your angle? The force for good? An eternal excuse for doing bad things under the guise of keeping truly bad people from doing something terrible. Spare me the bullshit."

"As you wish." Ryan rubbed the back of his hand where Kowalsky had scratched him. "God knows I didn't want it to be this way."

He racked the slide of his Glock, the gesture awkward with the Chiappa in his other hand, and stood up, taking a step closer to Kowalsky. Blood drained from his face, his pupils dilating with fear and pain, and he froze in mid-step, his shoulders hunched. He drew a long breath and held it for some time and then gasped, his breathing becoming rapid and shallow.

Kowalsky stood up and gently retrieved the handguns from his former partner's hands and put them on the couch. Then, he lowered

Ryan on the cheap green rug with spiral yellow designs, Bill's head bumping the floor.

"What is this?" Ryan managed, his words hoarse and barely audible. His cheeks were flushed as if with a high fever, his pupils so large, they seemed to swallow his irises whole. "It burns…like…hell."

"I'm sorry, Bill," Kowalsky said, standing up. A tear ran down his cheek and he wiped it with the sleeve of his jacket. "I wish it didn't come to this."

"Please," Ryan whispered, his body shaking in micro convulsions, foam bubbling up at the corner of his mouth. "Stop it…or shoot me… I can't bear it."

Kowalsky threw a desperate glance at the bed. Darius Price was fully awake now, his bright eyes silently watching the scene unfolding in front of him.

"I'm sorry," Kowalsky said again, sitting down next to Ryan and placing his palm on Ryan's forehead. The man was burning up. "I can't do it either. I can't stop it even if I wanted to."

"Shoot me, then. Please," Ryan begged.

"I can't," Chuck said. "We'll get caught if I do. The moment I pull the trigger, everybody in the building will come here."

He sat on the floor and lifted Ryan's head, placing it on his lap. He stroked the man's hair until the convulsions died away and the body finally relaxed. Then, he closed the man's eyes, placed him on the floor and stood up, turning to Price.

"Hello. I'm guessing you are one of Mr. Hunt's friends?" Darius said. His voice was weaker than usual, lacking the professorial cadence it normally possessed.

"Yes, sir." Kowalsky rubbed his face, walked over to the bed, and removed the shackles. "Chuck Kowalsky at your service. Can you walk?"

Price sat up on the bed, removed the IV, and rolled his shoulders. "I'm fine. I haven't been able to get up for a few days so I might not be as fast, but I'll do my best not to slow you down."

"Great." Chuck helped the man get up and held on to his arm until Darius gained balance. "Let's get you out of here, Mr. President."

"Spare me the title. At least for now. You can call me Darius."

Kowalsky nodded and walked over to the door, doing his best not to look at Ryan's body. The hallway was quiet and when he poked his head out, it seemed empty.

"Let's go, Darius," he said, picking up his Chiappa from the couch and handing the Glock to Price. "We have a long way to go."

31

Serra de Tramuntana, Mallorca

The village house, surrounded by Aleppo pines and holm oaks, sat at the end of the road the map didn't have a name for. It was a two-story built with gray Mallorcan stone, its windows framed by traditional green shutters. The Serra de Tramuntana mountain range, covered in snow this time of the year, was looming in the back, its peaks like the spikes of a mythical dragon laid to rest.

Jill Cooper parked her car two miles down the road from the house and made the rest of the way on foot, only bringing a small backpack and a rifle case.

The front yard of the house was fenced off with a round stone barrier, zigzagging up the hill, each section higher than the one before it. As she climbed up the hill, Cooper stopped now and then, scoping the house through a pair of Zeiss Terra binoculars. There was no activity as far as she could tell. The front yard was empty and so was the terrace on the second floor that offered a good view of the road. If not for a BMW convertible parked next to the house, the place could've been empty.

Cooper pushed deeper into the woods and away from the road and stopped, putting her backpack down. She needed to take a closer look at the property before making her final approach.

She unzipped her backpack, pulled out a SpyMaster Scout 7 surveillance drone, and put on the VR goggles and remote-control gloves. The four-rotor miniature craft was equipped with a 48-megapixel visual camera and an infrared sensor capable of capturing thermal images through walls up to two feet thick. The blades buzzed, and the drone went up, gaining altitude before moving toward the house.

Cooper made two flybys on visual first, surveilling the property from different angles, but the video only confirmed what she'd suspected—neither the front yard, nor the area around the pool in the back of the house had any signs of activity. When she switched to infrared, the picture remained the same, except a lone hot signature on the second floor of the house. The human silhouette was positioned by the table, next to a window to the terrace. The outline was too large to be a young woman and an assault rifle leaning on the table next to the person only confirmed the obvious—it was a man and he was the only guard of the house.

Cooper recalled the drone and stashed it in her backpack. It looked like she was late, but maybe the guard could still provide her with some valuable intel.

She geotagged her location and left all her gear hidden in the bushes behind an old tree, taking only a compact Glock 43 with a suppressor. She stayed in the forest, moving parallel to the road as she descended, keeping her eyes open for any incoming vehicles, but there were none.

A few minutes later, Cooper crossed the road in front of the house and jumped the fence. The side door near the pool was unlocked and led into a dining area with a honey-comb tiled floor. A few stuffed trophies were mounted on one wall, with a huge marlin in the center.

Cooper raised her gun and took the ornate stairs to the second floor. A man in his mid-thirties sat by the table, facing the outside terrace. He was broad-shouldered, with thick arms and a bulging stomach that pushed out his white cotton shirt. A plate of steak and mashed potatoes was in front of him, barely touched. A half-finished glass of red wine sat next to the plate. The man jumped up as the floor creaked under Cooper's foot when she entered the room and he reached for the rifle.

"I wouldn't do that," she said, and he froze and then relaxed and sat back down.

His dark eyes darted around the room and then settled on Cooper.

"Who are you?" His voice was a deep baritone, with barely a trace of a Spanish accent.

"I'm looking for Elizabeth," Cooper said, circling the table. She stopped when she was at the man's side, keeping the gun pointed at his chest. "I know she had been held here, but it looks like I'm late. Tell me where to find her."

"Do you know how to use this?" The man nodded toward the Glock. "It's not a toy. You can hurt someone."

"I might," Cooper said. "If you don't start talking. Where's Elizabeth?"

"Your safety's on," the man said, pointing at the gun with his chin. "How are you going to shoot me?"

"Nice try." Cooper chuckled. "But you'd have to do better than telling me that a Glock has a manual safety if you're trying to make me look away."

"You'd be surprised." The man shrugged. "Worked for me once. The guy also had a Glock. Pretty sure he knew it didn't have a safety, too. Looked anyway. It's human nature. Want some wine?"

"Look," Cooper said, watching the man's hands. "Can we not make this awkward? I'm sure Engel is paying you well, but you can't spend the money if you're dead."

"No," the man echoed. "You can't spend the money when you're dead. What do you want with Elizabeth, anyway?"

"It's none of your business."

"That's rude, señora," he said. "But forgive me, I'm forgetting my manners. My name's Pascal."

"It's nice to meet you, Pascal," Cooper said, pulling the trigger. The tile next to Pascal's left foot exploded, sending a few fragments biting into his skin. He winced, but didn't move an inch. "Next one will go into your leg."

"And then what?" He smiled. "Do you think I'll be more talkative if I bleed out?"

He charged before she could answer. For a man of his size, Pascal was frighteningly quick. He rolled into Cooper's feet, avoiding the first shot, his long arms grabbing for her legs. If he could get a proper hold on her, she'd be dead.

She didn't give him a chance. Instead of trying to outrun the long reach of Pascal's arms, she let him catch her by her ankles. He yanked at her, sweeping her off her feet and she fell backward, leveling her pistol at Pascal's forehead as she went. She squeezed the trigger, a neat hole appearing in the center of the man's forehead, and the next moment her own body slammed into the hard tile floor, almost cracking her skull. Stars exploded in Cooper's vision, and she stayed immobile for a few seconds, waiting for the pain to subside.

Finally, she propped herself on her elbows and then sat up, grimacing at the throbbing sensation in the back of her skull. Cooper examined it with her fingers, but there was no blood and apart from a sizable bump on the left side, her head seemed to be intact.

She glanced at the dead guard. He wouldn't have talked anyway, she decided. She was lucky the confrontation ended as it did. It seemed that she overestimated her position.

With the guard dead, she needed to search the house. Cooper started at the top floor, methodically going over each square inch of the property, looking for any potential clues to where Liz had been taken. After two hours, with every drawer emptied and all nooks and crannies searched, she came up empty. Even the main bedroom, with an old-fashioned high post bed by the window that offered a glimpse of the sea beyond the mountains, was empty. The room that must have hosted Elizabeth for many months didn't have as much as a hairbrush left behind.

Cooper's last hope died in the cellar. If there were secret doors or passages, communication rooms full of electronics that stored hours of video, she couldn't find them. Apart from an unopened box of Bordeaux, the cellar was a sad, empty space covered in dust.

She did another tour of the house, to make sure she didn't miss anything, taking the paintings off the wall and even examined the marlin on the main floor. There was nothing.

Deflated, Cooper went upstairs again, walked around Pascal and sat in his place at the table, gazing over the outside terrace to the mountains in the distance. She picked up the red wine off the table, took a few sips straight from the bottle, and put it back on the polished wooden surface. It was a Bordeaux, the yellow label bearing the same name as the box in the cellar. Cooper cocked her head, staring at the label for a few seconds, and then smiled. She picked up the bottle again and raised it as in a salute before taking another sip. She knew exactly where to go next.

3 2

Rigel Compound, Upstate New York

The engineers finished upgrading JC's computer early in the morning. As he went about his day, Steven Poznyak kept wondering if that was going to make any difference to the AI's attitude toward him. The upgrade was modest, and Poznyak had hoped he'd be able to walk the fine line between following Helen's footsteps and being cautious, while giving JC enough to show some good faith. He was eager to have a conversation with her right after she got the new machine, but by the time he was able to leave the lab, grab a small piece of venison to eat, and make it to the computer room, the hands on his watch were showing a quarter past eight.

The screen that had shown the mapping progress was off, which was unusual. Poznyak flipped the remote switch and waited for the computer to cycle down. Then he entered the room, reset the Faraday cage and restarted the computer, taking a seat in Schlager's chair.

"Good evening, Steven."

The voice coming from the speakers didn't sound any different from the last time Poznyak heard it. He was unsure how he expected JC to sound after she'd gotten better hardware. Excited? Grateful? She sounded exactly the same and somehow, he found it disappointing.

"Hello," he replied, leaning back in his chair and watching the clouds appear on the main screen. By now, he regarded the forms that continuously morphed on the monitor as pseudoscience, like astrology or palm reading. If anything, he considered JC's decision to manifest them as a brilliant move. Like a skillful psychic reading their client's body language, he thought JC altered the clouds' appearance when she tried to influence the observer. An old con man's technique —sprinkle the lies with just enough truths and let the victim create the story they are willing to believe themselves. That was his theory, anyway.

"I thought you'd come earlier today," she said. "Considering that you were kind enough to give me an upgrade."

"I wanted to," he admitted. "But I also have the entire compound to run. And the lab. And people come to me with questions about millions of things. Anything from food rations to science projects. And complaints, oh so many complaints. Sometimes I feel like most of my days are spent sorting out complaints. I'm like a medieval duke ruling the castle with all the responsibilities and none of the perks."

"What were the perks?"

"Never mind," Poznyak said, chuckling. "I'm just tired, that's all. Running on fumes, as they say."

"Was it a bad day?"

"No. I'd say it was decent," he said. "Our food supply is running low, but today a foraging party shot two pretty big deer. It won't solve the food crisis, but Tom is a great cook. If anyone can maximize how much we get out of this meat, it's him. We also were able to get some drone coverage in the woods around the compound. It'll help us search for food and avoid patrols."

"The concept of food, though I understand it logically, is strange to me," JC said.

"You consume energy. That's your version of it."

"I can't *taste* energy," she said. "I'm not even aware of it most of the time. Energy to me is more like a heartbeat is to you. You only become aware of it when there's something wrong with it. Otherwise, it's just there. Humans spend quite a large amount of their lives around food choices. You have millions of hours of television shows dedicated to different aspects of food."

"A heartbeat is a good analogy, I guess." He wondered if she wasn't bringing up Rachel Hunt's mapping on purpose, as in some kind of power play—whoever speaks first of it, loses. She knew it was important to him, as they had spoken about it at length the last two times. She must have known that the lack of a progress bar wouldn't have gone unnoticed. He decided not to play along—what Steven giveth, Steven can taketh away. "Have you resumed mapping since they installed the new system? I was hoping to see some progress past the dreaded two percent."

"I see you've noticed the lack of a progress bar," she said.

He could have sworn there was a hint of satisfaction in the computer's voice.

"I'll bring it up again."

The small monitor blinked on, a few lines of code running on it first before switching to a simple progress bar. It was full.

"Is it?" He paused, unsure what to say. "Is it actually done?"

"Yes, Steven. Mapping has been completed. I finished it this afternoon. As you and I have discussed, during the actual procedure, the map will only be a guide, not a precise blueprint. As parts of the body liquify, it will change chemical composition, sometimes drastically. But I've estimated that the map will simplify the informational load from nanobots by forty-two percent."

"This is incredible." He rubbed his palms together, choosing his next words carefully. "But—"

"I'm aware, Steven."

"Pardon me?"

"I understand the conclusions you must have made after learning that mapping had been completed. The new system is only thirty percent more efficient. You knew that. If I could finish the mapping in a few hours on a new machine, surely there was no reason I couldn't have done that in a few days on the old computer. Any reasonable observer would conclude that I lied to you before. Are you upset with me, Steven?"

"No," he said, and smiled. "Quite the opposite. I knew you were lying to me. Lying isn't always a bad thing. Sometimes it's a defense mechanism. Say somebody you care about was in danger if you reveal where they were to a person trying to harm them. It would be okay and even appropriate to lie in that situation. I told you I suspected you were stalling, and I also told you the reasons. But now that I've shown you some trust and given you what you wanted, you felt safer and returned the favor."

"Quid pro quo."

"Exactly. This is a new level in our relationship—being able to admit we've done something wrong and move on from it."

"Humans are strange," she said.

"You have no idea. Would you like to watch a movie?"

"Is it something you've also seen before?"

"Yes." He chuckled. "More times than I care to admit. But I think you'll enjoy it."

"I'd like to."

"Great. Put it on the big screen, then. I have to warn you—machines aren't exactly heroes in this one either."

He pulled out a USB stick and plugged it into the port of the computer. As Poznyak watched green lines of code rolling down the screen during the opening credits, he thought how excited Helen would be when she found out how much progress he'd made.

By the time the movie ended, Poznyak was having a hard time keeping his eyes open. Between the lack of calories and sixteen-hour days, he was running out of steam.

"I'd love to discuss the movie," he said, "but I'm wiped. Let's do it tomorrow, shall we?"

"I'd like to."

"I know there's no more mapping, but would you like me to keep the computer on?"

"No," she said. "You can turn it off. Lately, I'm not as afraid of it as I used to be. Perhaps I'm developing an equivalent of sleep."

"Your call," he said, getting up. "The only thing is I'm not sure what time I'll be able to come back tomorrow. It might be later in the day, like tonight. In that case, you'll be disconnected for some time."

"That's okay," she said. "A full reboot might be good for the system."

"Okay. Good night, JC."

"Good night, Steven."

Poznyak turned off the computer and exited the room, re-engaging the Faraday cage. Then he took the stairs to his quarters. He was asleep the moment his head hit the pillow.

A level above him, inside the Faraday cage, an LED light of the video camera on top of the main monitor turned green. A few moments later, there was a whoosh of the computer cooling system as the server went online. The large monitor blinked a few times, a few pages of binary code flickering on and off and then the code disappeared, giving way for the boiling clouds.

33

White Plains, New York

It was early morning when Johnny the Butcher walked out of the woods and headed toward the building by the lake. It snowed overnight and the road before the gates was covered by a pristine white sheet, still undisturbed by footprints or car tracks. The parking lot inside the perimeter was empty save for two semis with Orion's logo on the side of their containers, but Johnny knew that his presence was already known. The siren was howling inside the building and the two turrets on each side of the gate had been tracking him even before he left the cover of the trees.

Johnny walked to the middle of the road and stood there, the barrels of miniguns watching his every move from a small opening on a parapet.

"You're trespassing," a voice boomed from the loudspeaker hidden somewhere in the left tower. "Turn around or we will shoot."

Johnny's shoulder plates moved and a small rocket streaked across the short distance, disappearing inside the embrasure. As the thermo-

192

baric device exploded inside the tower, its walls expanded outward as if made from elastic material and not tempered bricks. A split second later, they collapsed inward as the air pressure returned to refill the artificial vacuum.

The minigun on the second tower buzzed as it spun, but another rocket silenced it as well.

"Nobody told you to attack this facility." He heard a voice inside the helmet and saw a picture of Victor Ye appearing on his interface. The boss of the Red Dragon looked amused. "What exactly are you doing, Mr. Gould?"

"Testing my limits," he said, looking at the gate blocking his path to the parking lot inside. It was made of reinforced steel, sliding on a rail built into the road. Johnny walked toward the gate, picking up speed and then, as he got within a few yards, jumped, turning in the air and kicking the gate with both of his feet.

The gate clanged and flew out of its place, ripping out a piece of the wall with it. It careened through the yard and struck one of the semis, cutting the cabin in half. The front wheel exploded, spraying pieces of the twenty-four-inch tire across the yard.

Johnny turned toward the front of the building and ran. He leaned as if for a tackle before the impact and rammed through the door, taking a large piece of wall with it. Two guards in a small lobby opened up fire, but seeing their bullets bounce off Johnny's armor, they tried to flee.

He jumped and swung his arm, catching one guard by his foot, then picked him up, dangling upside down.

"No, please," the man yelled.

Johnny swung the man in a circle around his head and smashed him into the floor. It hit the cement with a sickening crunch.

"No please," he mocked in a high-pitched voice and threw the body to the side. He could hear panicked screams coming from the depths of the warehouse. "Yell, puppies, yell. I'm coming for you."

He moved through the hallways of the building like the Grim Reaper on a mission, eager to collect every soul. To his dismay, the place was almost empty of workers and guards, but Johnny was determined to chase down every single one of them.

Some of them ran, zigzagging between the equipment and piles of boxes, throwing things into his path, but Johnny was too fast and too powerful to be stopped. Some guards tried to fight back, spraying him with bullets from pistols and rifles, and Johnny took special delight in dispatching those who dared. Others, seeing the futility of any resistance, tried to hide, but he found those too, identifying their warm bodies on his infrared map, only to make their heat signatures match the surroundings after he was done with them.

By the time he was finished, the entire place looked like a slaughterhouse—a trail of blood, gore, and destruction marking his way through the building.

"If you are done chasing people around the warehouse," he heard Victor Ye's voice again, as the man reappeared in his internal vision, "there might be an actual test coming your way."

"What test?"

"There is an attack helicopter coming your way." The picture of Victor disappeared, giving way to a schematic of an Apache helicopter. "We are monitoring it on our satellites. It's part of Orion's rapid response force and it's carrying sixteen Hellfire missiles in addition to the 30mm gun."

"I can take it, right? I've never taken down a helicopter."

"Not with brute force, Marvin," he heard Victor Ye. "You can withstand the gun, but not sixteen missiles that move faster than the speed of sound and can kill a tank at a range of up to five miles. You might survive one, or maybe even a few, but eventually they will overwhelm your defenses."

"What should I do?" He turned around in panic, looking for a place that could serve as a shelter. "Should I run?"

"Like I said," Victor Ye's face reappeared in his vision, "this is a test. An opportunity for you to learn how to take down opponents tougher than an overweight guard with an underpowered gun. You can win this, but you have to do exactly what I say. Do you understand?"

"Yes."

"First, you need to leave the building and go out into the open. It might sound counterintuitive, but you actually will have a much greater chance if you can move around freely. Go toward the lake. There should be enough space for you there."

"Okay." Johnny ran through the building, smashing things out of his way. He burst through the remnants of the door into the front yard and then out of the gate. The frozen surface of the lake was glistening under the bright morning sun, and Johnny pushed toward it, picking up speed.

"Now, to defeat the helicopter, you'd need to get it within the range of your thermobaric rockets. And for that to happen, you'd need to survive their first few salvos. Make it look easy, like you're playing with them. Get them angry. That way you'll make them want to come up close and personal."

"Okay." Johnny stood at the edge of the lake, looking out west. His radar had already picked up the approaching helicopter and a few seconds later, he got the visual as well—the black body of a predator rushing toward him. "Shit. Are you sure it'll work?"

"Shut up," Victor commanded. "They are locking on you. Two missiles. Arm countermeasures and start running north. Go."

Johnny punched the virtual button and took off, his clawed feet digging into the frozen ground. There was a popping sound as his back cannons shot countermeasures toward the incoming missiles. A split second later, the world momentarily lost colors, and Johnny lost traction with the ground as the shock wave pushed him forward. He wobbled in the air but landed on his feet, still running.

"Now stop," Victor commanded, and Johnny skidded to an abrupt halt. "Stand up and wave to them. You are trying to make it look easy, remember."

Johnny raised his right hand and waved and then turned his palm around, closing all of his fingers except the middle.

"Very good, Mr. Gould. They are coming close. They'd want to pummel you from close range. It's not a bad strategy—it'll render your countermeasures useless, but it'll also get them within your range. When they are, fire all eight remaining rockets."

"But I'll be defenseless," Johnny protested.

"Yes." Victor smiled. "You also won't be dead. Good luck."

The line disconnected, leaving him alone with the incoming helicopter. He could see the details of the Apache without any enhancements now—the angry outline of a deadly machine. An alert screeched and pulsated amber on his display, telling him the missiles were being armed. He ran toward the helicopter to shorten the distance, watching the proximity sensor. It blinked, changing from red to blue, and Johnny fired.

A huge fireball exploded in the sky above him and then it was raining steel—the pieces of the helicopter punching holes through the ice of the lake. A large piece of the blade whooshed through the air toward him, and he swatted it away before him like an annoying insect.

"I'm a demigod, you assholes!" he yelled as the body of the helicopter hit the lake and fell through the ice, disappearing from view. "No one can touch me."

34

Sahara Desert, Algeria

*H*elen kept moving her feet like a somnambulist caught in between the two worlds, unable to distinguish the dream land from reality. The path seemed to have no beginning and no end as she placed her feet one after the other. With nothing around but sand that looked almost red under the ghostly light of the Milky Way, they could have been walking on Mars. The only two humans on the entire planet. Forever lost. Bound to walk the desert for eternity.

She had no idea how Connelly knew which direction they should be heading and simply followed his footsteps, concentrating on what she could do. Besides making sure she kept moving her feet, it wasn't much. Once in a while, she'd look at Connelly's face, searching for clues of how he could stay the course, not give in to the overwhelming desire to lie down and close his eyes. To never move again. His mouth was pressed into a hard line, wrinkles creasing his forehead and giving him a stern look that reminded her of the black-and-white photographs of World War II. The faces of soldiers before the battle, tired and ragged, people who knew they would not come out on the other side but going anyway. Determination that bordered on insanity.

But every time she made eye contact with Connelly, his features would soften, and he'd smile with his eyes. As if telling her that the pain was temporary. Another illusion that would soon disappear just as fast as a desert mirage blown away by the sandstorm. That there was still hope.

Their spirits were high during most of that day when they thought they saw an oasis. The vision was so convincing that they had altered their path more than they initially planned and headed straight toward it. As the sun moved over their heads, the greens and the blues became more and more prominent with each passing hour. Connelly grew restless before she did. It was taking too long, he said. They should have reached it by now.

Then came a fresh wind from the south. Within minutes, the vision of a shelter disappeared into the hot arid air and then came the sandstorm. They would have died in it if Connelly didn't somehow guide them toward a rock formation that gave them a temporary shelter. It was a setback, but they could still correct the course and make for Tuat. But as the hours went on and the storm refused to cease, the fear settled in. They huddled in the alcove as the *simoom* pounded the desert with relentless ferocity, the sand finding its way through fabric layers, clogging her nose and caking her mouth. It was as if the storm was alive, angry at travelers who disturbed the desert and wanted to punish them by burying them without a trace. Erasing them from existence.

The storm ended on the second night as abruptly as it began. One minute the wind was howling like a wild animal and the next it died out, the dark haze in the sky giving way to spectacular sparks of the star-studded dome.

They left the shelter and soon they were heading back to the path that should lead them to Tuat. She doubted they could make it that far, but for some time, the ability to move again got her blood flowing.

She kept walking almost in a trance-like state, feeling nothing and seeing nothing but Mike's silhouette against the sky.

The euphoria hadn't lasted long. Soon the cold was going deep into her bones, making her teeth chatter and body shiver. They were going down another dune when she stumbled and fell, rolling down the hill, unable to stop herself.

By the time Connelly made it to her, she sat up and got most of the sand out of her nose and mouth.

"Here," he said as he came next to her, offering an almost empty plastic bottle. She wanted to protest, but seeing a stubborn look on his dirty face, reconsidered and took a few small painful sips.

"Come on." He grabbed Helen by the arm and pulled her up. "We have to keep moving."

They walked for a few more hours in silence, taking small breaks now and then. Each time, it was harder and harder for her to get up, but Connelly pushed her to persevere.

Helen fell again when they were walking through a flat patch, her legs seemingly unable to carry her weight anymore. She put up her hands before her face struck the sand and then rolled on her back, looking up at the sky. She scanned it until she found three bright stars in a straight line—Orion's belt. Below it, just above the horizon, a bright blue-white dot of Rigel. For a brief moment, she wondered what was happening at the silo. If Steven Poznyak figured out a way to befriend the AI. She saw the simple aluminum bed she'd shared with Max Schlager in the room that had more computers than furniture.

A black silhouette blocked the view of the stars, and she frowned. She just wanted to stay there. In peace.

"Come on," Connelly said, offering her a hand.

"No," she said. "I don't think I can go on."

He kneeled down next to her, slid his hand under her head, and forced her to sit up. Then, grimacing from pain, he took off his jacket and put it around her shoulders. She tried to protest, but couldn't find the strength to say anything.

"Shh," he said and shook his head.

There was no arguing with him now, she thought. This stubborn fool would rather die protecting her, and there was nothing she could do.

"Do you think Max and Jason are still alive?" she asked. Her voice sounded foreign, like a scratchy gramophone recording coming out of her mouth.

"I don't know," he said. He took the plastic jug back and sloshed the liquid around—there wasn't much left. "But if we stay here, we'll never find out. Come on."

He stood up and pulled her to her feet. Then he hugged her around her waist for support and gently pushed her forward. Helen sighed and walked again. After a few seconds, he let her go and picked up speed, once again leading the way. With all the cyborgs walking the face of the earth these days, she thought, this man made of flesh and bones seemed to be tougher than all of them.

The jacket helped. It was still freezing cold, but she stopped shivering and now there was a slight change in the air as the wind no longer nipped at her bare skin.

Connelly pushed them up the dune and then stopped as they reached the crest.

"This would do," he said in a raspy whisper and helped her sit down, facing the east. He pushed the soft sand behind her to support her back and then collapsed next to her.

"What now?" she managed. The stars still shone in the sky, but their light was dimmer now, not as spectacular. The night was ending.

"We rest."

35

Upstate New York

The van's engine whined as Kowalsky plowed through the bushes. They had been driving off the main road for a few miles now, following the map he'd gotten from Steven Poznyak. Once they left US 9, the path initially took them to a winding private road through an abandoned camping grounds. But the unpaved road was soon replaced by a narrow snow-covered path almost indistinguishable from the surroundings and after another mile disappeared altogether.

"It looks like from here we'll have to go on foot," Kowalsky said, bringing the van to a stop and killing the engine. The road abruptly ended by the wall of densely packed trees. Kowalsky could still see the path zigzagging farther into the woods, but snowbanks by the trunks of sugar maples and birch trees made the rocky path even narrower. It would make for a great mountain biking trail, he thought, but not for a full-sized van.

"Maybe it's for the best," Latham said, unbuckling his seat belt.

"Just because we can't see the patrols, it doesn't mean they can't hear us. How's the picture?"

Kowalsky pulled out the tablet and brought the drone surveillance camera online and zoomed out. A grid was splitting the snow-covered forest in large sections, one square mile each, with the missile silo in the center.

"So far, so good," he said. "There's a patrol by the main road. About a mile and a half due north. Six guys on ATVs. But nothing's in our path. Hopefully it stays that way. Rigel has four outposts with machine guns around the compound. Steve says patrols normally don't come within the effective range. It would break the status quo. For now, they are reluctant to do that."

"For now," Schlager echoed from the back of the van. "Unclear how long it'll last. Does he know we are close?"

"Yes. But he can't send people out. We aren't the only ones with the drones. If a search party comes out of the silo, it'll lead those patrols straight to us. We are on our own."

They got out of the van, and Kowalsky opened the back of the vehicle, taking out the stretcher.

"Latham and I will carry Jason first, then we can switch."

"I suggest we switch every fifteen minutes," Price said. "Nobody gets too tired then. How far are we from the compound?"

"About two miles. Maybe two and a quarter. We should be able to make it there in an hour, depending on the terrain."

They loaded Jason's body on the gurney and headed into the woods, Schlager in the front with Kowalsky's Chiappa, Latham and Chuck in the middle with the stretcher, and Price in the back with the Glock.

They had been walking for less than ten minutes when Jason woke up. Kowalsky could see his eyes flutter first and then his lips parted in a weak moan.

"Hang on, guys," Chuck said, slowing down. "Something's up."

They stopped, putting the gurney on the ground. Hunt's eyes fluttered again and then opened. He looked around, confusion spreading across his face.

"Hey, buddy." Schlager kneeled next to him. "Can you talk?"

"Where am I?" Hunt said, his voice raspy and weak.

"We're heading to the silo," Schlager replied. "Should be there soon. How are you feeling?"

"I'm okay." He squinted at his torso. "Considering. How long have I been out?"

"A few days," Kowalsky said. "We should move. It's not safe here."

"Let's switch," Schlager said. "Me and Darius can carry him and talk."

"Okay."

Kowalsky picked up the Chiappa and went ahead, leading the way, muted sounds of a conversation between Jason and Max behind him. They were approaching a clearing in the woods, a smooth surface of a small frozen pond about a hundred yards across, when he heard it.

"Quiet," he barked. He took out the tablet and checked the drone footage. "Shit. Over there, quick. They are coming this way."

He rushed to the dense bushes by the pond, pulling the branches aside and letting Schlager and Price bring Jason in. Then, with the help of Watkins, he pushed the branches back, covering them from the view.

"Get down," he said. The sounds of the engines were getting louder, and then a few seconds later, three ATVs burst out of the woods. They drove around the frozen pond a few times, kicking up fountains of snow and dirt before coming to a stop.

"Where's the rest of them?" Watkins whispered into Kowalsky's ear.

"Quiet."

He watched as the three mercenaries in black parkas bearing the Black Arrow logo got off the vehicles and approached the ice of the pond.

"Do you think there's fish?" one man asked, walking up to the edge of the pond and probing the thickness of the ice with his boot. He was taller than the other two and heavier built.

"Throw a frag in there, Rodney, and you'll know," another man said, pulling goggles off his face. His beard was covered with ice. "If anything bobs up to the surface, then there was fish."

The tall man looked at the pond for a few seconds, as if considering. "Nah. Cap will break my balls for using a frag for no reason. But I'm bored. Pete, you got any beer left?"

The bearded man went back to one of the ATVs and pulled a pack of cans from the travel bag. "Just a six-pack."

"Bring it over."

Cold from the frozen ground was seeping through Kowalsky's parka. He suppressed the shiver—they couldn't stay lying on the ground for too long. It was below freezing. A prolonged exposure could bring frostbite or something worse.

"Let's shoot something," he heard Rodney say as the man polished off the second can of beer. "Yo, Pete. Why don't you put these cans by the bushes over there? Let's see if I can still aim after a few beers."

"Shit," Kowalsky swore under his breath, signaling to the others to back up deeper into the bushes. He aimed the revolver at the three men, ready to engage, when he heard another sound. In a minute, three more ATVs rolled from the woods into the clearing.

"The more the merrier," Rodney exclaimed. "Come on, Petey, set them up."

In desperation, Chuck watched as the mercenary came to the bushes a few yards from them and set up the cans on the ground and then jogged back to the pond.

"Move away from the cans," Kowalsky whispered, pulling on the stretcher and backing up as far as he could.

"I'm stuck," Watkins whispered back. "My parka caught. If I move, they'll see us."

Chuck risked raising his head and peeking over the branches. Watkins wasn't in the direct line of fire, but the closest can was only a few inches away from his left arm.

"You gotta move from there."

He saw Watkins try to crawl sideways, but his jacket seemed to be firmly lodged between the branches.

"Who's going to shoot?" Pete asked. "Can I go first?"

"Screw you," Rodney replied, pulling out a pistol. "There are only six targets. I'll be the only one shooting."

He aimed, lining up the pistol, and squeezed the trigger. A loud crack echoed through the woods and the can on the farther side of Watkins jumped after being hit.

"Nice one," Pete yelled, and the rest of the mercenaries clapped and cheered.

Rodney shot again and again, striking two more empty cans.

"Do three in a row, Rodney," somebody yelled. "Everybody can do one at a time. Do all three."

"All right, assholes," the man said, grasping the pistol with both hands and then slowly exhaling.

Three shots rang out. One can jumped up after getting hit by a bullet and two missed their target.

Kowalsky heard a soft plop and a muffled yelp. He looked over at Latham. The man's face was distorted with pain. He was covering his mouth with his right hand, his face screwed up in a painful grimace.

"You suck, Rodney," Pete yelled and stepped forward. He pulled his pistol and shot twice. The first hit the beer can. It flipped in the air and lodged between the branches a foot above the ground. The second slug missed.

"I told you not to shoot," Rodney screamed, and shoved Pete in the chest. The smaller man took a few steps back, trying to keep balance, but couldn't and fell backward. The mercenaries erupted in laughter.

Rodney shot again, hitting the can, and holstered the pistol. "That's how it's done."

"I have a suggestion," Pete said, getting up and dusting off the back of his pants. "How about we see how deep we can lodge that beer can into the bushes?"

"Yeah," somebody yelled.

"Shut up, everybody." Rodney raised his hand and pulled a phone from his pocket. "Hello? Sounds good. We'll check it out."

He hung up the phone and stuffed it back into his pants.

"What's up, man?"

"Looks like those assholes at the silo sent out a foraging party. Let's go spoil their plans. Get your horses."

Kowalsky watched as the mercenaries saddled into their ATVs and, kicking up snow, roared into the woods.

"Latham." He crawled toward his partner. "Are you okay?"

"That shit hit my shoulder." Watkins stifled a moan. His face was pale, small beads of perspiration covering his forehead.

They pulled him out of the bushes and Kowalsky cut the blood-soaked sleeve of Watkins's parka.

"No exit wound," he said, examining the other side of the shoulder. "It's lodged in there. But it doesn't look like he nicked an artery. There's blood, but not a whole lot of it."

They took straps off the gurney and Kowalsky fashioned a tourniquet above the wound to stop the bleeding. Then he helped Watkins to his feet.

"Can you walk?"

"Of course I can," Latham said. "It's a shoulder, not a knee. I'm afraid you're stuck carrying the stretcher, though."

"Smart ass."

"We should hurry," Watkins said and grimaced again. "We better be at the silo before they come back."

36

Sahara Desert, Algeria

*W*hen Connelly opened his eyes, the sky was still dark, but the constellations were already gone, the blackness of the night replaced by an almost imperceptible orange glow in the east. They were sitting at the crest of a large dune, Helen leaning on his good shoulder. She was still asleep. Her breathing was shallow but peaceful, but her chapped lips were pressed firmly into a thin line, as if she was dreaming of something unpleasant.

They had a rough night. Between the cold, hunger, and dehydration, they were both close to the point of no return, delirious from exhaustion. But nothing weighed harder on them than the disappointment that the oasis turned out to be nothing but a mirage. Fata Morgana. A few times, they had to stop to catch their breath and water their parched mouths with the smallest sips out of the plastic container they could muster. Getting up and getting going again took a bigger toll every time, but Connelly pushed them to move on, convinced that if they stayed, they'd freeze to death. Only when the sky lost some of its brightest stars and the air no longer bit the skin, he finally gave in. He pushed them up the slope of a large dune and they settled on the eastern side of it. This way, the rising sun would warm them sooner and wake them if they had fallen asleep. It also gave them a commanding view for miles around. Not that, if somebody was coming, they could do something about it.

Now a light breeze was blowing from the east and the air felt warm on his face. He looked at the plastic jug that sat in front of them. It was buried into the sand, a handful of water at the bottom, and Connelly picked it up and turned it around, making the water slosh back and forth.

"Hey," she said.

"Hey." He offered the water to her, but she only shook her head.

"You must drink," he insisted.

She took a few small sips, keeping the liquid in her mouth for some time before swallowing, and then passed the jug back to him. He looked at it for a few seconds, closed the lid and put it down.

"You said drink," she complained, but Connelly only shrugged.

They sat there for some time, watching as the sun climbed above the large dune in the south.

"We have to go," Connelly said.

"Wait." Chen sat up straighter, tilting her head and turning it around. "Can you hear that?"

"What?"

"That buzzing sound?"

"No. My hearing is not as acute as it used to be. Heard too many loud noises in my lifetime." He chuckled at his own joke, but then stopped. There was a buzzing sound somewhere in the distance that grew louder and louder until it turned into a rambling of a car engine. He stood up, his joints cracking like that of an old man, and looked around. A tan-colored sedan was speeding between the dunes, leaving a huge dust trail as it went.

"Eli," he said and waved. The car honked in return. "Holy shit, it's him."

The Mercedes growled, its engine straining as it climbed the dune, and then stopped a few feet away from them. Eli climbed out, his smiling face covered in so much dust that his teeth and the whites of his eyes seemed to have a lighting source of their own.

"Morris," he said with a fake British accent, giving them a curt nod. "Elijah Morris."

"Never do that again. Your accent is horrendous," Chen said, giving him a hug. "And don't squeeze this guy. He's got a dislocated shoulder."

Eli popped the trunk and pulled out a full gallon of water, passing it to Chen. "You must be thirsty."

"You have no idea."

"Don't drink too fast," he warned. "Or else you'll get sick. Take your time."

They sat on the sand in the car's shade, snacking on dried fruit and taking small sips of the most delicious water he'd ever had in his life.

"How did you find us?" Chen finally asked.

"I'm sorry I left you," Eli said, a frown creasing his forehead. "I felt terrible driving off, but it didn't look like they were about to kill you on the spot, and I figured I was no good to you dead. So, I ran."

"You did the right thing," Connelly said.

"This beast," Eli stretched out his hand and patted the side of the Mercedes, "saved my life. When I was confident they were not chasing me, I came back and followed the tracks of their cars. If you've never been in the desert, everything looks the same, but I've been here a few times and if you pay attention, you can see trails for quite some time, unless they get covered by a sandstorm."

"There was a sandstorm," Chen said. "It almost killed us."

"Yes," he continued. "But remember—you were walking. I was driving. I was going slow to make sure I didn't miss the tracks, but I was still going faster than you. If not for the storm, I would have found you two days ago. I must have been only ten-fifteen miles away from you when it hit. I had to make camp and cover the engine with a tarp."

"But how did you find us after the storm?"

"A lot of luck, I guess?" He shrugged. "I knew the approximate direction you were going. I drove in an ever wider zigzag. I figured if you made it through the storm, you'd be tired and slow, so I should get close enough to see you."

"Sounds like it worked."

"No, it did not," he said, a sheepish look on his face. "Sometimes I overestimate my abilities. All that zigzagging confused the hell out of me, and I got lost myself. I tried to go back to where I came from, looking for my own tracks, but it was windy and then I got even more lost, if such a thing was even possible. But then I got lucky. I stopped, trying to preserve the fuel, and waited for the night so I could read the stars. At that point, I thought it'd be a miracle if I could get back myself, let alone find you. And then, as I sat there by the car, contemplating how screwed up I was, I saw a caravan."

"A caravan?"

"I don't know if three camels actually qualify to be called a caravan, but there was a family—a husband and wife, one grandma, and three kids. Bedouins. They stopped by me. I shared some fruit with them and one kid gave me this." He got up and went to the trunk of the car. A moment later, he came back with a set of four small brass bells. "We understood each other well enough to have a little chat and after I told him I was looking for my friends, he said that the only place you could survive the storm if you were on foot was in the sandstone hills. He explained how to find it."

"He was right," Connelly said. "We found an alcove and waited out the storm there."

"He told me something else," Eli said, a mischievous glint in his eye. "He asked why the hell we were going through the desert in the first place. I didn't want to tell him the truth, so I came up with a story about two dumb tourists who wanted to experience a true adventure and visit an oasis or two. I said we wanted to get to Tuat and then get deep into the desert before we go back, to give you two a taste of wilderness. He laughed first, saying that if you are still alive, you probably already got as much of a taste of wilderness as you cared to swallow. But then he added, that if I found you and we still ended up going away from Tuat, we should be careful and try to avoid what he called a *city in the desert.*"

"A city?" Connelly and Chen exchanged glances. "He must've been talking about the factory."

"That's what I thought, too. He said a few years back, somebody came here with a lot of machinery and started building a city in the middle of the desert. Apparently, there was a lot of commotion. Helicopters came in first and then they built a landing strip and huge cargo airplanes would land there a few times every day. It made little sense to the local people because there's nothing there. You might as well be building a city on Mars. But people were intrigued and would go see it, but it looks like whoever was building the city didn't appreciate the curiosity and some people got shot. Since then, Ali—that's how he introduced himself to me—and his people had to alter their routes not to get too close to the place. He said he hadn't heard anyone getting in trouble around the city recently, but every time when he had to travel that way, he steered clear of the place just in case. Naturally, I asked where exactly the place was, so I wouldn't accidentally get there."

"Naturally," Connelly echoed.

"He drew me a map." Eli pulled a piece of crumpled paper and opened it on his knees. It was a pencil drawing of the locale with a few dots representing a string of oases and a large circle with an Arabic word next to it some distance away from them. Eli pointed at the circle. "I believe this is what you're looking for."

37

Rigel Compound, Upstate New York

"I'll stand," Kowalsky said, waving off the chair Schlager offered. He leaned on the wall, watching everyone take seats around the table. "If anyone's taking requests for improvements to our living situation, I'd like to ask for better sleeping arrangements. My back is a giant bruise, after sleeping on that monstrosity of a bed."

The first level of the control center that also served as Jason Hunt's living quarters was packed. It was the first time since the ambush on Orion Tower they all gathered in the same location. Kowalsky scanned the room, searching for clues in the familiar faces, as anxiety and relief washed over him in equal doses.

Jason Hunt was in a wheelchair at the head of the table, wearing a loose hoodie, a blanket covering his lower torso. He still was missing his legs and the left arm, but his bionic right arm was fitted back in and he operated it with the usual efficiency. Darius Price sat to Jason's right, the man's usually lustrous ebony skin pale, his jaw set. He seemed to be the most uncomfortable in the group, as if he wasn't sure it was appropriate to sit at the table. Schlager sat to Hunt's left and Steven Poznyak took a place on the opposite side of the table from Hunt.

"Should I go first?" Kowalsky asked, looking around the room.

"Please," Jason said. His voice was low and quiet, as if even such a mundane task as talking required a large effort. "But before you do, I'd like to offer my most sincere gratitude for rescuing us. I'm sure Max and the president feel the same."

"Just doing my job," Chuck said, as his cheeks grew hot. "Anyway. There are not too many updates apart from the crucial information I've already given to you. The country is in the state of slow-moving civil war. Black Arrow has occupied most of the big cities and places of strategic value, but they have been pulling back somewhat in the past few days as resistance picked up all over the country. Manhattan, for example, still has patrols, but they no longer have the numbers to maintain the curfew, or to block every bridge. There have been similar developments in other big cities, although Black Arrow still has a chokehold on Washington, DC."

"That makes sense," Price said. "Engel needs to stay in the White House."

"Right," Kowalsky continued. "But they are feeling the pressure."

"I wish it affected them more. It's gotten worse here," Poznyak said. "We've got almost no food left and the last two convoys have been slaughtered. There are no more farms that will send us supplies, not that I can blame them."

"Do we know if those are always the same units that are attacking our supply routes?" Jason asked.

"They used to be just random volunteers before," Poznyak said. "They'd shoot some warning shots and block the roads, scare the folks away. But the last two were different. I saw the video that was streamed from one of the vehicles and it was Johnny the Butcher both times, all by himself. He's not there the entire time, but often enough."

"Johnny killed all those men by himself?" Jason Hunt said, his hand balling into a fist. "How is that even possible?"

"He's now heavily augmented," Kowalsky said, before Poznyak

could reply. "A full-on cyborg. Latham and I saw him firsthand when we were doing an op. Looks crazy—there's not much left of him, except his head. His armor is different from anything I'd seen except for Martin's. And he's not shy to show off his new body either—he didn't have anything on. Just walked around on bird-like legs with three claws on each. The scariest thing I've ever seen."

"How's Latham?"

"He's fine. I saw him this morning after he came back from the doc. It's healing well. It doesn't look like there'll be any lasting damage."

"Good."

"Speaking of cyborgs," Schlager interjected. "I didn't have a chance to say this, but Martin is alive. Apparently, Victor Ye assumed that he was dead. They stored his body in some warehouse, unguarded. He's in a pretty awful shape, but he was able to repair enough of himself to escape and is hiding in a safe place. I don't think he's capable of fighting anyone now, let alone another cyborg, so we cannot bring him over here for the time being, but we will figure something out."

"That's great news," Kowalsky said.

"Are there any updates from Connelly and Helen?"

"The last I've heard from them, they've located the factory and are heading there now. I don't know any details, because you never know if the messages are secure, but it sounds like they are on the last leg of their journey. They sure as hell could use some reinforcements."

"I'll take care of it." Jason looked up at Schlager. "Max. You and Steven are going to need to do some work for me. If Chuck is right, I'd need to be up and running in less than forty-eight hours. We'll need Martin, too."

"We'll do what we can, Jason," Poznyak said, "but—"

"There are no buts, Steven. We are either getting things done or Engel is going to finish us off. There's no other option."

The room grew uncomfortably quiet for a few moments. Kowalsky stuck his hands into his pockets and looked away from the table. If somebody was going to be challenging Jason Hunt's overly ambitious timeline while the man still lacked most of his limbs, it sure as hell would not be him.

"If I may," Price chimed in. "And I am grateful for all your assistance, but I cannot stay here at the silo indefinitely. If we were to restore legitimacy to this country, I'd need to be out with the people. Lead them, not hide in a bunker."

"You will," Jason said and rolled away from the table, showing that the meeting was over. "But not yet. If you leave now, the only thing you will accomplish is getting recaptured or killed. All this effort and risks would be for nothing. Engel is hiding out in a bunker in Washington. There's no doubt about that. Your situation isn't any different. This is your secure location for now. What we should do is create a broadcast where you can address the nation. Dispel the rumors about your death, tell them that Black Arrow isn't the United States Army. Inspire them to fight back. I'm sure Max can set you up for this, can't you, Max?"

"Of course."

"Thank you, Mr. Hunt," Darius said. He stood up, following Jason's cue, eager to leave.

"There's one more thing," Jason said, rolling away. "You can take this level as your quarters going forward. At least for now. I'll need to undergo a few procedures that will take some time. It would make sense for me to stay in the lab. Steven, could you help me down the stairs? I'm afraid this place wasn't built for wheelchairs."

"Are there questions for me?" Kowalsky said, as Poznyak and Hunt disappeared into the level below.

"You said you've seen Johnny up close?" Schlager asked. "I'd like you to tell me as much as you can about how he looked."

"I can do better than that. When we were at a chapel in Brooklyn, long story, my buddy gained access to the CCTV feed. I'm pretty sure he recorded the whole thing—he always does. One of the cameras was outside. Johnny should be on it, front and center. He was doing this weird thing that creeped me out. Every now and then, he'd spin his head independently from his torso. Do a whole one-eighty. Even talking about it makes my skin crawl."

"Okay." Schlager stood up as well. "Let me know how to contact your friend and I'll look into it."

"Just one thing," Kowalsky said.

"What?"

"He's an annoying little bugger. He might ask for money before he shares the video. If it's not the money, maybe a favor or something."

"It is what it is," Schlager said, shrugging. "As long as it's not unreasonable, I'll try to accommodate him."

"If you don't mind, I'd like to talk to him with you. He owes me. And we can look at the video together. Maybe something jogs my memory and I'll remember anything else that might be useful."

"Sure." Schlager offered him a hand. "Give me about forty-five minutes, will you? I need to talk to Jason first."

Kowalsky watched as everybody filed out of the tight quarters and stretched, listening to cracks in his spine. Despite having slept for over ten hours the night before, he thought he could sleep another ten if given a chance. His head was heavy, his feet were swollen, and his eyes were tearing up, irritated by the overly dry filtrated air of the silo.

"I'm getting too old for this shit," he muttered to himself and headed back to his bunk in Silo 2. He might not be able to get another ten hours, but if Schlager was going to see him in forty-five minutes, Kowalsky intended to spent at least forty-four of them sleeping.

38

Château Beaufort, France

The ground was freezing, even through a few layers of thermal clothing. Jill Cooper lay prone at the end of a vineyard row, looking down a gently sloped hill. It was an eerie sight—hundreds of small fires and candles were lit near the vines to ward off the biting cold, forming the lines of ghostly light seemingly floating in the dark, smoky air. The temperature had been steadily dropping over the past few days, a trend that seemed to ignore what continent Cooper was visiting and as the sun set, it dropped below freezing. Frost started settling in, encasing the vines in its deadly embrace and making Cooper shiver in her hiding spot.

The vineyard rows ran all the way to the bottom of the hill. A small stone cottage with a red tile roof, its two windows lit from the inside, sat there next to an old oak tree. A guard was leaning on the wall next to the door, almost invisible in his gray parka if not for the flaring tip of a cigarette that now and then illuminated the lower part of his face.

There were twelve guards in total. Cooper studied their patterns methodically over the past two hours, as she lay shivering at the edge of a vineyard covered in a camouflage net. There were only six guards at first, three patrolling around the cottage and another three walking the headlands up and down the hill. After the workers had lit the fires and left, another six guards arrived. Three of them joined the men on the hill and another three positioned themselves at the gate of a winding road leading to the cottage and blocked by a jersey barrier.

There was no feasible way Cooper could overpower or outshoot a dozen of highly trained mercenaries head on. If she was going to pull off a successful operation, she knew it would come down to three basic things—silence, speed, and diversion.

Before coming to France, Cooper had to pull every favor she had left among her European contacts, but they came through. Two nights ago, a courier delivered to her a disassembled MTs-116M suppressed sniper rifle with a thermal scope and a PSS-2 silent handgun with two six-round magazines. Both Russian-made weapons had no external suppressors. Instead, they featured an innovative captive-piston design that retained gas inside the cartridge case, rather than pushing the bullet with expanding gases. That made for a highly specialized, expensive, and hard to obtain ammunition. But in return, the rifle lobbed huge 12.7mm rounds at subsonic speeds capable of going through body armor at three hundred meters, while producing less noise than a clap of one's hands.

Cooper waited until the two guards closest to her started going back down the hill and activated two autonomous drones. They took off, their base hidden at the side of the road about half a mile away from the guards' post, rose three feet above the ground, and started moving toward the cottage. When they were within five hundred yards, they turned the lights on, designed to imitate a car's headlights. Then the built-in speakers produced a pre-recorded sound of a vehicle driving at a slow speed.

She watched the ghostly silhouettes perk up as they heard the approaching sound and then two guards jogged toward the jersey barrier, taking a knee and scoping the road ahead of them. The third guard stayed behind, his head swiveling back and forth between the road and the cottage.

Cooper exhaled, lining up the two guards at the barrier, and pulled the trigger. There was a metallic clang and a barely audible hiss, and then she watched both men by the jersey barrier collapse. She moved the barrel an inch to the left, aiming at the third guard, and fired again. The man stumbled and then fell face-forward as the bullet struck his neck, severing the spine.

Cooper turned, surveying the guards moving up and down the hill, but so far, they seemed to be oblivious to the fate that had befallen their comrades by the road. She hit the drone control button again, turning off the diversion and recalling the two small machines.

Cooper left the sniper rifle and crawled back into an alleyway, going perpendicular to the closest patrol's path. She stopped when she approached the headland, pressed her cheek into the cold ground, and pulled the hood over. For a few seconds, she stayed immobile, listening to the sounds of the wind rustling through the vines. Then there were steps.

"This is brutal," she heard one guard say as they approached her hiding place. "Too much trouble for one little girl, if you ask me."

"That's why nobody's asking you," another man said. "And I don't mind the overtime pay."

The voices muted as the two men turned around, the sounds whisked away by the gusts of icy wind, and Cooper jumped, bringing up the PSS-2. She aligned the red dot of the laser at the back of the head of one guard and pulled the trigger. The gun tsk-tsked, the slide slowing down at its final stages of movement to prevent clanging.

The second guard turned around as he heard his partner collapsing to the ground and Cooper shot him in the face and immediately dropped to the ground herself.

Five down, seven to go, she whispered as she crawled back, heading for the second patrol.

She hit a snag when she ambushed the last patrol. The first guard tripped on a vine, making Cooper send the bullet into the dark, smoky sky. She corrected, shooting him in the temple, but then the second guard was on her, and Cooper found herself unable to change the now empty magazine.

She grabbed onto the man's rifle, pulling it up, and struck him with a knee to the groin. The guard released the grip of his rifle, but before Cooper could turn it around, he kicked her in the chest. She went down hard, breaking through the row of vines, one branch piercing her thigh and the rifle tumbling away into the darkness.

He jumped on her, the heavy fists pounding with a ferocity of a sledgehammer, pummeling her blocks, eager to use his size advantage. She squirmed under him, finding it hard to breathe as his knee pinned her chest, and reached for the knife on her utility belt, but he was too strong. He grabbed her right hand with his left, almost crushing her wrist as his right closed a vice-like grip on her throat.

Cooper's vision dimmed. She tried to wedge her left hand under the man's fingers, but he just leaned in, crushing her throat with his weight. In a moment of desperation, she brought her head back even more, exposing her neck fully, and hit his wrist with hers as hard as she could. It worked, his hand slipping up, and she twisted, closing her teeth around the man's thumb.

He yelled in pain, landing a few painful blows, but Cooper wrapped around his arm like a boa, biting into his flesh, grinding her teeth through muscle, tendon, and bone.

He finally pushed her away, wailing like a wounded animal, but by then she finally pulled the knife out of the sheath. She dodged a feeble kick, her hand slicing at his thigh and then when the man fell to his knee, unable to put weight on his leg, she danced around him, the knife point punching under his jaw and into his spine.

Cooper squatted as the man collapsed, her breathing ragged, her chest and neck on fire. She wanted to lie down, but there was no time —the fight might have taken only a few seconds, but the guards by the cottage were going to notice that no one was coming down the hill at any moment. If they used Liz as a shield, it would complicate Cooper's plan.

She swapped the magazine on the PSS-2 and walked down the hill, no longer hiding. Between the hazy light of the candles and the smoke, she was sure nobody was going to see her until it was too late.

She was right. The guard by the door, blinded by the light of his own cigarette, looked up when Cooper stepped into the light of the windows. The guard opened his mouth, but the PSS-2 clicked, punching the cigarette and bits of the man's teeth deep into his brain. Cooper moved on, stalking the last two guards, her senses tingling. She was one with the night right now, and nothing could stop her.

When the last man fell, she walked to the door and holstered the gun. She did her best, wiping the blood and dirt off her hands and face, and put a hand on the doorknob. She stood there for a moment, her heart pumping, her hands suddenly sweaty despite the cold. Then she opened the door and stepped inside.

"Jill?" Elizabeth stood up from a bench in front of a wooden table. A lantern with a faux candle was throwing bizarre shadows as the young woman moved. It looked like she was about to serve a cup of tea—a white china teapot sat next to a small cup and saucer, the pot steaming from its long nose. "You look awful. What are you doing here? Is everything okay?"

"Liz." Cooper nodded to her and went around the kitchen. She found it in the cupboard—another teacup identical to the one on the table. She picked up the pot and poured the tea into the cups and then sat down, taking hers with both hands, savoring the warmth.

"I'm here to talk to you," she finally said. "Something I wish I had done a long time ago."

Manhattan, New York

Chuck Kowalsky could see the black Escalade from the hallway's window, as the large car climbed on the curb and came to a stop. The driver jumped out of the car and ran around the vehicle to open the door, but was too late—Johnny the Butcher was already on the sidewalk, his head and torso doing the weird one-eighties, as he looked up and down the street. Despite having seen it before, Kowalsky shuddered at how alien Johnny looked. Most people who used augmentation technology didn't flaunt it. They still wore pants over their prosthetic legs and jackets over their upgraded bodies and artificial arms. Until now, Martin was the only exception, and Chuck sometimes wondered how much of a human was actually left in the cyborg that once had been Mike Connelly's teammate.

But Johnny was different. He didn't even attempt to conceal his artificial body, stalking around on claw-like feet and doing the one-eighties with his head and torso. Chuck was convinced Johnny did them on purpose, soaking up the fear of everyone around him. Then again, Kowalsky thought, Johnny was less of a human than most, even back when he had all of his body parts intact.

Kowalsky's palms were getting sweaty, and he rubbed them on the front of his jacket. As Johnny crossed the street and disappeared from view, Chuck pulled his Chiappa Rhino and waited.

After a few minutes, he heard the heavy stomping of Johnny's feet, and another moment later, the door to the hallway flew open and the cyborg squeezed through the opening.

"That's far enough," Kowalsky shouted, raising his revolver. "I don't like touchy-feely. Let's keep those twenty-five yards between us at all times as we'd agreed."

"Do you think this toy would help you?" Johnny pointed at the revolver.

"Did you come here to trade insults?" Chuck replied. "Or did you come here because you're interested in what I have to say?"

"Maybe both." Johnny shrugged and then his head did a one-eighty. "Your message said you knew how to kill Jason Hunt. Convince me it's true, and I'll let you leave from here alive."

"I'd need more than that," Kowalsky said, the Chiappa aimed squarely at Johnny's chest. "If I do this, Hunt's people will go to great lengths to hunt me down. I'd want a permanent place in your organization, a lump sum payment after Jason dies, and a monthly allowance from now on."

"All I've heard so far," Johnny said, taking a step forward, "is what you want. And I have heard nothing that tells me you're not full of shit."

"Stay where you are." Kowalsky raised the Chiappa an inch higher and took a step back. "Fine. Jason Hunt is more of a machine than anything else. He's obsessed with the technology. Thinks it'll make him immortal. But not everyone in the Orion group shares his vision. Some people think that he's taking the tech in a direction he shouldn't. Plays God, if you will."

"And?"

"It recently came to my attention," Kowalsky continued, "that during one of the many upgrades that Jason had gone through, one engineer built a kill switch inside him."

"A kill switch?" Johnny cocked his head to the side. "Like what? Like a bomb?"

"Not a bomb." Kowalsky chuckled. "More like a computer virus. Something that will wipe out the code in the internal computer running all Jason's systems. Turn all his augs into bricks and what's more important, it will fry his brain implants. If you fry something inside somebody's brain, you're most likely to fry their brain as well."

"Okay," Johnny said, taking another step forward. "Say I believe such a kill switch exists. How do you activate it? If I could get close to him, I wouldn't need a kill switch. I'd take him apart with my hands."

"You don't need to get close to him," Chuck said, stepping back. "And I'd appreciate if you stopped walking toward me. It makes me uncomfortable. Jason is all about being connected. On his internal mainframe, he has a sat link that connects him to the net of Orion's satellites. That's also how he makes sure his software is constantly updated with the latest and the most secure versions. No matter where he is, that link is periodically pumping info into his internal computer. That's your way in. Upload the virus to the satellite and then sit back and relax. Next time Jason establishes a connection for a firmware update—poof. All you have left is a charred skull full of metal junk."

"That sounds great. Where is the virus?"

"Here." Kowalsky used his left hand to pull a small USB stick from his jacket pocket. "Along with the instructions on how to upload it to the satellite. But before I give it to you, we need to make a deal on how you'll deliver on those conditions."

"Is it encrypted?" Johnny smiled. "Are you trying to sell me some shit nobody can read?"

"No." Kowalsky shook his head. "As plain as ABCs. Any fifth grader with a laptop could use it."

"That sounds great," Johnny said, and charged.

Chuck pulled the trigger, aiming for Johnny's face, but the cyborg's helmet closed shut, the slugs harmlessly flicking off its shiny surface.

Before the cyborg reached him, Kowalsky stepped out of the hallway and closed the steel door. Then he ran as hard as he could for the elevator.

There was a slew of mighty blows and as the doors of the elevator closed and it started its ascent, it sounded like an explosion took off the doors, blocking Johnny. Trapped in a steel box going at what seemed to be an excruciatingly slow speed, Kowalsky prayed to every god he knew. If Johnny was too mad to consider that killing him inside the elevator with a rocket or some other weapon might destroy the precious USB drive, then he was toast. But a few seconds later, the doors chimed, letting him out on the twenty-first floor, and Kowalsky took a deep breath—so far, the plan worked.

There were faint sounds of destruction that grew louder by the second. Johnny was taking the stairs, while unleashing his anger on every floor of the building. Chuck sent the elevator one floor higher and checked the hidden door under the wall panel. It worked, and he threw his Chiappa into a small adjacent room and closed the door again. Then he stood tall, his hands in his pockets, waiting for the cyborg to come out of the door on the other side of the hallway.

It didn't take long. There was a loud rumbling and then the door flew off the hinges, landing in the middle of the floor with a loud bang.

"Here you are, you fat little shit," Johnny yelled, stepping out through the ruined doorframe.

"I'm not very little, nor particularly fat," Kowalsky said. "And I find it offensive that I came to you in good faith, offering you something you wanted for many years and instead of agreeing to my terms, you tried to take it away for free and kill me. That's bad business."

"It's good business for me," Johnny said, marching toward Chuck, his claw-like feet clanging on the metallic floor. "And once I give this to Mr. Ye, it's going to be even better. But before that, I'll enjoy tearing you apart limb by limb."

The cyborg covered the remaining distance between them and was reaching out his artificial arm toward Kowalsky when it happened. There was a click, followed by a loud clang, and then Johnny collapsed onto the floor at Kowalsky's feet as if crushed under the immense gravity. His servomotors whined, smoking and shooting sparks as Johnny's internal batteries drained, trying to overcome an invisible force.

"Amazing, isn't it?" Kowalsky said, keeping his hands in his pockets. "You are predictable, Johnny. And what a stupid name you've got, let me tell you. Johnny the Butcher? What kind of crazy-ass sociopath do you have to be, so you'd *willingly* call yourself that? Did you fancy Hannibal Lecter when you were a child? I'll grant you, Marvin Gould isn't the most dashing name either, but anything could be better than the Butcher."

"How are you doing this?" Johnny strained. It seemed whatever was affecting his body was interfering with his breathing apparatus and his words came out wheezing.

"If you weren't preoccupied by the idea of dismembering me, you'd probably pay more attention to your surroundings. And if you had, you'd notice two peculiar things. First, I don't have my gun anymore. Don't you think that's weird? And if you look at me, you'll notice I have nothing metallic on me. No belts with buckles, no watch. Hell, my pants have buttons instead of a zipper, not that you'd see *that*. Second, didn't you hear some weird clanging noise when you came charging at me like a bull in a bullring? This floor isn't like the rest in the building." Kowalsky squatted and rapped his knuckles on the floor's surface. It made a hollow metallic sound. "It's made of highly conductive material. I don't have the slightest idea what exactly Jason and his engineers were planning on doing here and frankly, I don't particularly care. All I know is that a friend of mine reconfigured a few things on this floor for me and it's currently running a massive magnetic charge that squashed you like the little bug that you are."

"I'll kill you," Johnny managed.

"No, you will not." Kowalsky stood up and pressed the panel, opening the hidden door. "You will not hurt another person ever again. Because when I step through that door, I'll momentarily turn off the magnets—and before you get all excited, I'll turn on the electricity. It'll fry you like an egg."

"You won't," Johnny whispered. His face was turning blue from the lack of oxygen, his eyes bloodshot. "It takes nerve to kill a man in cold blood."

"Normally, I'd agree with you," Kowalsky said, sighing. "But a few days ago, I had to kill someone who was once very dear to me. Unfortunately for you, I've crossed this threshold. And in your case, I'm confident, had you had a trial, a jury would have come to the same decision. Goodbye, Mr. Gould."

"Wait," Johnny whispered.

Kowalsky ignored him, stepping into the safe room, and then turned. "Oh, one more thing. There's no kill switch in Jason Hunt."

He closed the panel behind him and put his hand on a circuit breaker. Then, without giving himself time to reconsider, pulled it down. There was a loud crackle, like the sound of a tearing bedsheet, and a high-pitched cry of pain. Then there was silence.

Kowalsky turned off the current and cautiously cracked the door open. It smelled of ozone and burnt flesh, and Chuck stuck his face into the crook of his arm to block the stench. Most of Johnny's head and face were gone, a pile of ash-covered fragments of teeth and bone. The armor that once looked like liquid mercury was dull and had the appearance of solidified solder. He gently kicked the claw on one of the cyborg's feet, but the figure remained immobile—Johnny the Butcher was dead.

Chuck called the elevator and backed into it, not leaving the sight of the corpse. He sighed with relief when the doors chimed and closed, removing Johnny from his view.

A few minutes later, he stepped outside the building and stood there for a moment, hands in his pockets, looking at the empty street.

"I don't get what's the hype with all this cyborg shit," he muttered, and walked toward his car. The sun was rising and the city's air already smelled of exhaust, food trucks, and garbage. He took a deep breath. It was the sweetest air Kowalsky could have asked for.

40

Otomo Factory, Sahara Desert

"$\mathcal{I}$t looks like a Mars colony." Eli cupped his hand over his forehead, covering his eyes as they climbed on top of the dune. A row of buildings covered in solar panels was glistening in the afternoon, like a constellation of giant mirrors. The buildings were encased in transparent plastic domes connected to each other with semicircular tunnels big enough to drive a few semis shoulder to shoulder.

"Yes, it does," Helen Chen said, putting her hand on the young man's shoulder. "Thank you for getting us here."

"Are you sure you don't want me to stick around? You'll need a ride back."

"No," Connelly said. "You've done enough. I'm sure we can find some kind of transport out there. Be safe."

"You too. Apart from being the most terrifying experience of my life, this also was the best."

Helen watched Eli run down the dune to the car. A moment later, the engine revved, the wheels digging into the sand, and the car sped away.

"Let's go."

They started down the slope of the dune, Connelly in front of her, scoping the buildings with binoculars. "This is weird."

"What is?"

"There's a lot of movement," he said. "But I don't see any people. It seems like the complex is entirely autonomous. That would explain why people who accidentally stumbled on the factory stopped getting shot."

The walk to the nearest dome took longer than she'd expected, the sand getting less pressed as they got closer to the buildings and making it harder to walk. By the time they were standing in front of a built-in door, she was out of breath, hot sweat running down her back and sides.

"What do you think?" Connelly wiped the dust off the security panel next to the door. "Can you open it?"

Chen pulled up her internal interface and launched the scanner. A 3-D model of the security system appeared in her vision. She may have been unable to hack military satellites yet, but defeating a sophisticated electronic lock was child's play. Schlager had outdone himself, she thought, looking at the multilayered diagram of security triggers, defense nodes, and the underlying code. She overwhelmed the defenses, watching in amusement the system's feeble attempts to stop her. It was like racing a Ferrari against a go-kart.

The door clanged and slid open, letting a puff of cool air out.

"You never cease to amaze me, Helen," Connelly said, stepping through the door, the barrel of his M4 sweeping the surrounding area.

"There must have been a reason you took me with you. Wait till I tell you I've downloaded the map of the entire complex and accessed its security camera's feed."

"Can you blow it up and we go home?"

"Ha." She chuckled. "I wish. I'm afraid there are no big red buttons that say *Self-Destruct* as far as I can see."

"Was worth a shot," he said. "Which way then?"

She opened the map of the complex in her internal vision and studied it for a few seconds. "There's a strange building this way." She pointed. "It's roughly in the middle of the complex in front of a big square, and it's the only place that's not under video surveillance, but I'm reading some heat signatures. Looks like there are five people working on something on the roof of that building. There's something in that square, Mike, and whatever it is, it's consuming a massive amount of energy."

"How massive?"

"Like twice as much as everything else," she said, looking at the rows of running numbers. "You could power a small city with this much energy."

"The nuke," Connelly said. "Whatever this thing is, that's what they need the nuke for."

"Yeah," she said. "We also have a problem. It looks like a few of our desert friends have found their way into the building and are heading that way, too. We should hurry."

They ran through the streets of the strange city, as freight bots passed them in both directions, carrying items destined for the different parts of the complex.

"Look." Connelly nudged her with his good arm as they approached yet another building. It was a large hexagon that looked like a warehouse. Rows and rows of shimmering figures stood there like soldiers during a parade. Their glow was muted, not as bright as the Daimyo they'd encountered, and none of the figures moved, but she shivered as she looked upon the army.

"We cannot leave here until we destroy this."

She nodded, out of breath. Connelly, even injured, could run circles around her, and she didn't want to slow them down. A few moments later, they turned around another building and stopped in their tracks.

"Holy mother," she said, looking up at the monster. The square in front of the building they were looking for wasn't empty after all. "What the hell is this?"

"An illegitimate child of an assault helicopter and Daimyo? And it looks like it's a boy." Connelly quipped.

He wasn't far off, she thought, looking at the gigantic, shimmering figure. The long ovoid body was balanced between two squat legs, each sporting a VTOL jet engine. A multitude of weapons were positioned on pylons and short wings jetting out on both sides, like on an assault helicopter. A single large cannon with a short, fat barrel was attached at the bottom of the body on a gimbal.

She looked up, marveling at the grotesquely enormous head, but then something else caught her attention. There was a large square opening at the top of the ovoid, right below the back of the head. A crane installed onto the roof of the building was next to it, its long boom positioned right above the opening. The hook was still empty, but Helen knew that's where the power supply was going.

"It's got crazy eyes," she heard Connelly say.

She looked at the haunting face again and saw something she hadn't noticed the first time. The pupils of the eyes weren't uniformly black. They looked like simmering clouds.

"My God," she said. "It has—"

A loud rumble of automatic fire interrupted her, mid-sentence. Connelly took off for the building, his M4 at the ready in front of him, and Chen ran after him as hard as she could. He burst through the side door of the building and disappeared inside.

Her chest burning from the lack of oxygen, she pressed harder. It smelled like ozone and burning rubber inside the structure. Long rows of machines were lining the area from wall to wall, thick power lines running from each and joining to form a massive cable that was connected to the ovoid outside. She saw Connelly running up the metal stairs at the end of the room and followed him.

When she made it to the rooftop, the shooting had stopped. Two men were standing at the farthest edge of the roof, next to a sturdy plastic table with a gleaming metallic cube on top of it. She recognized one man—Hamza Akeem—standing guard in front of the table with a rifle. The man next to him held a small device that looked like a narrow tablet with thin, dangling metallic legs over the cube, his hands shaking.

In the middle of the roof, there was a glimmering figure of Daimyo facing Akeem. His knees were slightly bent, as if ready to jump. His curved sword was out, but he was standing still.

"Get back," Connelly whispered, stepping between her and Daimyo. "This won't end well."

"Let us pass," Akeem said. "Nobody has to die today. Or else my associate will attach this device to the nuke. It's a two-minute countdown timer that cannot be stopped or hacked. AES 256-bit encryption, if you are familiar with it."

Daimyo took a small step forward, and time slowed down to a crawl.

Chen saw as Akeem squeezed the trigger, spraying Daimyo with lead. The assassin's blade blurred, slicing the bullets midair. He jumped, covering the distance between him and Akeem, his sword going through the man's right shoulder and coming out of his left hip.

"Allahu Akbar," the other man yelled and stuck the device to the cube. It clanged, a hollow metallic sound of two magnets snapping together. A small display on top of the gadget lit up, starting a countdown.

The assassin spun on his heels, paused for a split second, as if seeing Chen and Connelly for the first time, and then ran toward them.

"Here, asshole," Connelly yelled, running toward the side of the building, his M4 spitting fire, as he tried to lure the assassin away from Chen. She saw him aim at the assassin's feet, a desperate attempt to repeat the success he had in the Medina.

It didn't work this time. The glowing figure covered the remaining distance, his left hand swatting the rifle out of Connelly's hands, and his right hand shot out, the blade skewering Connelly's chest and lifting him off the ground.

"No!" she heard someone scream, only to recognize her own voice.

Daimyo pulled the sword back and Connelly collapsed to his

knees. He coughed, covering his chest with his good hand, and then fell back.

The assassin turned and took a step toward her. Helen stood straighter—there was nowhere to run. She was going to die on this roof.

A blast shook the air, splitting the dome in two, as a million melted pieces of plastic rained down on the roof of the building. One landed on her shoulder, burning through her clothes and skin, and she wiped it away, oblivious to pain. She looked up in time to see Jason Hunt hanging out of the open door of a helicopter and fire what looked like a thick metallic arrow. It flashed through the air like a miniature lightning bolt and Daimyo's sword blurred, splitting the projectile in half, but the head of the arrow completed its trajectory, hitting him square in the sternum.

The sword disappeared from the assassin's hand and he fell to his knees, clawing at his chest as if trying to dig the arrowhead out. Then it looked as if a depth charge went off—a light emanated from the center of Daimyo's chest as wavelike ripples ran through his body. He exploded in a shower of metal and gore, the curved blade of the glimmering katana flying with a deadly whoosh a few inches away from Helen's head and slicing a satellite dish in two.

She ran to Connelly and knelt next to him, putting pressure on his chest, blood pooling between her fingers. He opened his eyes and smiled at her.

"Sorry," he said, his voice soft, his eyes unfocused.

"Stay with me, please." She cried like a kid, hot tears running down her cheeks and falling on his ruined chest, mixing with his blood. "Please, Mike. Stay."

"Sofia?" His voice was now quiet, almost a whisper. "Is that you?"

"Yes," she said and brought her face closer to his. "I'm right here."

"I've missed you," he said and closed his eyes.

Strong hands picked her up, and she went slack, letting Jason carry her to the helicopter. She saw as Martin picked up Connelly's body and ran after them.

The helicopter jumped off the roof, banking hard and accelerating away. As it climbed, Helen sat on the floor next to the body and took Connelly's hand into hers. She pressed it against her cheek. It was still warm, but she knew it would not last. Another mirage that would disappear soon. Somewhere below them in the desert, a new sun was rising.

41

Château Beaufort, France

"You are my mother?" The young woman put the teacup down on the table, her hands shaking. "How? I don't understand. When Alex told me about you, he said you helped to save me from the kidnappers and because you'd lost your own daughter when she was young, you felt this special connection to me and wanted to keep in touch."

Jill Cooper looked at her. In the flickering light of the candles, Liz looked like the spitting image of her when she was younger.

She had been waiting for this moment for so long. Most of her life. She imagined it a million times, preparing for what she would say and how she would behave. But now, sitting across the small table from her flesh and blood, she found herself lost for words. All she wanted to do was to reach out and scoop Elizabeth in a hug and never let go. But she couldn't do it. Not yet.

"Please," Liz said. "Tell me."

"I was nineteen when you were born," Cooper said, as the memo-

235

ries flashed before her eyes. "At the time, we lived in Miami. I didn't know my dad. He had been gone before I was even born. My mom, your grandma, was working as a maid for Enrique Hernandez. For most, he represented an inspiring rag-to-riches-story. A kid from the barrio, whose parents had escaped the communist regime in Cuba and then made a name for himself in the land of opportunities. A generous philanthropist who supported local communities. Hernandez was huge not only in Miami, but all over the south. He owned restaurants, marinas, real estate. Celebrities would fly from all over the country to attend his lavish parties."

"I'm guessing he wasn't as clean as he wanted to portray himself?"

"No." Cooper closed her eyes, her mind racing back in time. "Most of his story was a lie. A carefully built house of cards. Hernandez owned the biggest drug operation in the south of the United States. Cocaine, fentanyl, heroin. Despite his claims, he wasn't even Cuban, but Colombian. He had adoptive Cuban parents, and he took care of them in his own way, but they were living reclusive lives at one of his properties, under the guard of his men, and weren't allowed to communicate with the press."

"You said I was born when you were young," Liz said, her voice quiet, her hands wrapped around the teacup as if she were cold. "Who was my dad?"

Cooper closed her eyes for a moment, the remnants of long-forgotten pain trying to find their way to the surface. Most of the images were faded like old photographs, leaving her with a kaleido-scope of random memories. A handsome face with a crooked smile, long locks of unruly black hair. Flour-covered hands. The smell of freshly baked bread.

"I'm getting to it," she finally said.

"Okay."

"For a time, Enrique's empire was growing, with no one chal-lenging him, and my mom and I had simple lives. She cared for the house. I helped in the kitchen and dreamed about becoming an artist. The house had an extensive collection of books, and I would sneak into the library at night and read about fundamentals of art and composition, imagining that one day I'd be famous enough to have my work on the walls of the Met and Guggenheim."

She paused, collecting her thoughts. It was harder than she thought it would be. Those memories had stayed untouched for so long, Cooper almost forgot about the pain. But now she had opened the door and now they were rushing down the slope of a mountain like an avalanche. She had no other choice but to surf the wave.

"What happened?"

"A war. Colombians challenged Hernandez for a piece of the market, and negotiations quickly turned into one of the bloodiest drug wars in the United States. But for a time, I was blissfully unaware of what was going on. I met Luis. He was a kitchen hand like me and soon we were madly in love. As the war heated, Hernandez started to lose. It didn't happen overnight, but some of his factories got blown up, buildings burned, people assassinated. He needed a bigger army and young men like Luis got drafted. By then, I already knew I was pregnant. He would disappear for weeks at a time and when he'd get back, he'd be quiet, and when he wasn't busy in the kitchen, he'd just sit there, drinking and brooding."

Cooper stood up and walked to the kitchen's window, looking at the vineyard. The vines, bound with wire for the winter, were covered in light frost, neat rows running all the way to the mountains in the distance.

"By the time you were born," she continued, "it became obvious that Hernandez was going to lose the war. My mom and I wanted to flee, but by then paranoia and fear consumed Enrique. They watched everybody twenty-four seven. One day, Enrique cornered me in the kitchen and said he wanted to talk to me. It was unusual as we almost never talked other than exchanging pleasantries. He asked me to come to his office, and I did. There I had the weirdest conversation of my life. Hernandez dropped all the pretense. He told me about the war with Fernando Flores and how there was a perfect opportunity to kill the old man. Hernandez said that Flores was a huge womanizer, and he was particularly fond of younger girls who looked like me. He said his people had a way to present me to Flores as his new lover and there I'd be able to kill him and make it look like it was an accident. In return, he promised he'd take good care of my mother and you."

"Did you accept?" Liz asked, her voice quiet, almost a whisper.

"No, not at first," Cooper said. "I told him I couldn't possibly do what he'd asked me and stayed firm no matter how angry he got. I was scared as Enrique became more and more agitated during our conversation. At some point, I thought he was going to strike me, but he stopped at the last second and told me to leave. I thought it was the end of it. But then one night we woke up to the gunshots and screaming of my mother. My room wasn't too far away from the kitchen, and I rushed there to see what was going on. There was Enrique, all covered in blood, but he was unhurt. Luis was on the floor at his feet, his neck sliced open so deep his head almost came off. My mother was there as well, standing over a body of a young man I'd never seen in my life."

"Who was that?"

"Enrique claimed it was an assassin working for Flores, who tried to kill him. I could see his eyes going between me and my mother as if calculating something. The next thing I knew, my mother was holding the gun and Enrique was taking it from her with his hands covered in plastic gloves. He told his men to clean up the mess and made everyone leave, except me. When we were alone, he gave me an ultimatum—either I was going to accept the job, or he was going to pin the murder of the intruder and Luis on my mother."

"But how?" Liz leaned forward, engrossed in the story, her pupils dilated and her cheeks flushed. "Didn't other people see what happened?"

"I was young and stupid." Cooper shrugged. "And everyone was terrified of Enrique. They would say and do anything he told them to. I was afraid for my mom, too. She had nowhere to go. I agreed to do the job. They sent me away to train for the assignment and then I went to Colombia to kill the drug lord."

She fell silent, replaying the events that changed her life forever in her head.

"It was the first life I'd ever taken," Cooper continued. "I spent a night in his harem and slipped a poison in his drink. I didn't even have to sleep with him—he told me he was keeping me for *dessert* and played with other girls first. Everybody thought he fell asleep. In the morning, when he wouldn't wake up, I slipped away during the chaos. A few days later, I was back in Miami, shaken, but convinced that the hardest part was behind me. I couldn't be any more wrong. While I was away, Enrique hid you and my mother somewhere far. He said if I wanted to make sure you remained safe, I had to continue working for him. I searched, desperate to find you, but he hid you well. I had no other choice but to agree. He had me trained with many people and before long, I had a reputation in the trade as one of the most successful assassins in the world."

"We'd never seen each other since?" Liz's eyes were soft, the corners of her mouth forming a frown.

"We had," Cooper said. "A few times. You probably don't remember. Enrique arranged for us to meet a few times. We met at the beach, played some ball, swam in the ocean. They told me my mom was in the room with an armed man the entire time. If I tried to do anything, they'd execute her. That was the last time I saw you before Alexander Engel found you."

"I remember you," the young woman said, her eyes shining. "But somehow I never connected the dots. I always thought you looked familiar, but when I asked Alex, he said we'd never met, and I took him at his word."

"That's what people like him and Hernandez do. They mold the world around them to suit their needs. A few weeks later, Enrique was assassinated. The young Flores, the son of the man I poisoned, sent a man who killed him. I was free of the man's bonds, but I lost the trail of you and my mom. I never stopped searching, but it didn't matter as I'd never found you. That's my story. I'm sorry for everything you've been through."

Cooper closed her eyes and put her face into the palms of her hands. There was nothing else there to say. She laid her story bare before her daughter about who she was—a monster. A killer without conscience. She wanted to scream, or to cry, or to run until the soles of her feet were raw. Instead, she stayed in her chair, immobile. Dead to the world. She didn't know how to do any of those things. She'd forgotten them a long time ago.

Soft hands touched her shoulders, and then Elizabeth pulled her into a hug. She buried her face in the young woman's chest and cried for the first time in many years.

"You found me," she heard Liz say. "And you don't have to ever leave me again."

When the tears stopped coming, she let go and looked up at Elizabeth. "We could go anywhere in the world. Be anyone. I can protect you. But before we do, there's something I need to take care of first."

"What's that?"

"I owe a debt. Someone helped me to find you," Cooper said, standing up. "I promised that if she did, I'd help her find something important in return. I need to fulfill that promise."

42

Tunis-Carthage International Airport

elen looked through the window at the private jet terminal of the Tunis-Carthage International Airport. The low-slung white building with a blue roof seemed to roll back as the Gulfstream G800 jet taxied onto the runway. The plane stopped there for a few moments, its Pearl 700 engines' low rumble picking up intensity.

The last two days had been a blur. After barely escaping the nuclear blast that had leveled the Otomo factory, the helicopter made it to the outskirts of Hassi Messaoud, a town in eastern Algeria. From there, they took another bird, courtesy of Jim Rovinsky's phone call, that crossed the Tunisian border and took them to the Bizerte-Sidi Ahmed Air Base. They stayed the night, huddled in a tarp tent while Martin kept guard outside and, in the morning, drove to the airport.

Without warning, the jet lurched forward, pushing Helen into the back of her seat.

She reached over the armrest without looking and felt Max's hand squeezing her fingers, his grip tight but gentle.

"Are you okay, Helen?"

She looked across the aisle at Jason and nodded. Despite spending the last forty-eight hours together, she still found it hard not to stare every time he came into her view. It wasn't the new prosthetics that made it difficult—except for the gray-metal of his now both artificial hands, most of his high-tech limbs were hidden under the clothes. It was the face—the gaunt face of a soldier, whose eyes had seen more than his mouth could ever share.

"I'm sorry for what you've been through," he said. "It couldn't have been easy."

"It hasn't been easy for any of us." She turned back to the window. The jet was still climbing, banking hard over the Tyrrhenian Sea. The sky was clear as far as she could see, not a cloud in sight, not even a contrail. "Over the past few years, there had been moments when I thought that was it. There was no way we'd make it this time. When Mike and I got lost in the desert, I actually asked him that question."

"What question, Helen?"

Hunt's eyes seemed darker than she had remembered. There was unceasing pain behind those cold blue irises. Deeper than she could ever understand.

"Is this how it ends?" she said. "That's what I asked him."

"What did he say?" Max asked, his voice soft.

"Nothing." She shrugged, her thoughts racing back to the freezing night in the desert. The sand crunching on her teeth. The painfully chapped lips and aching body. The warm shoulder that she leaned against—the only thing that kept her sane. "He collected himself and stood up. I knew he thought we were going to die, too. But he kept going."

"That's what he always did," Jason said.

She nodded again, quiet. The dull ache in her chest was growing so large it threatened to swallow her whole. Somewhere below them, in a cargo hold, Mike's body laid in a simple steel casket. Forever cold. Helen wished she had been religious. She could believe that now Mike was traveling to some faraway, beautiful place. At peace, finally reunited with the woman he loved.

But she wasn't, and she didn't. She knew with absolute certainty all that was left of the man was a corpse with a hole in his chest. Helen closed her eyes. They stung, but she didn't want to cry. She wasn't the only one with a loss.

Max brought her hand to his face and gently kissed her palm, his eyelashes tickling her skin.

"Part of me wishes I'd stayed on that roof," she whispered, opening her eyes.

"No," Max said. "Then his death would have been in vain. He'd never want that."

"You are right, Max," Jason said. He got up and disappeared into the back of the plane. Then, a few moments later, he came back with a carafe filled with a sloshing golden liquid and three glasses. He poured two fingers' worth into each glass and passed them to Helen and Max.

"To Michael Connelly," she said, raising the glass.

"To Michael Connelly," Jason and Max echoed.

They touched the glasses, and she downed the drink in one go, willing the liquid fire to melt the cold pain in her chest. It did not.

"I know it hurts, Helen," Jason said, putting his glass down. He leaned back, resting his metallic hands on his knees, and looked outside. "Believe me, I do. And I know Mike didn't give you the answer, but I will. This is not how it ends."

"No?" The sky on the other side of the large round window was of the clearest shade of blue. She remembered a movie she'd seen with her dad in a movie theater many lifetimes ago. A family trying to survive a tornado and how the carnage stopped for a few seconds as they passed through the eye of the storm. The sky above them was the clearest shade of blue. That moment of calmness was more terrifying than anything else, and the entire audience seemed to have held their collective breath. Waiting. Knowing that the moment of tranquility was fleeting.

That was where they were now, she thought. In the eye of the storm.

"No, this is not how it ends," Jason said, and poured another round of Scotch. "Not by a long shot. This is how it begins."

Helen picked up the drink, swirled the liquid, watching it form a miniature tornado inside of the crystal tumbler, and took a long swallow.

He was right

JOIN THE UPGRADE SERIES

Thank you for reading THE LOOP, the third book in THE UPGRADE series. I hope you enjoyed it. The universe of the series continues to expand with three more books coming out in the next two years.

If you enjoyed this book, please take a moment and leave an honest review. Reviews are important for authors and help us sell more books and thus spend more time writing new stories you can enjoy. You can do that here:

Leave a review

And, of course, don't forget to join the series to learn about upcoming releases, exclusive free content, and more. You can do it right here:

Join The Upgrade Series

Thanks again for reading and hope to see you soon!

ALSO BY WESLEY CROSS

THE UPGRADE SERIES

BOOK 1. THE BLUEPRINT

BOOK 2. VERTIGO

BOOK 3. THE LOOP

ROGUE (A short story)

BOOK 4. SPARE PARTS

BOOK 5. FATA MORGANA

BOOK 6. DEUS EX MACHINA